RED DOG

Other Books by William C. Dietz

THE WINDS OF WAR SERIES
Red Ice
Red Flood
Red Dragon
Red Thunder
Red Tide
Red Sands
Red River
Red Dog

AMERICA RISING SERIES
Into the Guns
Seek and Destroy
Battle Hymn

MUTANT FILES SERIES
Deadeye
Redzone
Graveyard

LEGION OF THE DAMNED SERIES
Legion of the Damned
The Final Battle
By Blood Alone
By Force of Arms
For More Than Glory
For Those Who Fell
When All Seems Lost
When Duty Calls
A Fighting Chance
Andromeda's Fall
Andromeda's Choice
Andromeda's War

RED DOG

WILLIAM C. DIETZ

Wind's End Publishing

Cover art by Damonza

ACKNOWLEDGEMENT AND DEDICATION

RED DOG would have been impossible without the technical advice I received from Vietnam War Chinook pilot Jim Weatherill, a true American hero.

During Jim's combat tour he was awarded the Air Medal, which is given for single acts of heroism or meritorious achievement in a combat zone.

More than that, Jim was subsequently awarded <u>thirty</u> oak leaf clusters, each representing <u>another</u> air medal.

Jim was also the recipient of an Army Commendation Medal for meritorious service, plus the Broken Wing Award for the emergency landing that followed an engine failure.

Jim is also an accomplished writer, who in partnership with his wife Anne, wrote *THE BLADES CARRY ME.*

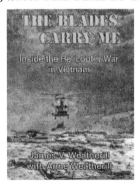

THE *BLADES CARRY ME* is the hair-raising account of Jim's exploits in Vietnam, as well as the touching story of what life was like for Anne back in the United States.

"BLADES" is a must-read.

And now, with *WHEN PATHS CROSS*, Jim brings his writing talent to fiction.

Highly recommended!

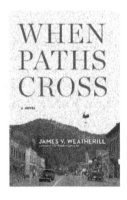

This book is dedicated to Jim, and all of the other pilots who flew helicopters in Nam, thank you one and all.

TABLE OF CONTENTS

SYRIA

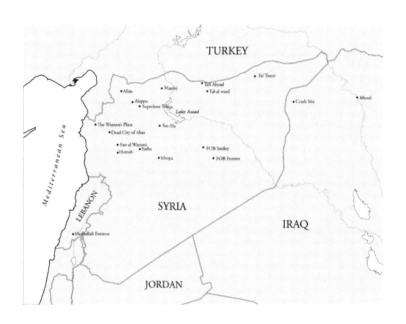

TURKEY

- Tal Tamir
- Tell Abyad
- Afrin
- Manbij
- Tal-al ward
- Aleppo
- Crash Site
- Mosul
- Superbase Tabqa
- *Lake Assad*
- The Women's Place
- Sur-Na
- Dead City of Abaz
- Fan al Wastani
- Sarba
- Hamah
- Ithriya
- FOB Smiley
- FOB Foxtrot

Mediterranean Sea

LEBANON

- Hezbollah Fortress

SYRIA

IRAQ

JORDAN

CHAPTER ONE

Northwest, Syria

The CH-47D Chinook helicopter was passing through a mountain pass in the coastal Al-Ansariyyah range as it came under fire. There was no way to know by whom, because it could have been ISIS, al-Qaeda, Iranian regulars or bandits. And that didn't matter.

What mattered was that the Chinook had been hit. And, thanks to the audible alarms and the read outs in front of her, army Captain Marie Soto knew that the port engine was failing and the heavily laden helo was losing altitude as a result.

"I think the bastards are firing *down* on us," co-pilot Jonny Lee observed. "And they hit one of our transmissions."

Chinooks have *five* transmissions, all connected by drive shafts. That made for a lot of moving parts and a lot of things that could go wrong.

"Yeah, more like two or three of them," Soto replied, as the second engine lost power.

"We're taking fire from both sides," her crew chief warned. "And trailing smoke."

Soto's job was to maintain control and keep her passengers alive. "We're going down Chief. Pass the word. Get the APU (auxiliary power unit) started Jonny! We don't have time for the checklist. Pull the fire handles and follow me on the controls."

Lee ran the engine failure list from memory. Engine condition levers, generator switches, fuel pumps and many more. Each item required a visual check and acknowledgement.

The ground was coming up fast. Soto managed a quick warning to the crew and passengers. "Hang on! We're going in hard."

Soto could see her landing spot through the plexiglass under the yaw pedals. Draw a horizontal line and tip it down 70 degrees. That was the correct glide angle.

Soto caused the Chinook to flare and nearly stop. But the landing area fell away and the front wheels hit hard. The helicopter skidded and the slowing rotors slammed into a boulder.

The impact threw the helo's passengers around as the rotors pounded to a stop.

"Let's shut this thing down," Soto said calmly. "The last thing we need is a fire."

Crew Chief Alma Alvarez was back in the cargo area. The sound of her voice carried all the way to the cockpit. "Check the people on either side of you! Help them if they need it… And get out of the helicopter *now!*"

The Chinook was carrying forty-nine soldiers plus crew. Alvarez gave instructions to her crew as passengers left via the rear hatch. "Pull the guns. I'll bring the grenade launcher. We'll return the ammo. This is tango territory. Who knows what sort of riff raff the crash will attract."

The passengers were replacements for casualties or people who had rotated out. That meant they weren't a coherent unit. Some were 11B infantry, but most were techs, medics, and mechanics.

That was irrelevant, however. "Every soldier, a rifleman." A phrase coined to convey the concept that army personnel are warriors first, regardless of their MOS (military occupational specialty).

With only a few exceptions, they were armed. That's why Captain Roy Preston felt good about the group's capacity to defend itself.

But Preston *didn't* feel so good about his ability to lead them. He was a supply officer after all. But he'd been through officer training, and that would have to do.

And, when a master sergeant stepped up to salute him, Preston knew that his ass was golden. "Sergeant Clay, sir... What's the plan?"

Preston grinned. "I'm no expert Sergeant, but I'd say we should establish a perimeter ASAP. I would appreciate your help."

"No prob, sir. We've got some noncoms. I'll appoint four squad leaders, divide the troops equally, and give each squad a quadrant to protect."

That was when Soto arrived. She was wearing a tac vest and carrying an M4 carbine. "Have we got injuries?"

"Nothing serious," Clay answered. "Some lacerations, contusions and sprains. No purple hearts."

Soto nodded. "Good. I heard you mention a perimeter. My crew pulled their guns. Please site them where you think they'll be most effective."

"Will do," Clay replied. "I'll let you know once I've had a chance to look things over. Can we expect air support?"

"We can," Soto replied. "Two A-10s are on the way."

"I'll tell the troops," Clay volunteered. "That'll be good for morale." Then he left.

"We lucked out," Preston said. "It's clear that Clay knows what he's doing. And, we had a pro in the cockpit. The landing sucked but I'll take it."

Soto laughed and offered her hand. "Marie Soto."

"Roy Preston. You go clockwise, and I'll go counterclockwise. Let's see what kind of condition our condition is in."

The first thing Soto noticed was how arid the countryside was compared to the fertile land on the west side of the mountains.

Still, judging from the presence of an old farmhouse, and a rusty water tank, it appeared that someone tried to grow crops there. Tried and failed.

Then Soto paused to eyeball the slopes above. The Nikon binoculars were part of her personal survival kit, and powerful in spite of their diminutive size.

The tan colored rock was home to fan-shaped scree fields, a scattering of wind twisted trees, and at least two mountain goats. *Is an observer looking down on us?* Soto wondered. *While his posse comes our way?* Soto saw a momentary reflection, and knew the answer.

"Excuse me, ma'am," a private said. "Your crew chief sent me. We're taking everything off the Chinook. Should we store it in the farmhouse?"

"No," Soto replied. "That's the first thing the tangos will fire on if they show up. Divide the stuff by four and establish separate dumps."

Just then a mortar round landed on the house, exploded, and hurled debris in every direction. The soldier stared at her. He said, "Yes, ma'am," and ran off.

Soto took off at a jog and circled the perimeter to the point where Clay was dispatching runners hither and yon. A round landed on the Chinook, exploded, and triggered a fuel fire. There was a loud *WHUMP*, flames shot straight up, and debris cartwheeled through the air. "They didn't waste any time," Clay observed, as Soto knelt next to him.

"I think they have an observer on the mountain," Soto told him. "He's walking the rounds in. They assume air support will arrive soon, and want to score on us before that happens."

"Let's hope the zoomies put the pedal to the metal," Clay replied. "In the meantime, let's circle the perimeter. When the shelling stops, the tangos will attack. Warn the troops."

Soto wanted to find a hole and crawl in, but knew the sergeant was right, and forced herself to scuttle from position to position spreading the word. Most of the soldiers were busy scraping out firing positions and stacking rocks.

Soto was inspecting her third defensive position when the shelling stopped. A reedy cry of *"Allahu akbar!"* (God is most great) was heard, accompanied by the chatter of automatic weapons, and the realization that the attackers were closer than Soto had assumed.

The enemy fighters rose from the ground like wraiths, each wearing a homemade ghillie suit, and charged. Not everywhere, but at a single point on the perimeter, where they hoped to break through. The target was twenty yards to Soto's left.

"Hold your ground!" she yelled. "Don't leave your positions!"

Otherwise, a reserve force could surge in to take ground, Soto thought. *Who are these bastards? Somebody knows what they're doing.*

A series of explosions marched across the ground outside the perimeter, and Soto saw an arm somersault through the air, as Alvarez fired her M79 grenade launcher.

The weapon had been a favorite in Vietnam, and was still in use, even though six shot launchers were available. *"Morir hijos de puta!"* (Die mother fuckers) Alvarez shouted, while bullets kicked up geysers of dust all around her. That's when Lee tackled the crew chief from behind and most likely saved her life.

The grenades did the trick though, and tangos fortunate enough to survive the barrage of grenades went flat, and tried to disappear. Clay was on-scene by then shooting enemy fighters with a machine-like efficiency.

Soto's HOOK 3 radio burped static. "Wizard-Two-Two, this is Dozer and Vapor in from the north with guns, rockets, and bombs. Pop smoke to mark your perimeter. Over."

Soto hurried to respond. "This is Wizard-Two-Two… Welcome to the hood. Standby. Radios are in short supply. I'll pass the word. Over."

Dozer's reply was drowned out by the roar of twin turbofan engines as a "Hog" roared overhead, quickly followed by its twin.

It appeared that the tangos knew what was coming because some of them popped up and ran. "Aimed fire only!" Clay bellowed. "Conserve your ammo!"

Soto's runner ran hunched over as enemy bullets snapped past him. Purple smoke, the only color the Chinook carried, billowed in his wake. "Standby Wizard-Two-Two," Dozer said. "Daddy gonna mow the lawn. Over."

What followed was a textbook example of what air support could do. Rockets flashed off rails, and gravity bombs tumbled through the air, soon followed by the unmistakable roar of GAU-8/A Avenger rotary cannons. A single gun run was sufficient to silence the battlefield.

"Hey Wiz," Dozer said. "Sorry we can't linger. But we've got a customer east of here who wants your leftovers. A QRF (quick reaction force) is headed this way, ETA three hours. *Hasta la vista.*" And with that, the planes banked then flew east.

Soto noticed that the shadows had grown longer and the light was starting to fade. Shit, shit, shit. Night was about to fall. Would the tangos try to creep in under the cover of darkness? Probably. Soto went looking for Preston and Clay. The captain was nowhere to be seen. But the sergeant was making the rounds. "This is your chance to improve your firing position, son…"

"Two swallows of water Corporal, that's all you get, pass it along."

"What the hell? Who's the idiot who took a dump here? Order them to dig a pit toilet."

"Hello, Captain… Kudos to your crew chief. She has balls."

"I'm sure she'll be pleased to hear it," Soto replied dryly. "Where's Captain Preston?"

Clay made a face. "KIA, ma'am. He took a bullet to the head."

Soto winced. "How many?"

"Four killed and seven wounded. Two seriously."

Soto looked around to make sure that no one else could hear. "So, Sergeant… Based on your experience how bad will this get tonight?"

"Well, there's no way to be sure," Clay answered. "But if I had to guess, I'd say it's gonna be an eight, on a scale of one to ten."

"That bad?"

"Yeah, that bad."

"What do you recommend?"

"Ration water, feed the troops whatever we have, keep two thirds of our force on watch, establish listening posts, and redistribute the remaining ammo. Some people are short and others aren't."

Soto nodded. "As Picard would say, 'Make it so.'"

"I'm more of a STAR WARS fan," Clay replied. "But, yes ma'am."

The explosion caught Soto by surprise, and caused her to flinch. "Mortars," Clay said. "The tangos know the planes are gone."

Downed aircraft had a high priority with the folks at Central Command. And Soto took advantage of that to request a second ground support mission. "The tangos are pounding us with mortars. And there isn't much cover. Send more Hogs. Over."

"Roger that, Wizard. Prepare to mark your position with flares. Over."

A full twenty minutes passed before a plane roared overhead. "Wizard-Two-Two, this is Boots. I am an A-10 with guns, rockets and bombs. My wingman had to turn back, so I'm solo tonight, but ready to party. What you got? Over."

Soto couldn't help but laugh in response to the other woman's patter. "Boots, this is Wizard. We're surrounded. The tangos are firing on us with indirect. Flares are ready. Over."

"Light 'em up," Boots said cheerfully. "Then duck for cover. Over."

Soto turned to a runner. "Flares in five. Tell 'em."

The kid took off as Soto spoke. "We're short on radios, Boots. Give us five while we spread the word."

"Roger that," Boots replied. "In the meantime, I'll try to scare the shit out of them. Over."

The mortar fire slowed and stopped as Boots made low altitude passes over the area. The tangos, whoever they were, responded with small arms fire.

Soto had a high level of admiration for Boots, and her willingness to draw fire to protect the people on the ground, but couldn't help but worry. All it would take was what aviators called a "golden BB" to hit the Hog in the right place, and bring the flying tank down. A possibility that Soto, as a Chinook pilot, worried about all the time.

Boots was still at it when the runner returned. "All squad leaders have been notified, ma'am. And the countdown is underway."

"Boots, this is Wizard. You'll see the flares shortly. Make your first run when you're ready. Over."

"Gotcha Wizard," the A-10 pilot replied. "The groundfire is heaviest south of your position. I'll start there. Over."

A series of explosions, each marked by an orange-red flash of light, and a resonant *BOOM,* marched across the flat land to the south.

There was no way to accurately assess the damage inflicted by the gravity bombs, but given the massed groundfire originating from that area, Soto assumed that a whole lot of hajis were headed for heaven.

Then Boots switched her attention to the east. Rockets slashed in, flashes of light marked hits, and Soto saw a momentary billow of flame as a vehicle took a hit.

"Uh oh," Boots said. "I have multiple lock-ons. Firing flares… Too many… Punching out."

The explosion was so bright it illuminated the entire area. But only for a couple of seconds as fiery debris rained from the sky, hit the ground, and was lost in the darkness. "She-it," Clay said. "Did she make it?"

"Maybe," Soto said doubtfully. "And maybe not. I'll call it in."

The conversation with Central was brief. The relief force had come under attack, and though delayed, was still coming their way. There was no mention of sending more planes.

No further mortar rounds fell. Because they'd been destroyed? That's the way it looked.

But the exchanges of small arms fire continued, with Clay circling the perimeter, voicing the same mantra over and over. "Conserve ammo, conserve ammo, and—oh yeah—conserve ammo."

The sergeant had returned when Soto heard a whisper from her radio. "Wizard? Are you there, hon? Over."

"I'm here," Soto confirmed. "You're alive. Thank God."

"Yeah," Boots agreed. "I survived the drop and managed to hide the chute, but I have a problem."

"Which is?"

"My right ankle is sprained or broken. I can't walk, but I'm crawling your way. Don't amscray without me. Promise?"

"I promise," Soto said. "Where are you? Relative to our position? Over."

"East," Boots replied. "But don't send anyone after me. There're too many tangos. Over."

"I read you," Soto said. "Stay in touch. We'll monitor this channel. Over."

Soto heard a double click followed by silence. She turned to Clay. "I'm going after her. I think my copilot will want to go too. But I need an additional body. A man preferably. We might have to carry her back."

Clay eyed her. "No offense, ma'am, but what makes you think you can find her? It's pitch black out there."

"My copilot and I have night vision gear (NVG)," Soto answered.

"Okay," Clay replied. "In the meantime, what are we supposed to do for leadership?"

"You're it," Soto answered. "You know that. So, please find a volunteer."

"You're a better infantry officer than a pilot has a right to be," Clay commented. "Okay, I'll see what I can do."

It took fifteen minutes to assemble and equip the mini rescue party. The team consisted of Lee, a burly medic named Dix, and Soto.

The men had two pistols, each enabling them to fire one-handed if necessary. Soto was carrying her sidearm plus the M4. She led the way, with Dix in the two slot, and Lee bringing up the rear. He was in charge of their six.

Soto could see clearly but her surroundings had a greenish hue. Her radio was ready. "Boots, this is Wizard. There are three of us. We're coming your way. Over."

The A-10 pilot was whispering. "I told you not to send anyone. Over."

"Oh yeah," Soto replied. "I forgot. Sorry. Do you have night vision? Give me a landmark… Something to home in on. Over."

"There's an old truck directly in front of me. A flatbed, like a farmer might use. That's the good news. The bad news is that a haji is standing on it. Over."

"Got it… Keep crawling, but don't get too close to him. Over."

Soto heard two clicks and continued east. She heard voices two minutes later, knelt, and signaled the others to do likewise.

Three tangos crossed her path moments later headed north. They were chatting in a language Soto didn't recognize. It was sloppy, very sloppy, but that wasn't surprising.

Once the enemy soldiers were gone Soto waved the others forward. A section of stone wall blocked the way. Soto climbed over it. Another fifty feet of progress put her on a rise. And there, about a hundred yards away, was the truck. And sure enough, a tango was standing on it.

Soto had two choices. She could get close, climb up onto the truck, and try to kill the asshole with her knife. That might work if she was a green beret. But she wasn't, and almost certain to fail.

That left choice number two. Get as close as possible, shoot the bastard, and send the others forward to find Boots. In the meantime, she would take the lookout's place, and trust that a single shot wouldn't be enough for the enemy to home in on.

Then the three of them would hustle the A-10 pilot back to the crash site and relative safety. Perfect it was not. But after a whispered conference Dix summed the situation up. "It beats the hell out of doing nothing. Let's go for it."

It seemed safe to assume that the lookout didn't have night vision goggles. But the terrorist could have a day-night scope on his rifle, which would explain why he was holding the weapon up to his eye, as he scanned the surroundings.

That meant the Americans had to belly crawl forward to the outcropping of rock which Soto had chosen as her firing bench. Then it was time to place the M4 in front of her, snuggle up to the weapon, and fix the man in her crosshairs. *A headshot*, Soto decided. *So, he can't use his radio.*

She was dimly aware of gunfire to the west. A sure sign that the bad guys were still trying to break through the perimeter. Soto thumbed her radio. "Boots... Do you read me? Over."

"Five-by-five. Over."

"We're west of the truck. I'm going to smoke the guy who is standing on it. My two-man posse will come looking for you. Don't shoot them. Over."

"Roger that, over."

Soto took a deep breath, held it, and began to squeeze the trigger. She heard the report, felt the recoil, and prepared to fire again. There was no need. The tango collapsed.

"Go, go, go!" Soto whispered. The men took off. Lee led the way.

Soto was up and running too. Eager to get up on the truck where other lookouts, assuming there were some, would be able to see a figure standing there.

After scrambling up onto the truck Soto paused to listen. And, as far as she could tell, the solitary shot hadn't been enough to raise an alarm.

Time seemed to slow as Soto waited for Lee to report in. But it was Boots who spoke first. "You're directly in front of me," she whispered. "Keep coming. Over."

Lee responded with two clicks of his mike. Then there was silence except for the haunting cry of an Arabian wolf in the distance. The sound sent a shiver down Soto's spine. Predators were hunting, and prey were hiding. Such was the world that Soto lived in.

"Wizard," Lee said. "Don't shoot. We're a hundred feet east of you. Over."

Soto jumped to the ground and saw them appear. A diminutive figure flanked by two larger bodies. Boots was hopping along with help from the men. Progress was understandably slow. And there wasn't a damned thing anyone could do about it.

With Soto leading the way the foursome made their way west. A flare lit the sky, the tempo of firing increased, and Soto feared the worst. What if she and her companions arrived only to discover that the crash site was in enemy hands?

Soto considered a call to Clay, remembered that the noncom didn't have a radio, and bit her lower lip. Helicopter pilot. What the hell was she thinking? Meteorology. Army weather girl. That would have been a great MOS. But no, she wanted to fly. Just like her dad.

Soto saw movement to her right, knelt, and signaled the others to do likewise. The enemy patrol consisted of six men walking single file. Soto was reminded of officer training. "One grenade'll get you all!" That's what the instructors liked to yell.

But Soto didn't have a grenade. All she could do was pray that the tangos didn't spot the group of Americans.

As with so many prayers, Soto's went unanswered. A haji yelled something and fired. The bullet kicked up sand next to Soto and she fired in return. Her slug knocked the man over as the other tangos brought their weapons to bear.

But Lee and Dix had dropped Boots by then and were firing their pistols. The fusillade was poorly aimed, and half the bullets missed their targets, but the rest hit flesh and bone. Two men fell, two fired in return, and a third ran.

Soto felt something nip her left shoulder, switched to the three round burst mode, and fired. The M4 produced very little recoil. As her slugs took a haji down, the other man jerked, as Lee and Dix emptied their backup pistols.

Soto turned. "Was anyone hit? No? Then let's haul ass."

"Specifically, *my* ass," Boots added. "Come on boys, get me to the Tabqa air base, and I'll buy the drinks."

"Enough said," Lee responded. "Come on, Dix… Let's move."

The next thirty minutes were anything but easy for Boots and the two men. There were gullies to traverse, rocks to avoid, and the continuing threat of being intercepted by hostile forces.

But as the sounds of fighting diminished Soto had reason to be hopeful and fearful at the same time. Had the attackers been beaten off? And disappeared into the night? Or were they inside the American perimeter looting bodies?

Finally, when the foursome was about a thousand yards from the crash site, Soto ordered the others to take a break. "I'm going to get closer. And, if it looks like it's safe to do so, I'll make contact. Otherwise, I will return here."

"That's a good idea," Lee allowed. "I'd rather be shot by the enemy."

On that note Soto made her way west, pausing every few yards to look and listen. And that paid off when a male voice said, "Help me carry this shit… It's heavy."

Soto felt a surge of excitement. "Attention inside the perimeter! This is Captain Soto. Four of us are coming in. Do you read me?"

"There was a pause followed by the now familiar sound of Master Sergeant Clay's parade ground voice. "Listen up! Friendlies approaching from the east. Weapons tight!"

Soto used her radio to call Lee and give the all clear. Clay came out to meet her. "Welcome back, ma'am. We heard shots fired in your direction, and feared the worst. Did you find her?"

"We did," Soto replied. "She has what may be a broken ankle, but she's gutsy as hell, and hopped all the way. Give me a sitrep."

"The reaction force arrived and kicked ass. A first lieutenant is in command. We were about to send a patrol out to find you."

"Thanks," Soto said. "So, what's the plan?"

"The plan is to pack up and get the hell out of here," Clay said with a grin.

"Works for me," Soto replied. "Where are we headed?"

"Tabqa airbase."

"That's where I hang my helmet," Soto told him. "Let's get this show on the road."

It took thirty minutes to load people and gear aboard a motley collection of fighting vehicles which included two American MRAPs, a German DURO transport, a French Griffon VBMR, and the war weary Humvee that led the way.

Soto managed to find a spot to sleep in the Griffon. The M4 was wrapped in her arms and her head was resting on her escape and evade bag. It was lumpy but that didn't prevent Soto from falling asleep. She remained that way for most of the long, three-and-a-half-hour trip.

Then a loud voice woke her up. "We're about to arrive at Superbase Tabqa. Our convoy will be required to stop outside the wire, where we will deass the truck and line up for a security check. Please have your ID Card and or transfer papers out, ready for inspection. Welcome to Tabqa."

The ensuing process was a pain in the butt, but necessary, and Soto spent the time shooting the shit with Boots. The A-10 pilot was from Alabama, and looking forward to some time off before returning to duty.

That was when Soto noticed the cowboy boot on the pilot's left foot and pointed at it. "Aha! Your callsign. How do you get away with it?"

Boots batted her eyes. "That depends on who's asking. Men are easy."

"But now you'll have to wear standard issue."

Boots laughed. "Don't be silly. I have backups."

Once the security check was complete the airbase swallowed the convoy whole. Soto had been stationed at Tabqa for three months by then, and knew some of its history. The Syrian airbase had been held by the Islamic State (ISIS) for a period of time, before losing a hard-fought battle to the Syrian Democratic forces or SDF, an alliance of Kurdish and Arab Militias backed by the U.S.

Then U.S. special forces took over and used Tabqa to support a variety of initiatives in the region. As WWIII started and Iran pushed into Iraq, millions of dollars' worth of equipment and defenses had been poured into the so-called "superbase," which soon became a home away from home for thousands of U.S. and Allied troops.

The Allies ate pizzas, hot dogs and hamburgers at American fast-food restaurants and bought electronics, T-shirts and groceries from a huge exchange. Then, when called upon to do so, they ventured forth to fight an ever-changing lineup of terrorist organizations and Iranian militias. The emotional whiplash was difficult to cope with, but beat the alternative, which was life at a Forward Operating Base (FOB).

The sun had broken company with the eastern horizon by the time Soto and her former passengers were admitted to Tabqa and deposited outside the base's security center.

After checking to make sure that the dead were being handled properly, and that the wounded soldiers were receiving care, Soto said goodbye to Boots.

The A-10 pilot was loaded onto a medical Humvee bound for the base hospital. She waved. "Remember! I'm buying."

That left Soto and Lee to hitch a ride to the patch of bone-dry ground assigned to Charlie Company, which was part of the 1-167th General Support Aviation Battalion (GSAB). On a good day Charlie Company boasted 20 UH-60 Back Hawk utility transport helicopters, and 12 CH-47D Chinooks.

Soto heard the percussive sound typical of Chinooks and looked up as a so-called "fat cow" came in for a landing.

The D's shared the same airframe with previous models but had more powerful engines. A Chinook's triple-hook cargo system could carry up to 26,000 pounds of cargo externally, including a 40-foot cargo container, like the one dangling below the incoming bird.

"That's Cooper," Lee shouted, as the container landed. "He has a nice touch."

The company area included two dedicated helipads, eight CHUs (Containerized Housing Units) for people to sleep in, and a ninth for the headquarters company's use.

It was generally referred to as the "Bermuda Triangle" because of the way reports, requisitions, and inventories went in and never came out.

Soto and Lee passed in front of his hootch, agreed to meet at the DFAC (*dee-fack*) (Dining Facility) later, and agreed that they were lucky to be alive.

Soto arrived at her quarters to find a note taped to the door. It was short and not especially sweet. "Captain Soto will report to Major Albro immediately upon her return."

Who the fuck is Major Albro? Soto wondered.

She sighed, unlocked the door to her "slot," and stayed long enough to shed her M4 and E-bag. Then it was time to visit the communal restrooms located at the center of the area, and trudge over to the headquarters trailer, where Albro was likely to be.

After pulling the door open Soto stepped into what felt like an icebox. The army had generators. BIG ones. So, there was no need to get sweaty. Not inside the wire.

Corporal Hayes was flying the front desk. "Good to see you ma'am; I'm glad you're okay."

"Thanks Hayes. Who is Major Albro? And why does he or she want to see me?"

"Major Albro is our new company commander," Hayes replied. "As of yesterday."

"What happened to Zensky?"

"They sent him to an outfit in Saudi Arabia."

"*Why?*"

"That's above my paygrade," Hayes responded. "But I heard he's getting some sort of a bump."

"Okay, thanks. Is Major Albro in?"

"Yes, ma'am. I'll let him know you're here. There's coffee on the table, along with some doughnuts."

Soto was drinking tepid coffee, and halfway through a chocolate covered doughnut, when Hayes sent her in. She took three steps forward, came to attention, and saluted. "Captain Marie Soto reporting as ordered, sir."

Albro was seated behind an army-issue field desk. He wore his hair high and tight, his eyes were like chips of obsidian, and his mustache was so thin it could have been penciled on. The salute resembled a wave. "At ease, Captain. I'm glad that you and your copilot returned safely. That said, your helicopter was destroyed."

"Yes, sir," Soto responded. "We were shot down."

Albro was toying with a pen. "Yes, let's discuss that. I'm sure you're aware of the fact that a Chinook can fly at 18,000 feet. But, according to what air traffic control told me, you were flying at a very low altitude. So low that the enemy was able to fire *down* on you. Why was that?"

Soto's eyes were fixed on a point above Albro's head. "We had orders to stay low so that Iranian radars, located three hundred miles to the east, couldn't detect us. Sir."

Albro tapped the desktop with his pen. "That's the way of it, isn't it Captain? There's always a good reason why the helicopters assigned to you crash. Two dead stick landings according to your file."

"Three now, sir."

"Don't be a smart ass," Albro said thinly. "I won't tolerate it! And it's unbecoming. Do you read me?"

"Sir, yes sir."

"Work with me, and I'll work with you, Captain. For the good of the company and the battalion. Have a complete after-action report on my desk by 1300 hours. Dismissed."

It was hot outside. A Blackhawk clattered over Soto's head as jets roared down the adjacent runway and shot into the sky. That's where freedom was. And that's where Soto wanted to be.

CHAPTER TWO

Superbase Tabqa, Syria

It was 0127. Engines roared as a pair of fighters took off. Master Sergeant Felix Bone barely noticed. He was standing in front of his hooch, his pack resting on the ground, as he waited for the duty truck to arrive. That's when the latest mission would begin.

Bone felt numb. Not excited. Not frightened. Just numb.

He was forty-seven years old and had been in the army for twenty-nine years. During that time Bone served in Iraq twice, fought in Afghanistan *three* times, and been part of raids in a long list of ugly places. All he knew was war.

The plan was to retire once he had thirty. But then World War III came along, and Bone received a notice informing him that his enlistment had been extended "…Until the end of the war, or for as long as the army requires your services."

Not that it mattered, because Bone was up to his ass in debt, and couldn't afford to retire. Or serve stateside, because he'd lose his combat pay if he did.

The pile of unpaid debt was partly his fault. The speedboat was a mistake. He used it what? Three times a year? And was paying three hundred bucks a month for it.

But his wife Yolanda deserved most of the blame. She refused to work in order to homeschool the kids. All three of whom required food, clothes, cell phones, lessons and allowances.

So, as Bone stood in the cold waiting for the truck to arrive, he was thinking about money instead of the mission. That was a rookie mistake. *Focus*, Bone told himself. *Money won't matter if you're dead.*

Headlights appeared and swung around to pin him in their glare. The M939 truck's diesel engine roared as the 5-ton came to a halt. *It's showtime*, Bone thought. *Strap it on.*

"It" was the master sergeant persona that Bone had developed over the years. Gruff, fearless, profane and competent. Like in the movies. *Why?* Because it worked, that's why.

Bone threw his pack up to Corporal Levy, one of the so-called "Boneheads" who were members of the noncom's private posse, and covered his six. 'How's it hanging, Corp?" Bone inquired, as he climbed up into the back of the truck.

"Long and strong, Sarge. Here's your coffee. A Grande, two sugars, no cream."

"Thanks, Levy... You're okay for a Yankees fan. Move over Sergeant Olson... I thought you were sick."

"Naw, genital herpes don't count as being sick," the other noncom replied.

"That'll teach you to hump air force wrench turners," Private Hiro commented primly. "What the hell did you expect?"

The banter between the Boneheads elicited chuckles from the other members of the team, all of whom were Army Rangers, and happy to have some entertainment.

The truck took a series of turns before stopping in front of a trailer in officer country. Lieutenant Pete Sully climbed over the tailgate. He was an experienced leader, for which Bone was thankful. Newbies, even Ranger newbies, could be dangerous.

Sully took a look around. "Really, Sergeant Bone... Is this group of miscreants the best you could do?"

Bone shrugged. "They're gnarly, sir. But they're Rangers."

Olson said, "Hooah!" And the rest of the men replied in kind: "HOOAH!"

The whole thing had a ritualistic feel, with each member of the team knowing what to expect, and how to respond. *There's comfort in that*, Bone mused. *And they need it. No, we need it. Because this fucking war is grinding me down.*

A Sikorsky UH-60 Black Hawk helicopter was waiting on Pad 4, rotor blades turning, as the team arrived. Sully led the team to the side door where the bird's crew chief stood ready to welcome the Rangers aboard.

All of them knew the drill. The Rangers took seats, settled in, and ran last minute checks on their weapons and gear. Each man had a radio, headset, and boom mike.

Roughly five minutes passed before the Black Hawk took off and Sully began the inflight briefing. The team had heard it the day before. But Sully believed in the old axiom: "Tell 'em what you're going to tell 'em, tell 'em, and tell 'em what you told 'em." Bone agreed.

"Okay," Sully said. "Here's the skinny. We're headed for a village called Sarha. It's located about seventy-five miles southeast of Tabqa, which means this will be a short flight.

"According to the latest Intel, Sarha is home to about six hundred people—the power is out—and has been for a long time. The population is neither hostile nor friendly. They can best be described as survivors who have been able to coexist with a variety of terrorist groups over the last ten years. Al-Qaeda is the latest.

"Our job is to snatch an al-Qaeda commander, and failing that, to smoke the bastard. We aren't sure how many fighters he has, but estimates run from twenty to fifty. I'm hoping for twenty.

"As you know, this bird is noisy as hell. So, we're going to land two miles outside of town, and hoof it. Our night vision gear will be critical. Please don't be the idiot who falls into a dry wash and breaks an ankle. If you do, we'll leave you there, and pick you up during the exfil. Are there any questions?"

"Yes," a private named Perez said. "Is it too late to join the Coast Guard?" That produced chuckles all around.

"Okay," Sully said. "Let's keep it simple. In, grab, and go. Then back to base for a nap. Nothing to it."

That too was part of the script. The kind of optimistic bullshit that leaders always offered at the beginning of a mission. Bone knew that, because when he was in command, he did the same thing.

And, every once in a while, the rosy predictions came true. *I hope this is one of those times,* Bone thought.

Since Sarha was only 75 miles from Tabqa airfield, and the Black Hawk could do more than 180 miles per hour, their travel time would be a mere 25 minutes, give or take.

Thanks to their skill, and night vision gear, the pilots put the twelve-thousand-pound helo down with a gentle thump. "Have a nice stroll," the pilot said over the intercom. "And be sure to give an hour's warning for the exfil."

The Rangers understood. The bird would be vulnerable if it remained on the ground, and would run out of fuel if it remained aloft. So, the crew would return to Tabqa and a hot breakfast. "Have some bacon for me," Sully replied. "Crispy please."

"Done," the pilot said. "See ya later."

The Rangers hit the ground, hurried to exit the landing zone, and waited for the bird to take off. Engines roared, rotor blades clattered, and the Hawk was gone.

"This is Red-Dog-Six," Sully said. "I'll take the point with Three. Maintain visual contact with the man in front of you, but don't bunch up. Red-Dog-Nine will be eyes on."

Bone was Red-Dog-Nine. And, as second in command, it was his job to walk drag, so that both halves of the team would have leadership if the column were cut in two.

Bone had responsibility for monitoring the team's six as well, a process that involved pausing to look and listen, before hurrying to catch up.

Sometimes, on good days, a patrol like theirs would have an MQ-9 Reaper circling overhead. But the demand for Predators was high, which forced Central to ration the drones, depending on the priorities at the time.

"All right," Sully said. "Keep your head on a swivel, and let me know if you spot something of interest. Oh yeah, and I'm told that venomous Palestine vipers are active at night. Don't step on one. And if you do, don't scream. Noise travels in the desert."

"Or, put another way," Levy said. "Die quietly."

"Cut the crap," Bone said sternly. "Come see me when this is over."

Levy was a certified Bonehead, but that didn't give him the right to mouth off, and Bone would find a shit detail that had the corporal's name on it. The patrol headed south.

***

Sarha, Syria

It was a luxurious house by local standards in that it had three bedrooms, separate dining rooms for men and women, and a Honda generator powerful enough to support a small refrigerator and some lights.

One of the bulbs threw a circle of buttery light down onto the table in front of al-Qaeda Commander Amer Atwi. A laptop was positioned in front of him, and on it was the outline of what Atwi hoped would become an agreement between al-Qaeda and the Islamic State of Iraq and Syria (ISIS).

The opportunity was huge. Both al-Qaeda and ISIS had lost their leaders during the last month. One had been killed by an

Allied "Flying Ginsu" drone, which was equipped with deployable blades, and the other dropped dead of a heart attack.

The result was a momentary vacuum which Atwi hoped to take advantage of. The essence of his plan was to engineer a merger between al-Qaeda and ISIS, thus creating a new terrorist organization with the power required to accomplish what neither organization had been able to achieve alone.

And there was a great deal to recommend the idea. Both al-Qaeda and ISIS were Sunni. Both hoped to establish a conservative Sharia-based government which would govern the entire Muslim world.

But there were differences too. ISIS leaders had criticized al-Qaeda for its lack of a coherent purpose which, in their view, was to take and hold territory. Because nothing less than that would signal legitimacy to the western world.

Meanwhile al-Qaeda argued that the best path forward was to punish the enemy the way the United States had been punished on 9/11. Then, having weakened the *Kafirs* (disbelievers), strategic goals could be accomplished.

But surely those differences could be resolved. Or, so it seemed to Atwi and a man named Hatem Chalibi, the ISIS commander with whom Atwi had been communicating via the worldwide *Hawala*. (An informal transfer system used for financial transactions.)

Besides moving money, *Hawala* had gradually morphed into a secure communications network, and was frequently used for nefarious purposes.

Atwi's thoughts were interrupted as a middle-aged woman entered the room, bearing a tray loaded with a tea service and Syrian pastries. She was the owner's wife, and justifiably proud of her baking skills. "For you and your friend," she said. "You must eat to stay strong."

Atwi thanked her and glanced at his watch. Ten minutes. And then, if things went well, the effort to unify ISIS and al-Qaeda would begin.

***

North of Sarha, Syria

"Tangos at twelve o'clock," Sully whispered. "Down."

Bone turned his back to the team and took a knee. There was nothing to see but desert. How many fighters were there? Where were they based? And which group of assholes did they belong to? Questions chasing answers.

One thing was for sure however... A firefight would be disastrous even if the Rangers won. For one thing, the people in Sarha might hear the gunfire. And even a couple of casualties would severely weaken the team and force Sully to scrub the mission.

The officer was counting. His voice was little more than a whisper. "One, two, three, four, five, six in all—traveling east to west. Hold your positions."

The patrol had passed the Rangers by then. But Sully continued to wait. And, sure enough, *another* haji walked past. A tail-end Charlie on the lookout for anyone who might dash across the patrol's path after it passed. The L-T knew his shit, that was for sure.

"Clear," Sully said. "Let's go."

Bone followed the man in front of him. The patrol veered left and right as Sully led the Rangers between rock formations, and clumps of raetam—a flowering shrub found in many parts of the Middle East.

Then, after a quarter mile or so, Bone heard something completely unexpected. And that was the rush of flowing water. "Hold up," Sully whispered. "The dry gulch north of town is full of water. Standby."

Bone assumed the water was the result of a flash flood, born many miles away, and traveling downhill. To cross or not cross? That was the decision Sully had to make.

The wait seemed to last forever, but was actually less than five minutes long. "Okay," Sully said. "Bigfoot is taking a line across, and will anchor it on the other side. Put your Speedos on. Over."

"Bigfoot" was Corporal Murphy's nickname, and stemmed from his boot size. The Ranger was six-two, weighed two-ten, and if anyone could wade through raging flood waters, Murphy could.

Bone couldn't see much at first. But, as the column jerked forward, the situation became clear. Most of the team was on the far side of the watercourse by then, one man was halfway across, and two were waiting their turn. Bone stepped up to join them.

"Ignore the crossing," Bone told them. "Maintain situational awareness. This would be the perfect moment for the enemy to open fire on us."

Both soldiers turned their backs to the flood waters and made a show out of scanning the darkness. *They're thinking about what a jerk I am*, Bone mused. *That goes with the job.*

As the last man to cross, it was Bone's job to untie the rope from a rock before entering the thigh high water. It was unexpectedly cold. And after one end of the rope was freed, the current sought to push Bone downstream, making a straight crossing impossible.

But with a team of three Rangers pulling him in hand-over-hand, Bone made good progress, although a momentary stumble threatened to trip him up.

It would be a nightmare to try and exfil through the water while under fire, Bone thought, as he stepped on dry land. *The bird will have to pick us up somewhere between the water and town. And it's likely to take fire. Shit, shit, shit.*

"Good Bigfoot," Sully said, as if to a tame beast. "Form up, and let's get this show on the road."

***

Sarha, Syria

The meeting between Amer Atwi, and ISIS Commander Hatem Chalibi, had been underway for twenty minutes. Atwi had done most of the talking. Something Chalibi welcomed. "So," Atwi concluded, "the time is right for us to engineer a merger."

Chalibi took a sip of hot tea. "I think your proposal has merit. I have some questions however."

Atwi nodded politely. "Of course. Please tell me what's on your mind."

"Well," Chalibi replied, "senior though we are, we don't have enough clout to implement such a merger."

"True," Atwi conceded. "But we have access to those who have the necessary authority. Our job will be to champion the concept, and engineer the necessary consensus."

Chalibi nodded. "Yes, one step at a time. That's the way to go at it. What if we're successful? Who will lead the new organization? A person from al-Qaeda? Or someone from ISIS?"

Atwi produced a grimace. "That is the highest hurdle. For my part, I would be happy to accept a leader from your organization. That said, I fear that many of my peers will be unwilling to accept direction from anyone other than a member of al-Qaeda. The trick will be to find a man respected by both groups but beholden to neither."

Chalibi chuckled. "That will be difficult my friend... But things that come easily are often worthless. Let's create a list of potential candidates."

***

The northern outskirts of Sarha, Syria

It was pitch black, and since only a few residents had the money necessary to own a generator, lights were few and far between. But thanks to their night vision gear, the Rangers could see the one-story mudbrick houses and vehicles parked here and there quite clearly.

They could also see the armed fighters who were standing on flat roofs, lurking in doorways, and patrolling the streets. Bone figured there were roughly two dozen of them.

That number dropped steadily as the Rangers went to work with their recently issued Sig Sauer XM5 assault rifles. Each of which had a suppressor.

The tangos standing on the roofs were the first to die, followed by the lurkers, and those patrolling the streets. Was that all of them? Hell no... Not in Bone's opinion.

They were very close to the house where the meeting was taking place by that time, and about to make the final push, when a huge dog shot out of the shadows and attacked Sully.

The officer went down without firing a shot. Bigfoot shot the animal in the head, but it was too late. Sully's jugular had been severed, and he was bleeding out.

"The L-T is down and out," Bigfoot said. "I have his tag."

Bone swore. "The house is directly ahead. Follow me!"

A parachute flare went off, and lit the street while it drifted downwards. The surviving tangos began to fire at the Rangers *and* each other. That was because the al-Qaeda fighters didn't trust their ISIS counterparts and vice versa.

Bone expected a stray round to strike him between the shoulder blades as he ran a zigzag course toward the house. It was critical to reach the structure, snatch the target, and get the team off the street. Everything depended on it. A bullet snapped past his right ear. *I'm too old for this shit*, Bone thought, and forced himself to run faster.

***

Chalabi heard gunfire as his radio burped static. He picked it up. "Yes?"

"Kafirs have entered the village, *Qayid* (Commander). And they are headed your way. We are taking fire from others as well… We think they are al-Qaeda."

"Kill them," Chalibi snapped as he drew his pistol. The weapon was pointed at Atwi. "I was sent to learn the details of your stupid plan," Chalibi told Atwi. "You will find unity in *sama* (heaven)." Then he pulled the trigger.

A hole appeared at the center of Atwi's forehead, his head snapped back, and he fell sideways to the floor. Chalibi came to his feet as something heavy hit the front door. The woman appeared. "This way," she said. "Follow the stairs to the roof."

"I won't forget," Chalibi promised, as he headed for the stairs. They led up past the second floor and onto the flat roof. A three-way firefight was underway. Chalibi heard a loud *boom* as an RPG went off.

It was important to stay low, which Chalibi did, as he hurried across the roof. A neighboring house stood only a few feet away, and the roof was lower, giving the ISIS commander an opportunity to jump the gap.

Chalibi hit hard, rolled, and came up with his pistol in hand. There was no need.

A quick check revealed that the house shared a wall with a small goat shed. It was an easy jump down to the slanted roof, and from there to the ground. Then, after crossing the back yard,

Chalibi took shelter in the ruins of a Christian church. "I'm in the *Kafir* church," Chalibi told his men. "Join me here. We will fight."

***

"It was terrible!" the woman wailed. "They forced their way into my home, ordered me to make tea, and were sitting at my table when the shooting started. That's when one of the men shot the other man! That's him lying on the floor."

Bone took a moment to compare the dead man's countenance to the photo on his phone. "That's Atwi all right," Bone said. "Get a DNA sample, Levy... And search the house for Intel. Where's Olson?"

"On the roof, Sarge... That's where you sent him."

"Okay, good. He'll keep a lid on this shit. What are you waiting for? Move!"

Bone switched frequencies and thumbed his radio. "Centurion, this is Red-Dog-Nine, currently in command of Operation Zebra. Over."

"Roger that," a female voice replied evenly. "Over."

"Have you got my twenty? We're holed up in a house, and taking heavy fire. We need two uglies (Apache gunships) followed by a dust-off. Over."

"Hold one, over."

Machine gun fire raked the front of the house, causing the woman to scream, and Bone to go prone. "Red-Dog, this is Centurion," a male voice said. "We can spare one ugly. But, since there's only one fight, that's good enough. Right? Over."

"Very funny," Bone replied. "What's the ugly's ETA? Over."

"Four-five minutes. Sorry. Over."

Forty-five minutes was a fucking eternity. Bone sighed. "Thanks. Over."

There was a lot of house to defend. But, thanks to Sergeant Olson, the surviving team members were well positioned to keep the tangos at bay.

While making the rounds Bone learned that a Ranger named Carson had been killed, and a man named Tanaka was seriously wounded. *We're bleeding out*, Bone thought. *This is going to be close.*

And it was a close thing. But, thanks to the intramural competition between al-Qaeda and ISIS, neither organization was willing to let the other "win" by successfully overrunning the house.

So, each time one of the two groups was ready to attack, the other intervened, thereby taking pressure off the Americans.

Finally, after seesawing back and forth, the ISIS fighters got the upper hand, and were about to finish the fight, when the AH-64 Apache attack helicopter arrived. "Red-Dog-Nine, this is Banjo with guns, rockets, and missiles. Light some flares. We're incoming from the east. Over."

"This is Red-Dog actual," Bone replied, as a Ranger lit a flare. "Roger that, and welcome to the party. Watch out for RPGs. The tangos are all around us. Over."

"*Were* all around you," Banjo responded, as his copilot/gunner fired a salvo of Hydra 70 rockets from the ugly's hardpoints. Bright red explosions marched through the village, sparing only the house the Rangers had taken refuge in, and those adjacent to it.

RPGs streaked upwards. And the "dumb" weapons were a real threat because, unlike SAMs (surface-to-air missiles), RPGs couldn't be drawn off target by flares or chaff.

But it required a great deal of courage and skill to standup, aim a launcher at the sky, and hit a moving target. Fortunately, Banjo was able to finish his run untouched, turn, and start another run.

By that time Olson's sharpshooters had accounted for two of the RPG gunners, thus reducing the antiaircraft fire by half.

And, as Banjo fired the chain gun mounted between the aircraft's landing gear, 30mm shells probed the fiery wreckage left in the wake of the first attack.

"They're running like rabbits," Banjo observed. "I'll stay on station until the Crashhawk arrives. Over."

Bone knew that Blackhawk helicopters were often referred to as "Crashhawks" due to their tendency to crash for no particular reason. A real morale builder for the men on the ground. "Roger that," Bone replied. "Tango Mike (many thanks). Over."

Banjo was correct insofar as Bone could tell. The hajis had left.

So, with three Rangers to help him, Bone went out to find Lieutenant Sully and Private Carson. Their bodies lay where they'd fallen. With the care and respect due to fallen comrades, each body was loaded onto a blanket, and carried to the roof of the dwelling the Rangers had fought so hard to defend.

The Blackhawk arrived fifteen minutes later. The pilot followed the orange smoke in and landed on the roof. The trip to Tabqa was delightfully uneventful.

Once on the ground the Rangers were separated, put through individual debriefings, and released. "You did a good job," the captain in charge of Bone's hotwash told him. "I'm sorry about Lieutenant Sully. We all are. The Doc tells me that Tanaka will make it."

Bone was hungry and went to the DFAC the way he was, which was to say dirty and smelly. That sort of behavior was frowned on by some. But none of the people present had the stripes or the balls to approach the grim looking master sergeant and chew him out.

After eating his fill Bone made his way back to the company area, paused to shed his filthy uniform, and made his way to the showers. Then, back in his slot, it was time to check email. There were lots of them, but Bone read Yolanda's first:

"Hi Hon,

I hope things are going well over there.

The kids are fine, your mom says, 'Hi,' and the weather is sunny.

I do have some bad news tho—I missed three payments on the boat. We have to eat you know... And the bank took it back.

Later, when things improve, we'll buy another one.

Love, Yo."

Bone felt a sense of despair. "Later, when things improve..." When would that be? And why hadn't she told him about the missed payments? So, he wouldn't worry? Or because the news would piss him off?

Bone closed the lid. Should he call her? No. That would lead to a fight.

He went to bed. Sleep came quickly. But so did the dreams. And all of them were bad.

CHAPTER THREE

Superbase Tabqa, Syria

After three days of sleeping in, replying to interrogatories about the crash, and doing laundry, Soto was summoned to company headquarters for a meeting with Major Albro.

The meeting was scheduled for 0800. Albro arrived at 0823. Soto stood, and Albro said, "As you were. Sorry I'm late. The colonel's staff meeting ran long. Please join me in my office."

Soto could tell that something was up, but *what?*

Once inside the office Albro indicated a chair. "Take a load off. I have some news for you. Two CH-47Fs arrived."

Though not the latest models, the 47Fs were newer than the D lost in the crash, and Soto would welcome the additional horsepower, avionics and reduced maintenance.

It was as if Albro could read her mind. He smiled thinly. "Nope, no 47F for you!

"'Dead Stick Soto.' That's what the other pilots call you. And it would be nice to keep the new birds airworthy for a while. So, I'm going to give you another 47D. And a new assignment to go with it."

An enormous map of Syria occupied most of one wall, and Albro went over to point at a yellow pushpin. "This is FOB (Forward Operating Base) Smiley. You're going to ferry food, ammo, and personnel in—and take casualties out.

"That will consume most of your time and energy. But I'm going to send odd jobs your way every now and then too, so you don't get bored."

The statement seemed to demand a response so Soto nodded. "That sounds like fun, sir. Thanks."

Albro frowned. "Was that sarcasm, Captain?"

"No, sir," Soto lied. "I like to fly that's all."

Albro clearly had doubts, but wasn't willing to challenge her. "Good. Dismissed."

Soto found Jonny Lee where she expected to find him, which was lifting weights. He completed an overhead press and let the barbell fall to the mat. "Hey, Marie... What's up?"

"We have a new ride. Well, not a *new* ride, but a new *old* ride. And they have us down for a mission at 1400."

"Awesome. I'll gear up and meet you at the bird. Where is it?"

"In Revetment 7. Her tail number is 98-02022. They call her the '*Double Deuce.*' Find Alvarez if you can."

"I'm on it," Lee replied. "We'll meet you there."

A Black Hawk clattered overhead as Soto made her way to the row of revetments where the company's helicopters were parked. Those on base anyway, since most were out on missions, leaving only the machines slotted for night trips—or awaiting repairs.

The protective walls consisted of neatly stacked HESCO bastions, which were made of wire mesh, equipped with fabric liners, and filled with whatever was handy. Dirt and rocks in this case.

The HESCOs wouldn't protect the helos from mortar rounds, bombs, or missiles. But they were proof against small arms fire and adjacent explosions. And that was a lot better than nothing. When Soto arrived at slot seven, she stopped to look before circling the aircraft.

To the untrained eye the *Double Deuce* would look like every other Chinook 47D. But Soto saw things others wouldn't notice:

The fact that the port engine was newer than the starboard engine for example. Patches where bullets had penetrated the hull. And a section of new paint on the fuel tank fairing.

Soto had an almost sensual love of aircraft. She ran a hand across the faded likeness of two playing cards painted on the nose, paused to eyeball a dent, and spent a minute examining each set of landing gear.

The ship had flaws. But that was to be expected. The rear ramp was down. Soto followed it up and into the Chinook's cargo bay. It was empty at the moment. But it wouldn't be long before forklifts arrived towing trailers loaded with food, ammo, and anything else the FOB requested. Then the long narrow space would be loaded with up to 26,000 pounds of cargo.

Three machine guns were mounted aft of the cockpit. One at the crew door on the starboard side, one window-mounted weapon on the port side, and a third near the cargo ramp. *Gunners*, Soto thought. *Alvarez will take care of that.*

From there Soto entered the cockpit. Stale sweat was the overriding smell, with hints of window cleaner, stale food, flatulence, oil, hydraulic fluid, and fuel.

The combination of odors was not only something Soto come to like, but served as an olfactory record of what sort of missions the aircraft had flown lately. Which, judging from the lingering smell, had something to do with diesel engines.

Both of the pilot seats were not only worn, but dirty and saggy. The left seat, where the aircraft commander normally sat, was pushed way back—suggesting that the most recent occupant was a tall man. Soto sat down and went to work adjusting it to her five-foot, seven-inch frame.

Occasionally aircraft commanders would sit in the right seat while flying alone, because helicopters were less stable than airplanes, and helo pilots liked to keep a firm grip on the all-important cyclic stick, which was clutched in his or her right hand.

That kept the pilot's left hand free to manipulate the thrust lever, which controlled the blades' pitch angle, and to flip switches or turn knobs on the center console.

"So, whaddya think?" Lee inquired as he dropped into the righthand seat.

"I like her," Soto replied. "But that could change. Did you find Alvarez?"

"Yup. She was getting her hair cut."

"Did you ask about gunners?"

"That's affirmative. Al's going to find out if we can keep the people already assigned."

"That would be good," Soto commented. "Okay, enough screwing around. Let's check everything we can. Logs, the whole nine yards."

There wasn't enough time for a rivet-by-rivet examination of the fuselage and landing gear, but the pilots did the best they could, and passed a list of minor fixes on to Alvarez.

Meanwhile loading got underway, and Alvarez was everywhere, poking and prodding to make sure that the overall load was balanced and that the cargo would come off the *Double Deuce* in what the crew chief considered to be the correct sequence. And God help anyone who tried to shirk, scam, or bully her.

Thanks to Alvarez the final crate went aboard at 1330, giving Soto and Lee plenty of time to run through the preflight checks, check clearances, and talk to the tower. The *Double Deuce* lifted off the tarmac at 1402.

The first task was to make the journey from Revetment 7 to Helipad 2. And that was no small task for an aircraft that was nearly 100 feet long and 60 feet wide—with the blades turning. When Soto pulled up on the thrust lever, and pushed forward on the cyclic, the Chinook began to move. As she ground taxied to Helipad 2, Soto could feel the way the helicopter was loaded, and adjust her expectations accordingly.

Then after receiving a takeoff clearance from the tower, Soto brought the Chinook to a hover, checked the power level for each engine, confirmed that they were identical and tipped the nose down.

Using her left hand, Soto increased thrust, but not by much. The combination sent the *Double Deuce* skimming over the tarmac and into forward flight.

Then Soto went about the critical task of departing from a base with two very active runways. A jet flashed past the Chinook on the right and was gone in seconds leaving a trail of black smoke. Soto expected the resulting turbulence and made the necessary adjustments.

The *Double Deuce* cleared the airport less than a minute later and turned onto the course that would take them to FOB Smiley. "Smiley," Lee said. "Why 'Smiley?'"

"Lieutenant Smiley was killed during the first attack on the base," Soto replied. "From what I heard at HQ, the place is a real bullet magnet. Let's hope that the hajis are taking the day off."

FOB Smiley was located one hundred and thirty-five miles to the southeast, which meant it would take the *Double Deuce* roughly an hour to get there without pushing it.

It wasn't long before the Chinook was flying at 8,000 feet, an altitude above the reach of shoulder fired missiles, and well out of range of the Iranian Khordad 15 air defense systems located in central Iraq.

Soto knew Lee was eager to fly the Chinook, even if there wasn't much to do. So, she surrendered the controls to him, waited for the obligatory "I have it," and pretended to take a nap. Except the fake nap turned into a *real* nap. And lasted until Lee woke her.

"We're ten minutes out, Marie... I can see the base in the distance."

Soto opened her eyes and sat up straight. Lee was correct. FOB Smiley was located at the foot of a rock pinnacle too pointy for more than a couple of people to stand on. A supersized American flag flew from it and clearly served as a brightly colored "fuck you" for all the tangos in the hood.

And, as Soto accepted control, she could see the HESCO containers that defined the rectangular perimeter. Each corner of the compound was marked by a sandbagged observation tower. The single ECP (Entry Control Point) was protected by blast mitigation structures, and weapons emplacements. All of which was SOP.

What *wasn't* SOP, and was a reason for both pilots to laugh, was the huge smiley face located inside the wire. It had two boulders for eyes, plus a curved row of large rocks to represent a mouth, all painted bright white. A nice way to welcome incoming helicopters and ground support planes.

Judging from the smoke produced by a trash fire, the wind was blowing from the west. Something Soto would take into account as she landed.

Lee was on the horn with a guy who identified himself as Bravo-One-Two, and invited the pilots to "Come on down."

It was a routine landing. The *Double Deuce* threw a black shadow onto the LZ, and dust swirled, as the ground came up to meet them. There was a solid thump when the gear touched down.

Then it was time to run all of the checklist procedures before releasing her harness, putting her helmet aside, and following Lee through the right side door to deass the aircraft. If their job was over for the moment, Alvarez was just getting started, as a forklift prepared to climb the ramp.

A captain and an E-6 were standing about fifty feet away. The officer waved them over.

"Welcome to FOB Smiley! I'm Captain Hickok, aka Bravo-One-Two. And this is Sergeant Wilkins. She's in charge of logistics."

Soto introduced herself as they shook hands. "And this is Lieutenant Lee. So, if you don't mind my asking, what the hell are you doing out here?"

Hickok produced a boyish grin. "That's a good question. We ask it all the time. The official answer is to control the road that leads east to Iraq, which is a joke, because it would take a full battalion to do that.

"The second reason for our presence is to search for and recover downed pilots. And we're pretty good at that. Three for three so far.

"And, we suspect that the third mission is to give the tangos something to attack, so they leave other targets alone. They don't say that, mind you... But that's what we suspect."

Soto was surprised by the extent of Hickok's honesty. "How are you going to make major if you tell the truth all the time?"

Hickok laughed. "We don't worry about promotions out here. Our goal is to stay alive. And you guys are a key part of that. Water, ammo, fuel and food. That's what keeps us going. So, thank you."

"You're welcome," Soto replied, as fuel flowed from a bladder on the *Double Deuce* to one on the ground.

Orders were shouted as the forklift completed another trip. Wilkins was holding a stopwatch. "We're running twenty seconds late, sir. I'm going to have a word with the crew once this evolution is over."

Soto turned to Hickok. He nodded. "We time each turnaround. Our goal is to unload your bird in fifteen minutes. Who knows? Getting you in and out quickly could make an important difference someday."

Soto was impressed and grateful. It would be bad enough to land under fire, and sure death to stay for long, so the fifteen-minute limit could save lives. Hers among them.

The trip back to Superbase Tabqa was delightfully uneventful. And Soto was looking forward to taking the day off, as she descended to a hover, and scooted over the tarmac to Revetment 7. A fueler arrived a few minutes later. That was SOP to ensure that all aircraft were mission ready.

Soto was about to head for her hootch when a private arrived on a motor scooter. "Captain Soto?"

"That's me."

"I have a message for you ma'am, from Major Albro. Please sign my log."

A sheet of paper was clamped to a clipboard, and Soto scribbled her name into the box adjacent to her name.

"Here you go," the private said, as he gave her a sealed envelope. The scooter backfired as he drove away. The note was handwritten: "My office 1800 for a meeting. Maj. Albro."

Soto glanced at her watch. Shit. She had fifteen minutes to get there. Fortunately, Soto was able to flag down a security vehicle and hitch a ride.

The fact that Soto was three minutes late arriving in Albro's office earned her a frown. But others were present so Albro let the ass chewing slide. "Gentlemen, this is Captain Soto. Marie, I'd like you to meet Oscar Polat, and Master Sergeant Felix Bone.

"Mr. Polat is employed by Turkey's National Intelligence Organization, and Sergeant Bone is on detached duty from the Ranger battalion here at Tabqa."

Polat was thirty something, with a head of thick black hair, and fashionable stubble. And, judging from the look in his eyes, the Turk was busy removing Soto's clothes.

He came forward to shake hands. The accent was American. "You put my nation to shame, Major Albro. We have female pilots in the military, but none so beautiful."

Albro frowned. "Let's keep this professional. Commentary about Captain Soto's appearance isn't appropriate."

"Of course. It isn't," Polat said, as he continued to hold Soto's hand. "And that's why I won't mention her blue eyes."

The then Turk let go, which gave Bone the opportunity to shake Soto's hand. "It's a pleasure to meet you ma'am." And with that the Ranger returned to his seat.

"Alright," Albro said. "Mr. Polat, perhaps you'd be so kind as to describe the mission that you and the sergeant were ordered to carry out?"

***

Polat nodded. Would it be necessary to tell the *Amerikalis* the truth at some point? Maybe, and maybe not. In the meantime, his cover story would be enough.

"It's quite simple actually," Polat told them. "ISIS is holding one of our army officers hostage. My mission is to find the poor bastard and rescue him.

"I'm pleased to say that, thanks to your National Reconnaissance Office (NRO), we have what we believe to be Colonel Kaya's location."

***

Bone didn't like working for a Turk. Not one little bit. Not because Turks were Turks, but because they were iffy allies, who were often more focused on killing Kurds than Iranians. Take the Brits for example. You could count on them. But the Turks? Not so much. He cleared his throat. "When do we go in?"

***

"Tomorrow night," Polat replied. "The location is about a hundred and sixty miles northeast of here. We'll fly in, offload two HMMWVs (High Mobility Multipurpose Wheeled Vehicles) and take care of business. No fuss, no muss."

***

Bone had his doubts. What was it Lieutenant Sully said, just before the tangos killed him? "In, grab, and go ... Then back to base for a nap. Nothing to it."

Did Captain Soto buy it? He couldn't tell. Her face was impossible to read. Polat was right about one thing though—the woman was hot.

That reminded Bone of Yolanda. Some collection guy had been calling her day and night. Why wasn't the bastard out fighting for his country? Asshole.

***

Soto didn't like Polat. Not even a little bit. As for Sergeant Bone, time would tell. Based on appearances he looked like a real badass. But looks could be, and often were, deceiving. She cleared her throat. "You mentioned two Humvees. Do you plan to leave a security force behind? To guard the bird?"

***

"I'll take that one," Albro said. "We have detailed reconnaissance photos of the spot where you'll put down. The nearest village is ten miles away. So, no, the planners don't think you'll need a squad of gun slingers. But, if something unexpected happens, you can take off and land at extraction point two."

***

Unless they blow my ass out of the air with an RPG, Soto thought cynically. But there was no point in saying that, so she didn't.

The meeting broke up a few minutes later. Soto made a date with Bone to review the latest Intel in the morning, and returned to her slot to log some serious rack time, which she did.

After breakfast Soto briefed her crew on the mission, and concluded her comments with a warning. "Once the Humvees leave, we'll be on our own. Make sure we have bipods for the machine guns, lots of 40 mike mike for the launchers, and full-on E&E (Escape & Evade) packs. Oh, and check your night vision gear. You're going to need it. Crew call is one hour prior to take-off at 0100."

Subsequent to that Soto met Sergeant Bone at the underground Intel center on the west side of the airbase. They had to pass through two layers of security before arriving in front of a reception desk where an air force tech sergeant consulted her computer, confirmed their appointment, and sent them to a room where Senior Airman Eason was waiting.

He was pleasant, professional, and boring. The LZ that the planners had chosen was partially protected by a horseshoe shaped quarry. A dirt driveway led to a paved road, which led to a hamlet named Tal-Al ward.

According to Eason, a hostage was being held at what had been a commercial sugar beet farm prior to the civil war, but was currently occupied by ISIS fighters.

"You said '*a*' hostage, rather than *the* hostage," Soto observed. "Was that intentional?"

"Yes," Eason replied matter of factly. "*We*, meaning Allied intelligence, don't know who it is. But based on aerial photography, we know that a person wearing a hood was escorted into 'Building A.'"

"However," Eason continued, "the Turks claim to have humint (human intelligence) that indicates the hostage is a colonel named Kaya. All we have is their word for that though— because they refuse to share anything that might compromise their sources and methods. And, if our positions were reversed, we would do the same thing."

Soto looked at Bone and was fairly sure that he was thinking the same thing she was. The hostage could be anybody. Colonel Kaya? Maybe. Or someone else.

***

Bone focused his attention to the blowup on a wall screen. "Building A" was somewhat separated from the other structures, thank God. Would it be best to park the vehicles and sneak in? Or arrive with guns blazing? Each approach had advantages.

But one thing is for fucking sure, Bone decided. *I'm going to make the call. And if the Turk doesn't like it, he can kiss my ass.*

***

Bone and his team of eight Rangers boarded the *Double Deuce* at 1230. Soto and Lee ran their checklists and started the engines at 1245. Polat arrived sixteen minutes late, came forward, and tried to claim the fold down observer's seat in the cockpit companionway.

That pissed Soto off. "I'm sorry, Mr. Polat. But civilians aren't allowed in the cockpit. Please return to the cargo area. Thank you."

"How can I give orders from back there?" Polat wanted to know.

"I don't need orders," Soto replied. "Please leave the cockpit."

Polat said something in Turkish, which Soto assumed to be a swear word, and left. The pilots turned the cockpit lights off to prevent the ambient lighting from interfering with their NVG devices.

The Chinook took off three minutes later. The *Double Deuce* was doing one-seventy, which meant the Rangers would be on the ground in less than an hour.

Once clear of the superbase, there wasn't much to see other than large swathes of black, sprinkled with clusters of diamond-bright lights where the power was on.

The number of lights continued to dwindle until darkness cloaked the land. *Both literally and metaphorically,* Soto decided, as flashes appeared off the southeast. A battle was being fought for *what?* A hill? A fortification? A bridge? There were lots of possibilities.

As the distance to the LZ closed both pilots kept a sharp lookout for headlights, campfires, and anything else that might suggest that tangos were lying in wait for them.

But there weren't any. And, while that didn't necessarily mean it was safe to land, Soto felt an increased sense of confidence. "Strap in. Gunners will standby. We're four from dirt."

The U-shaped rock quarry was plain to see, and there was a flat area at the center of it. Soto brought the Chinook to a hover and let the helicopter down.

The gear on the port side made contact first, indicating the way the ground sloped, but they were down. And what had been Soto's helicopter now belonged to Alvarez.

The crew chief wasn't shy. Orders flew, tiedowns were released, and engines started. The roll-off took place five minutes later.

Both Humvees were heavily armed, one with a "Ma Deuce" .50 caliber machine gun, and the other with a Mk 19 grenade launcher.

Sergeant Bone, Polat, and three rangers occupied the lead vic, with Sergeant Olson and the rest of the team in the second. Engines roared and gravel sprayed as the Humvees departed.

Suddenly Soto, Lee, Alvarez and the gunners were all alone. Soto hoped so anyway. Because the "bird" was a huge sitting duck. The long wait began.

***

At his insistence Polat was seated up front next to Corporal Levy, who was driving. And that was fine with Bone, who was seated behind Polat, and ready to shoot the Turk in the head if that seemed necessary. "What happens in Syria, stays in Syria." That's the way Private Hiro put it. And Bone agreed.

The target was about five miles from the LZ. Levy had instructions to stop half a mile out, so that Bone and a Ranger named Tyson could advance on foot, and neutralize sentries if any.

Stars blazed above, the air was chilly, and Bone could see his breath. *Here I go again*, he thought. *Is this the one? Or, will I croak the way Patton did, from a blood clot? Focus, asshole. Or you'll trip over a rock and bust your head open.*

There were no sounds other than the rasp of Bone's breathing, the occasional rattle of a displaced stone, and the distant *pop, pop, pop* of a semiauto firing. Connected? No. Sound travels in the desert.

Bone could discern the shapes of farm buildings by then, what remained of them anyway, but no sentries. Were the hajis sloppy? Perhaps. Or well hidden.

The two men approached the farm in a series of short dashes. Run, pause, and scan. Run, pause, and scan. Nothing.

They arrived at a wall, followed it to a sagging gate, and slipped through. Lights? Nope.

Building A was a scant fifty feet away.

Bone advanced, M4 at the ready, head swiveling from side to side. The front door was open. That, more than anything else, served to confirm Bone's growing suspicion. Assuming the tangos had been there, they weren't anymore. He turned to Tyson. "Watch for IEDs." The Ranger nodded.

The Rangers entered with their tac lights on, swept the interior for targets, and came up empty. Bone thumbed his radio. "This is nine. The farm appears to be deserted. But you never know, so keep 'em peeled. Bring the vehicles forward, and keep the heavy stuff manned. Over."

The Humvees arrived two minutes later and took up defensive positions outside. Polat entered the building with a flashlight in one hand and a pistol in the other. There was no mistaking how he felt. "Shit! Shit! Shit! They left."

"That's how it looks," Bone agreed. "If they were here to begin with."

Polat crossed the room to a metal stove, where he paused to look for tripwires, before opening the door. Hinges squealed and there, glowing within, were red embers. "They were here alright," the Turk grated. "Search all the buildings. If you find something take it. I'll go through it later."

***

There was lots of trash of the kind that undisciplined soldiers leave behind. Empty cans, water bottles, and yes—candy wrappers. One of them caught Polat's eye. He bent to pick it up. The image of a wide-eyed little girl stared at him, with the partially ripped word "Alenka" down below the picture.

Polat knew those chocolate bars, and had eaten at least a dozen of them while stationed at the Turkish embassy in Moscow. *She was here*, Polat thought, as he stuffed the wrapper into a pocket. *Who else would have such a wrapper?*

The feeling of elation was short lived. Now the long tedious task of finding Hala Omar would start all over again.

***

A rock quarry near Tal-Al ward, Syria

Soto checked her watch for the umpteenth time. The ground party had been gone for half an hour. There had been no radio contact. Was that a good thing? Or, a bad thing?

Soto's thoughts were interrupted by Corporal Morales. "Mo" was a gunner, and stationed up on the cliff wall, with a good view of the paved road. "I see headlights, ma'am… One, two, three, four, five, six sets. All headed our way. Over."

Soto felt a stab of fear. What the hell? Was Mo looking at a column of incoming gun trucks? She thumbed her radio. "ETA? Over."

"Five minutes max. Over."

A gunfight was out of the question. Could she load the *Double Deuce*, and haul ass?

Nope. Not enough time. "Grab you E&E bags and form on Mo everybody… Hurry! Over."

There was a mad dash to grab bags and follow Alvarez over to the trail that led up to the ledge where Mo was glassing the highway.

Soto didn't need binoculars. The lights were plain to see. And they were stacked, meaning closed up, like cars in a presidential motorcade. Was that what she was seeing? A VIP? Traveling from one location to another under the cover of darkness?

That possibility was preferable to a convoy of gun trucks, but would be just as disastrous, if a sharp-eyed bodyguard spotted the Chinook. Then the brakes would come on, armed men would pour out of the vehicles, and swarm the *Deuce*.

Soto turned to Mo. "Where does this trail lead?"

"Up and out ma'am."

"Thank God for that. Get ready to take the point if we're forced to exfil."

"Roger that," the gunner replied. "But let's shoot the shit out of the bird *and* the tangos before we leave."

Soto realized that Morales was right. His M60 machine gun was sitting on a bipod and positioned to sweep the quarry below. "Good idea Mo... But stay off the bird unless the situation is hopeless."

"Can do," Morales replied. "I'll make those mother fuckers pay. Sorry, ma'am. I meant terrorists."

Soto laughed in spite of her fears, as the combined roar of engines was heard and the first vehicle approached. Its headlights probed the darkness ahead as it passed the entrance to the quarry and kept on going. The second vehicle was no more than fifteen feet back. And Soto figured the driver was focused on maintaining the tight interval rather than sightseeing. It passed too. As did the rest.

Finally, when the entire convoy was safely past, Soto realized that she'd been holding her breath, and let it out. "Okay, people... That was fun."

"I should have packed some extra skivvies," a gunner named Beeley said. Everyone laughed.

"Return to your original posts," Soto ordered. "And maintain situational awareness."

Bone called in five minutes later. "Wizard, this is Red-Dog-Nine. We came up empty. We are fifteen from your twenty. Over."

Soto felt a tremendous sense of relief. Now all she had to do was get back to base, grab some shut eye, and put the mission behind her. The worst was over.

CHAPTER FOUR

Northern Syria

After days spent locked in a filthy room, Hala Omar had been loaded into a van bound for what Commander Chalibi said would be "A more secure location."

For him perhaps, but not for her. She was on a journey from one hell, to another hell, sandwiched in between two smelly fighters.

Every now and then one of them would place a hand on a thigh. She would slap it and the men would laugh. Commander Chalibi included.

He was seated up front next to the driver, eating pine nuts out of a plastic bag, while an imam preached over the radio.

Hala knew it was her fault but felt sorry for herself anyway. It all began when she was sixteen. That was the year she and a team of girl gymnasts traveled to Moscow for a competition. They had no chance of winning of course, but saw the trip as a lark, as did their coaches.

During their time in Moscow the girls were introduced to many important people, including a Deputy Prime Minister named Toplin, who took a particular interest in Hala. Even going so far as to send her flowers the following day. An embarrassment the other girls would never let her forget.

And that was that, until six years later when Hala, as a foreign correspondent for Al-ikhbariah-Syria, the state-run news channel, was sent to Moscow. Shortly after her arrival Hala was invited to a cocktail party where she encountered Toplin for a second time.

He was even more important by then. A rising star and a possible successor to the president. Toplin was married but invited Hala to a private dinner anyway. And she acceded.

That was the beginning of what turned out to be a slippery slope. Toplin showered Hala with gifts, installed her in a fancy apartment, and gave her what every reporter wants most: access. To him, yes, and to others as well, which led to a series of noteworthy scoops. One of her stories ran in the *New York Times*.

But access came at a price. And Hala paid. First with her virginity, next with her integrity, and ultimately a loss of self-respect.

Then China started the war, Russia followed, and Toplin took over when the previous president died. Hala expected the politician to replace her with someone younger, *hoped* Toplin would replace her with someone younger, but he didn't.

"Why should I?" Toplin replied when asked. "You know my habits." Which was as close as Toplin came to expressing his attachment to her.

So, when the letter arrived from Hala's mother, informing her that her father was ill, and likely to die, Hala asked Toplin for permission to go home. He refused. "It's far too dangerous for you to visit Syria," he said. And that was that.

Or would have been if Hala hadn't decided to rebel. She had money saved up from her pay, plus an allowance from Toplin. And like any good reporter, Hala had a long list of contacts. One of them was a so called "guide," otherwise referred to as a "human smuggler."

His name was Dimitri Grankin. And, true to his word, Grankin transported Hala to Georgia, and from there to Turkey. That's where he sold her. Not to a sex trafficker, but to a representative of ISIS, who understood Hala's value as a hostage.

What would Toplin give in return for his mistress? Money? Weapons? Either would be satisfactory.

Hala was drugged in Turkey, and awoke in Syria, only to discover that she was Commander Chalabi's prisoner. *But not forever*, Hala decided. *My chance will come.*

***

Superbase Tabqa, Syria

Two days had passed since the failed mission, and Soto had been busy doing what helicopter pilots do, which is to fly helicopters. Now, after a routine flight to FOB Smiley, and a short hop to Sughra, Soto was standing in front of Albro's desk. Other pilots were invited to sit down. That was the rumor anyway.

"I need a pilot," Albro told her. "Lieutenant Brody was my first choice. But he's ill. So, I'm turning to you. Have you heard of the Citadel?"

All of the helo pilots at Tabqa knew about the Citadel. It was located to the southeast, almost out of range, and was subject to around the clock attacks from Iranian backed militias.

But that wasn't the hardest part of it. The Citadel had been used as a fortress for at least two thousand years, attacked hundreds of times, and had never fallen, according to local legends.

That was because there was no way to access the top of the four-hundred-foot-tall column of rock. Other than the two-donkey wide path that wound its way up to the maze of rooms officially known as FOB Foxtrot.

So, in order to deliver supplies, a Chinook pilot had to perform what was known as a "pinnacle landing" on a ledge located at the three-hundred and fifteen-foot level.

That meant maintaining a hover, while backing up to the point where the rear wheels came into contact with the ledge, and holding that position while the helo's cargo came off.

"Yes, sir," Soto replied. "I've heard of it."

Albro leaned back in his chair. It squeaked. "So, do you think Dead Stick Soto can do the job without crashing another helicopter?"

Soto had performed two pinnacle landings, both during training. And didn't want to perform another. But there was only one answer she could give. "Yes, sir."

"Okay then," Albro said. "Swing by the flight control office (FCO) for a briefing. The folks at The Citadel are expecting you to arrive at 1500. Dismissed."

Lee was in the DFAC having breakfast, and Alvarez was on a run. Both were carrying radios and agreed to meet Soto at the FCO.

Soto arrived first and was eyeballing a wall map when Lee arrived. "Here's where we're headed," Soto said, as she touched a red push pin. "The Citadel."

"Say it ain't true," Lee said. "I thought Backwards Brody owned that shit."

"He's sick," Soto explained. "And Albro chose us."

"Because we're expendable," Lee said.

"Maybe," Soto allowed. "But the helicopter isn't."

Alvarez entered the office. She was dressed in running gear and a shoulder holster. "What's up?"

Soto told her. "No problem," Alvarez said confidently. "The *Double Deuce* has the best pilots in the company. We can land anywhere, and we can do it ass backwards. Feel free to quote me on that."

"Thanks, Chief," Soto said with a smile. "Let's get our butts in gear."

It took two hours to take delivery on the supplies for FOB Foxtrot and load them properly. Which was to say, the way Alvarez wanted. "We need to distribute the load evenly," she insisted. "So, it'll be easier for the pilots to keep the bird steady."

Now, with a belly full of food, ammo and fuel, the *Double Deuce* was fifteen out from The Citadel, and Soto had butterflies in her stomach.

"Shit," Lee said, as the helicopter started to descend. "Some asshole or group of assholes are shooting at us."

Soto heard a series of pings as groundfire hit the fuselage. The Chinook was an enormous target. And that's where luck entered the equation. She could fire flares to pull a missile away. But bullets? Nope. All she could do was keep flying, and hope for the best.

Her gunners could respond however, and did, doing the best they could to suppress the groundfire.

The Citadel was an imposing tower of granite left standing after the relatively soft sedimentary rock surrounding it had worn away. Window-like openings were visible here and there, as were impact craters, and sections of a winding trail.

"Wizard, this is Foxtrot-Three. Be advised that it's hot as hell, we have an intermittent breeze from the west, and the usual light to moderate groundfire. Over."

Lee was handling the comms which left Soto free to fly. "Roger that, Foxtrot-Three.

"We have four cases of beer onboard, so you might want to suppress that groundfire if you're feeling thirsty. Standby... We're coming in ass first. Over."

Foxtrot-Three knew that of course. And could see it as Soto brought the helicopter to a hover, turning the behemoth to face away from the tower's west side, prior to backing up.

"Chief?" Soto inquired. "Clear left? Clear right?"

Alvarez was standing in the open hatch. She looked left and right. "You're clear," Alvarez responded. "But we're off target. Slide right until I say 'stop.'"

Soto did as she was told. "Okay," Alvarez said, "Stop! You're looking good. Back her up."

That was Soto's cue to add aft cyclic. Slowly, but surely, the *Double Deuce* backed up until the rear wheels were hovering four feet above the rock ledge. "Stop!" Alvarez instructed. "Now bring her down. Four, three, two, one, touchdown. Perfect!"

The task of pulling tons of supplies off the helicopter began seconds later. Soto's job was to keep the *Double Deuce* exactly where she was, butt down on the ledge, with her nose pointed west.

Even though Alverez had done her best to load the Chinook evenly, Soto could feel slight changes as pallets came off, and had to make tiny adjustments as a result.

Then there was the intermittent wind that threatened to push the helicopter back against the spire, unless Soto reduced power, so as to lower the helicopter's nose while the wind tried to lift it up.

Finally, after what seemed like an hour, but was actually no more than twenty minutes, Alvarez gave the all-clear. "The last package is off, ma'am... You are clear left and right."

Soto released a sigh of relief as she brought the Chinook up off the ledge and forward. Then it was a simple matter to add power and climb as more bullets pinged the hull. "Wizard, this is Foxtrot-Three. You *are* a Wizard! Thanks for the beer. Over."

"You're welcome," Soto said. "Anytime. Over."

"We made it," Lee said, as they left the ground fire behind.

"Yeah," Soto agreed. "Do you feel like flying?"

Lee smiled. "You know I would. I have the aircraft."

Soto took her hands off the flight controls. They were shaking. She managed to conceal them by folding her arms. Soto didn't know what was wrong with Backwards Brody, but was hoping for a speedy recovery.

***

The village of Sur-Na Syria

Hala Omar was being held in the village of Sur-Na in northwestern Syria, an area that had recently been overrun by ISIS *again*. The first time having been ten years earlier, before Kurdish forces, allied with a Sunni militia group, kicked them out.

And according to Adra, the woman who had been ordered to take Hala in, the situation in the village was bad. Very bad.

It was late afternoon, two guards were lurking outside the house, and the women were conversing in whispers. Adra's willingness to talk about the situation in Sur-Na stemmed from the fact that she recognized the reporter right away, and even remembered Hala's days as a gymnast.

"I'm so sorry you're here," Adra whispered, as she leaned forward over the table. "We are living in hell. My husband prefers to shave each day. Now he has to wear a beard, and I have to cover my face in public.

"Our schools are closed, the medical clinic is closed, and the houses that belonged to Sunnis were seized.

"But that isn't the worst of it," Adra added. "The *Shaitan* (devils) whip people for eating during Ramadan, and last week a man and a woman were executed for committing adultery.

"Plus, according to the rumors, seven hundred members of the *Egaidat* tribe were slaughtered when they refused to comply with Sharia law. We live in fear."

Hala knew that was true. She was allowed one walk per day, face covered, with a Kalashnikov toting guard following behind her.

The fear Adra referred to was visible in the way people refused to meet her gaze, hurried to complete their errands, and crossed the street to avoid contact with ISIS fighters.

Meanwhile, Sharia imams were not only calling people to prayer five times a day from the local minaret, but bleating propaganda in between.

The man in charge of all that was Hala's captor Commander Chalibi who, through his second in command Ferran Mostafa, ruled with an iron fist. And insisted on having dinner with her each evening.

For that reason, Hala was expected to be ready just after the *Maghrib* prayer at sunset, when she arrived home from the mosque. The ritual always started the same way, which was with a loud series of knocks on the front door.

Then clad in black from head to toe, Hala would be escorted to what had once been a Sunni family's house, where she would climb a flight of stairs to the flat roof. A well-set table would be waiting for her, along with a glass of iced tea, which in a community with limited electricity was a luxury.

Chalibi would typically arrive ten or fifteen minutes later. A habit that bothered Hala not at all. She was perfectly content to enjoy the sunset, and watch the swallows perform their daily ballet, as the stars appeared.

On that particular evening Chalibi was twenty minutes late, and arrived without an apology. "There's my little whore, delectable as always, just waiting to be fucked.

"I'm sorry to say that negotiations are painfully slow. In fact, it isn't clear if President Toplin knows about your present circumstances, or cares. Perhaps your skills are lacking and he has no reason to miss you."

That was typical of Chalibi. He liked to talk. And Hala knew how to play him.

"What are you asking for?" Hala inquired, as their dinners arrived. "Perhaps it's too much."

"Not so," Chalibi insisted, as he tucked into a serving of chicken *freekeh*. "All we want is one million U.S. A pittance as far as Toplin is concerned. Did you know that he's a billionaire? With money hidden in Allied countries?"

"That's what they say," Hala allowed noncommittally.

"Maybe Toplin's wife is the problem," Chalibi speculated. "Maybe she knows about our demand and wants you dead."

"Anything is possible," Hala allowed. "But that seems unlikely. No one in their right mind would tell her."

Chalibi nodded. "Right. Toplin wouldn't like that. So, whore, you sold yourself to Toplin. Why not *me?* I will pay you one American dollar."

The accusation was true. And it hurt. *But that's in the past*, Hala thought. *I will never sell myself again.* "No," Hala said. "Not for a dollar. Not for any amount."

Chalibi was visibly angry. Because of her defiance? Because he took her refusal personally? Both, Hala decided.

Fortunately, the hot tea arrived at that moment along with two desserts. The Yazidi slave girl was about to pour when Hala intervened. "Please allow me to do that."

Then she rose to come around and pour Chalabi's tea. The act of subservience was enough to calm him. *For the moment,* Hala thought as she poured. *But only for the moment.*

***

Superbase Tabqa, Syria

Major Albro liked to hold what he called "scrums," by which he meant meetings where pilots could discuss whatever was on their minds. A good idea in Soto's opinion, except that Albro preferred to run his mouth rather than listen.

That's why Soto chose to sit in the back row and surreptitiously play a game on her phone.

The topic of the day was the Chinook from Delta Company that had been shot down the previous day. Not by a surface-to-air missile, or an RPG, but by a Russian MiG-25 fighter flying out of Tabriz, Iran.

"MiG-25s have a range of 1,160 miles," Albro explained. "That means attacks on traffic in this area aren't likely since a Foxbat (NATO reporting name) would have to travel 500 miles to get here, and couldn't linger for long before returning to base. Isn't that right Captain Soto?"

The question caught Soto by surprise, just as it was supposed to, and heads swiveled as the other pilots turned to watch her squirm. Lee was seated next to her. He whispered the word, "Defenses."

That was enough to prompt Soto. "That's correct, sir. Assuming our fighters and SAMs failed to bring him down before he could get here."

Judging from Albro's frown he was suspicious. "That's correct. But, for those of you who have to fly missions into northeastern Syria, Mig-25s are a definite threat. Please keep that in mind. Now, on to the question of spare parts."

The scrum came to an end twenty minutes later. Soto and Lee were already on their feet when Albro made one last announcement. "Captain Soto, please report to my office. I have a pick-up mission with your name on it."

Soto groaned. "A turd is more likely. Don't go far Jonny. Oh, and thanks. I owe you."

It was a short walk to the command Conex. And, when Soto arrived, it was to discover that Albro was already present. A corporal cleared her into Albro's office. "Captain Soto reporting as ordered, sir."

Albro looked up from his computer. "Have a seat Captain, I'll be right with you."

Have a seat? Since when? Ah, Soto thought as she sat down. *The pinnacle landing. Foxtrot-Three said something nice.*

"Okay," Albro said, as he hit "Send." "Remember Mr. Polat? He's back... And he has permission to take a team of Rangers into southern Turkey looking for Colonel Kaya. Your job is to fly the team up to the border and drop it off. They'll drive from there."

"Sir, yes sir. Why not fly in? I'm curious, that's all."

Albro made a face. "Because the Turks won't allow it. Are they trying to hide something? Maybe. But, if so, that's above my paygrade. And the colonel cleared it."

"Have we got a day and time?"

"Yes, we do. Tonight at 0100. Master Sergeant Bone will command the Rangers."

Soto stood. "Yes, sir… He's the real deal."

"Good," Albro replied. "Watch your six."

Soto offered a salute, received one in return, and left. *It could be worse*, Soto decided. *All we have to do is drop them off. An easy day.*

***

The email was from Bone's mother. He couldn't believe his eyes, and went back to read the message again:

"Dear Felix,

"I'm sorry to tell you this, but Yolanda dropped the kids off yesterday, and plans to file for a divorce. She said that the bills are continuing to pile up, the bank is going to foreclose on the house, and the loneliness is getting to her. The bitch.

"Your brother is going to help me move your stuff out of the house and into a storage unit. He thinks you should file for bankruptcy, and I agree. Should we move ahead on that?

"As for the kids, they're extremely unhappy as you can imagine. But I'll do my best to care for them until you return. I raised you and your brother after all… So, I have some experience. Can you get an emergency leave? I hope so.

"BTW… Yo told me she's going on a vacay with some air force asshole.

"Love, Mom"

Master sergeants don't cry. But Bone did. Yo was a bitch, just like his mother said, but she'd been a source of comfort and joy at times. And she was the mother of his children.

So, he cried, wiped the tears away and swore he'd never break down again.

Mom was right. He should go home. And, given his situation, an emergency leave would be easy to get.

But that would have to wait. Bone was scheduled to fly out at 0100. And there was no fucking way that he'd leave Sergeant Olson and the other Boneheads with Polat.

So, Bone would be there for his men, even if he hadn't been there for his children, and would submit his request for leave as soon as he got back. *Man up, Bone... You can feel sorry for yourself later.*

***

Northern Syria

For thousands of years the town of Tell Abyad and the surrounding area had been ruled by the Romans, Byzantines, Sassanids, Umayyads, Abbasids, and the Ottoman Empire before being arbitrarily handed over to Syria by the French in the wake of WWII.

The Syrian civil war started in 2011, and Tell Abyad was captured by the free Syrian Army in 2012, only to be captured by al-Nusra Front and the ISIL in 2014.

Then Kurdish forces took control of the town only to be overwhelmed by the Turks in 2019, who remained in control. And that was where Oscar Polat wanted Soto to land.

Not in the town, but a mile south of it, since the Turkish government wouldn't allow American aircraft to land in their territory. Never mind the fact that both countries were members of the Alliance.

But that was fine with Soto, who had no desire to land in Turkey, and preferred to put down within the relative safety of the fort maintained by the Syrian Democratic Forces (SDF). An outfit that consisted of Kurdish, Arab, and Assyrian/Syriac forces.

It was however a distinctly American voice that greeted Soto over the radio. "Wizard, this is Snake-Six actual. Welcome to the hood. You should be able to see four white flares. Put down at the center of the square. Over."

"Roger that, Snake-Six… Will do. We're three from dirt. Over."

Once the *Double Deuce* was down Alvarez went about the job of unloading two Humvees.

Meanwhile Soto left the Chinook to stretch her legs and ran into Lieutenant Wilson, aka "Snake-Six." The Green Beret was clearly in his late thirties or early forties—which meant he had most likely been promoted from E-8. An increasingly common practice driven by the high mortality rate of special operations personnel, including officers.

Wilson had a firm handshake and a boyish grin. "I understand you're going to hang around for a day or two."

"That's right," Soto replied. "I don't know what you charge per night, but we brought two cases of beer."

Wilson laughed. "That's exactly what we charge! We'll keep that on the down-low however. Our Allies wouldn't approve."

"Good," Soto said. "Nor would my CO."

"Find me when you're ready," Wilson told her. "And I'll take you and your crew to our bomb proof guest suite."

"Please be aware that two members of my crew will be aboard the aircraft at all times," Soto said. "Don't shoot them."

"I'll pass the word," Wilson promised. Then, like a ghost, he was gone.

Polat and the Boneheads departed fifteen minutes later. Soto watched the taillights dim and then disappear. *Take care Sarge,* she thought. *And don't turn your back on Polat.*

***

Bone had to give Polat credit for one thing... The bastard had a good understanding of the Turkish mindset. Especially the military mindset. In their totality the Turkish armed forces were greater than those of France and Great Britain combined. With 570,000 people under arms before the war and more than 400,000 in reserve, Turkey's military was the Alliance's second largest standing force.

And Bone knew from personal experience that the larger something gets, the more bureaucratic it becomes, until written rules strangle personal initiative.

The answer? Cover your ass with paper. And that was why Polat was carrying a thick sheaf of identical orders from on high.

"You will under all circumstances render any and all assistance to Mr. Oscar Polat and his American security team by order of Hakan Aydin, Chief of the National Intelligence Organization of Turkey."

Just the thing to hand out to every corporal, sergeant, and lieutenant who wanted to protect themselves from criticism if something went wrong. And that was *all* of them.

So, each time the two-vehicle convoy came to a checkpoint, which was frequently, Polat would hand the person in charge a copy of the order, give them thirty seconds to digest it, and demand passage. It worked every time.

What concerned Bone was the iffy nature of the territory they were passing through. Though nominally under Turkish control, the situation was actually quite complicated, since ISIS and Kurdish militia groups still controlled certain villages.

That meant it would be easy for the team to blunder into a battle between the adversaries, take fire, and be wiped out.

Otherwise, their goal was to reach an ISIS safehouse where, according to Turkish intelligence, Colonel Kaya was being held.

The good news was that their destination was only fifteen miles from the border... And they were making good time. In fact, according to the map on Bone's tablet computer, they were only a few miles out. Bone thumbed his radio.

"We're close enough to walk in. Look for a place to stash the Humvees."

Corporal Levy was driving the lead vic. And it wasn't long before he spotted what remained of a barn, turned, and pulled in behind it. "How's this, Sarge?"

The derelict building would prevent a passersby from spotting the Humvees from the road. But that was all. Still, it beat the hell out of nothing, so Bone okayed it. "It'll do. Levy and Tyson will remain with the vehicles and come running if called.

"The rest of you will deass the Humvees, check your gear, and prepare to move out. I will lead the first fire team, and Sergeant Olson will lead the second. Do you have questions? No? Let's do this thing."

Each team member had a headset, radio, and night vision gear. And that was critical in order to navigate their way across open fields, over ancient stone walls, and through a large stand of trees. Polat was carrying a sexy FN 5.7x28mm, Belgian-made, submachine gun, and walking a few paces behind Bone. Did the Turk know what to do with it? Bone hoped so.

After twenty minutes of walking the safehouse appeared in the distance. The hum of a generator could be heard, lights were visible, and ISIS sentries were silhouetted against them. Stupid, but who said they were smart?

That's what Bone was thinking when a mortar round landed a hundred feet behind him and exploded. The first round was quickly followed by a second and third. Then, as a flare lit the area, the ISIS fighters opened fire.

The Rangers didn't need to be told. All of them dropped to the ground, elbowed their way toward cover where there was some, and returned fire. Bone thumbed his radio. "Red-Dog-Three, this is Nine. We're pinned down between mortar fire and the house. Bring the vic with the 40 mike-mike. Tell Five to kill the mortar, but to stay off the house. Over."

"Roger that," Levy replied. "On the way. Over."

More shells landed behind the Americans—only closer now. Each M4 had a flash suppressor, but the weapons did produce occasional sparks, which gave the mortar team a rough idea of where the *Kafirs* (disbelievers) were hiding.

One more adjustment and the shells will land on us, Bone thought. *We need to distract them.* "This is Nine... Throw flashbangs on five, run forward, and drop. One, two, three, four, five!"

Bone threw his grenade, came up off the ground and dashed forward. At least six flashbangs went off in quick succession, blinding the ISIS fighters, as the Rangers went prone.

The tangos would need at least thirty seconds to recover their night vision and would need some additional time to readjust the mortar. Meanwhile three short bursts from the American M4s cut two hajis down.

But at least a dozen tangos were still in the fight, and they fired long bursts from their AKs, hoping to luck out. That was when Bone heard the roar of an engine, headlights swept the area, and Levy's Humvee arrived.

Tyson was on the 40mm grenade launcher and knew how to use it. Explosions marched across the area in front of the safehouse. Bodies and parts of bodies cartwheeled through the air. Bone wasn't sure which blast killed the mortar team, but knew one of them had, because the weapon was silent. And, as far as Bone could tell, all the enemy fighters were down.

Bone stood, and was about to issue orders, when he heard the muted sound of automatic gunfire from the direction of the house. Flashes were visible as well. Bone yelled, "Follow me!" and ran toward the building.

The front door was ajar. Bone kicked it open and entered ready to fire. Bodies lay all about. And there, standing at the center of the room, was Oscar Polat with the submachine gun clutched in his hands. An ISIS fighter moaned and Polat fired a burst into him. The moaning stopped.

Bone looked around. "What the fuck happened here?"

Polat shrugged. "I was afraid that they would kill Colonel Kaya. So, while they were shooting at you, I circled around and entered through the back door.

"Two men tried to stop me. I shot them. That's when the fighters in the front room turned on me and I had to shoot them too."

Bone didn't like the way Polat had gone off on his own, but couldn't object, given the way the situation turned out. "And Kaya?"

"He isn't here," Polat said. "I don't think so anyway... But I'll check to make sure."

Sergeant Olson entered at that point. Bone turned to face him. "Set up a perimeter. Have someone bring the second Humvee forward. Assign two men to search bodies and gather Intel. I'll do the same in here."

Olson nodded. "Got it." Then he was gone.

Bone was carrying a camera on his tac vest and removed it. The first thing he wanted to get photos of were the documents spread out on the dining room table. They were in Arabic but that didn't matter. The Intel people would read them. Polat was doing the same thing.

Once Bone was done, he took a look around, spotted a leather briefcase leaning against a wall, and went to get it. By putting a dozen dirty dishes into the sink, Bone managed to clear a space in which to empty the case. A lot of it was worthless including a toothbrush, toothpaste, a comb, and some sort of medication.

But there were papers too... One of which was a hand drawn map with Arabic hand written notes, all in Arabic. The Intel nerds would love that. Bone photographed each one and made a mental note to package them. Once that chore was complete Bone began to search the bodies.

***

Polat was very disappointed. If Hala Omar had been held at the ISIS safehouse, she'd been removed, and taken elsewhere. Although it was Polat's opinion that she'd never been there. A certain informant would have some explaining to do.

In the meantime, Polat was aware of the documents the American had left on the kitchen counter and went over to inspect them. Polat could speak, read, and write Arabic which meant he could assess the haul quickly.

The material included a thick sheaf of ISIS operational orders, some personal correspondence, and a map. A very interesting map which, according to the notes scribbled here and there, referred to a large stash of ISIS gold.

Given the nature of his profession Polat was quite familiar with the fact that ISIS leadership was obsessed with obtaining and holding gold bullion. They believed that bank notes, which were originally backed by gold, had become worthless pieces of paper.

Polat felt a rising sense of excitement. Was the gold still where the map said it was? If so, an enterprising person such as himself could go there, and retrieve it. All while continuing to carry out his mission.

A careful search confirmed that the informant was wrong. There were no female bodies alive or dead in the house. That meant Hala Omar was still on the loose. So, the search would continue.

Then a terrible thought occurred to Polat. Once Master Sergeant Bone turned his photos in, American intelligence would learn about the gold. Polat had to stop that from occurring. But how?

***

South of Tell Abyad, in Turkish occupied Syria

After standing watch for two hours in the *Double Deuce*, Soto headed for what Lieutenant Wilson cheerfully referred to as "The Coffin," meaning a forty-foot Conex container that was buried under ground, and home to a team of twelve Green Berets, plus any transients who happened to pass through.

The fact that only half of the Green Beret team was present in the container helped a little, however the combined stench of smelly feet, unwashed bodies and MRE farts was hard to take.

But Soto was exhausted. So much so that she managed to ignore the fug, climb into a claustrophobic upper bunk, and pass out. And that's where she was when Lee came for her. He had to stand on the side of the lower shelf in order to whisper at her. "Wake up, Marie... They gave us a mission."

Soto tried to open her eyes. It felt as though they were glued shut. And her mouth was bone dry. "Mission?" she croaked. "What kind of mission?"

"An extraction," Lee replied. "A platoon-strength supply convoy was ambushed, cut into sections, and surrounded. The survivors managed to come together and lagger up in some ruins. A spirited defense plus two A-10s are keeping the tangos at bay. But somebody needs to pull them out, and we're the closest."

"Roger that," Soto said, as she sat up and hit her head. "Damn it... Prep the *Deuce*. I need to take a pee and brush my teeth."

The Chinook's rotors were turning by the time Soto climbed aboard. Alvarez was waiting for her inside the cargo area. "Drink this, ma'am. It'll get you going."

Soto accepted the mug, took a sip of the piping hot liquid, and swallowed. "Wow! That's good... What is it?"

Alvarez grinned. "Hot chocolate with a shot of peppermint vodka."

Soto gave the noncom a one-armed hug. "Thanks Chief. Tell the gunners to get ready. It sounds like we're in for a warm reception."

Mug in hand, Soto made her way forward to the cockpit, and side-slipped into her seat. "Any problems?"

"None," Lee replied.

"Okay. You're flying. Let's go."

Lee grinned. "Yes, ma'am!"

Soto spent the next ten minutes finishing her drink and coming up to speed. The ambush had taken place sixty-eight miles southeast of Tell Abyad which meant that the *Double Deuce* could reach the site in less than half an hour. She turned to Lee. "Have we got a contact?"

"Yes, call sign Lama-Four. Use the emergency freq."

"Lama-Four, this is Wizard. We are a Chinook inbound. Give me a sitrep please. Over."

There was a burst of static followed by the sound of a female voice. Sporadic bursts of gunfire could be heard in the background. "Welcome to the party, Wizard. Over."

"Hey there honey, don't you worry none," a familiar voice said. "This is Boots and Loco. Stash and Ripper were low on fuel, but we're in with guns, rockets and bombs.

"Put out red flares to mark your position. We'll mow the lawn, and Wizard will pull you out. Ain't that right Wiz?"

Soto couldn't help but smile. "That's right Boots. Get organized Lama... The less time we spend on the ground the better."

"And, speaking of ground, give me a flat spot. Remember, we're about one hundred feet long. Over."

Soto could see explosions up ahead, red flares, and crisscrossing tracer. "This is Boots… In from the east with rockets. Over."

Boots made a pass, followed by Loco. The pilots fired five Maverick air-to-surface missiles each. Explosions marched across enemy held territory. A sure way to put some heads down.

Soto turned the nav lights off. Lee chose to come in high to minimize ground fire. "I'm going to stay steep," Lee said.

Then he killed forward motion, and dropped the *Double Deuce* straight down, while centering the helo between the flares. Soto heard the *ping, ping, ping* of bullets striking the hull as the landing gear thumped down.

That was when Soto sensed motion to her left. A glance confirmed her worst fears. Lee had been hit and was slumped to the right.

Soto wanted to help Lee, but couldn't leave the controls, so she called a gunner forward.

He entered the cockpit and managed to pull Lee upright. He turned to Soto. "The L-T took a bullet, ma'am. He's dead."

Soto wanted to cry out, to scream, but couldn't allow herself to do that. Teeth gritted she called Alvarez. The crew chief was there, calm as usual, sorting people out.

The gunners were firing high, to avoid friendlies, and to keep the hajis from breaking through the steadily shrinking perimeter. The airframe shook as Boots and her wingman dropped gravity bombs to the west.

A staff sergeant appeared out of the chaos. A bloody battle dressing was wrapped around her head. "Lama-Four ma'am… We're loading the last KIA. I'll call the effectives in and we're out of here." Lama-Four eyed Lee, shook her head sadly, and left.

That was Soto's cue to check all of her gauges, and confirm that the *Double Deuce* could successfully get off the ground. "Boots, this is Wizard. I'm about to lift off. Over."

"No problem, hon… You go for it. Over."

Alvarez stuck her head into the cockpit. "Lama-Four is aboard. Let's haul ass. You're clear left and right."

"Clear left and right," the gunners confirmed, as they continued to fire.

"That was when Alvarez saw Lee. "No! Fuck *no!*"

Soto didn't reply. She was too busy. Bullets were still flying every which way in spite of the efforts by the A-10 pilots. And the volume of fire increased as the Chinook took off. The hajis could see victory slipping away and were determined to prevent it from happening.

One golden BB. That's all it would take to bring the *Double Deuce* down. Soto's entire body was straining with the effort of wishing the helo into the sky. *Come on, come on, come on. You can do it baby... You can do it.*

And the Chinook *did* do it. Soto turned toward the superbase. What she needed now was speed. All the speed the *Deuce* could give. "Tabqa air traffic control... This is Chinook nine-eight-zero-two-zero-two-two. I'm inbound with six casualties, ETA forty-five minutes. Please notify medical. Over."

"Roger that," a male voice said. "You're cleared for Helipad 2. Over."

Soto began to cry.

CHAPTER FIVE

South of Tell Abyad, in Turkish occupied Syria

Polat, Bone, and the rest of the Ranger team made the trip south without incident, and arrived at the Green Beret compound only to discover that their transportation was gone.

"Your Chinook was sent to some sort of shit show southeast of here," Wilson informed them. "But no worries. Central says the Chinook will come back for you the day after tomorrow."

"You must be shitting me," Bone said angrily.

"I wouldn't shit you," Wilson replied calmly. "You're my favorite turd."

"Sorry, sir, I was out of line."

"No prob," Wilson said. "Think of this as an all-expenses-paid vacation."

After a restless night spent in The Coffin, Bone arose eager to escape the Conex, and find something to eat. Polat was waiting for him. The Turk was all smiles. "There you are! I'm going into town for breakfast. Would you care to join me?"

Polat wasn't Bone's first choice of a breakfast companion. But the Boneheads were sleeping in, and he was hungry. "Sure, that sounds good. How will we get there?"

"In a taxi," Polat answered. "They're lined up outside the gate."

The Turk was correct. Seven sun-faded cars were waiting outside the compound. Some were tricked out with company paint jobs, and the rest were unmarked sedans of one kind or another. Polat chose one of the latter, gave orders in Turkish, and made small talk as the driver pushed through a herd of goats, crossed a shallow stream, and entered Tell Abyad.

After a further exchange in Turkish the car turned a corner and came to a stop in front of a restaurant with tables out front. Polat paid the fare, opened the door, and got out. Bone followed. "Let's sit in the sun," Polat suggested. "We'll be warmer that way."

And it was true. The sun was still rising and the air was cool. Later, around midday, the temp would be in the 80s. Polat chose a table large enough for four. "Have you had a Turkish breakfast? No? Well, it's always a good idea to secure a large table if you can."

The other customers were regulars for the most part, some of whom were clearly curious about the strangers, but in no way hostile.

The meal began with strong Turkish coffee, soon followed by a dozen plates and bowls. "We call it, *kahvalti*," Polat said. "And it's the most important meal of the day."

Bone soon found himself confronted by a bewildering array of bite sized delicacies including olives, cucumbers, cured sausage, eggs, several cheeses, tomatoes, fresh-baked bread and a choice of spreads.

Bacon and pancakes would have been preferable. But it wasn't long before Bone found himself enjoying the meal. Finally, with another cup of coffee in hand, he was feeling pretty good. "That was excellent. Thank you."

Polat smiled. "*Rica ederim*. That means, 'you're welcome,' in my language. Now, let's talk business."

Bone frowned. "Business? What kind of business?"

"The kind that involves breaking a few rules, and putting a lot of money in the bank," Polat replied. "Shall I continue? Or do you want me to stop there?"

Bone took another sip of coffee. His heart was beating faster. He had a need for money. Lots of it. But he wasn't about to sell his country out if that's what Polat had in mind.

"That depends," Bones said cautiously. "Can you give me some idea of what we're talking about?"

"Yes, I can," Polat answered. "Let's say that a group of bad people had something of value and hid it. But we discovered where it was concealed and took it. How would you feel about that?"

Bone frowned. "Which bad people? There are lots of them in Syria."

Polat chuckled. "True. I'm talking about ISIS."

"Okay," Bone said. "It sounds good so far. Which rules would we need to break?"

"The ones that say we should report such a discovery to our respective governments."

Bone considered that. What would the governments do with whatever it was? Fritter it away, that's what. Whereas he could help his mother and his kids. "So, tell me… What did ISIS hide?"

"Roughly nine million worth of gold coins," Polat answered. "We'll split it fifty-fifty."

Bone felt a surge of excitement. All of his problems would be solved! He'd retire the moment the army allowed him to, conceal his new found wealth by being frugal, and take care of his family. Bone raised his coffee cup. "Count me in Oscar… Here's to partners in crime."

***

The village of Sur-Na Syria

Hala Omar's days were nearly identical. Get up, take a sponge bath, attend *Fajr* (the sunrise prayer) return to Adra's house for breakfast, help with chores, attend *Dhuhr* in the early afternoon, perform more chores, and have dinner with Chalibi immediately after the *Maghrib* prayer at sunset.

Hala disliked the dinner ritual, yet looked forward to it at the same time, since there was always the possibility of news. The latest tidbit being the fact that one of Toplin's assistants had been in touch with Chalibi's representative, and ransom negotiations were underway.

That was a lose-lose situation insofar as Hala was concerned. Which would be worse? Being returned to Toplin? Or continuing to be held captive by ISIS? Both possibilities terrified her.

But of the two, Chalibi was the most pressing. With each passing day the ISIS commander's sexual advances were becoming more aggressive, and Hala knew it was only a matter of time before he would rape her. And why not? According to Chalibi's reasoning it was impossible to rape a whore.

That meant each trip to the ISIS leader's residence was laden with fear, and as Hala left Adra's house, she wondered if she'd be able to stall Chalibi one more time. Or would he attack her?

She could run of course. Would the guard with the scruffy beard shoot her? Or did he have orders to hold his fire? A dead hostage had no value after all. Not that such deliberations mattered because Hala knew the man could outrun her. An escape attempt would hasten physical punishment which might or might not include rape.

So, Hala entered the house the way she always did, with what felt like a pool of liquid lead in the pit of her stomach. The guard remained outside as Hala climbed the stairs to the flat roof where Chalibi was waiting. *Why?* He was usually late.

Chalibi rose from his chair and came forward to embrace her. His breath smelled of alcohol. "Welcome my sweet! I have news... President Toplin is going to send a representative to inspect the goods. That means our time together will end soon. But not before I enjoy your services."

And with that Chalibi began to rip Hala's clothing off. She tried to resist, but Chalibi was strong, and her efforts were futile. Hala was half naked when he pushed her onto the couch, and tore at the rest of her clothes.

Chalibi was panting by the time he stripped Hala's panties off and began to undress. "Spread your legs whore… I'm going to fuck your brains out."

Hala obeyed. But, as she did so, Hala slid the fingers of her left hand down behind the red velvet cushion. Was the steak knife still there? The one she'd planted there three days earlier? Yes! It was. Hala withdrew her hand as Chalibi landed on top of her.

The decision to surrender had been made a week earlier. Chalibi would have his pleasure. And would pay a steep price for it.

There was nothing subtle about the rape. It consisted of a forced entry followed by frantic pounding and gasps of pleasure. Timing was everything. *Now*, Hala thought. *When he's weakest. Get ready.*

Chalibi was stiff armed, and his eyes were wide, as the climax came. And it was then, at the moment of orgasm, that Hala stabbed him.

The blade plunged deep into Chalibi's neck, stopped only by the handle, as Hala jerked the weapon down.

Chalibi tried to scream but couldn't. He rolled off Hala and onto the floor, where he hurried to pull the knife out, only to release a gout of blood. It spread quickly to form a red halo around his head. Chalibi's life force faded from his eyes.

Hala sat up, swung her feet over onto the floor, and stood. She felt dizzy. *Don't faint. Not now. Be strong.*

There was blood on Hala's face and breasts. Her first task was to remove it. Then, after taking clothes from Chalibi's closet, she would dress as a man. After that? She would make decisions on the fly.

The Yazidi slave girl appeared on the roof. She stood and stared. "You did it! You killed him. Thank you."

Hala's plan didn't take the slave girl into account but should have. A stupid and potentially disastrous mistake. The Yazidi people were indigenous to Kurdistan, which included parts of Iraq, Syria, Turkey and Iran.

Since the spread of Islam in the 7th and 8th centuries the Yazidis had been persecuted by Arabs, and later by Turks, because some of their religious practices were deemed to be heretical.

Thousands of Yazidi women and girls were forced into sexual slavery. And there, standing in front of Hala, was one of them. A girl of what? Fourteen or fifteen? *I never thought about her*, Hala realized. *I was too focused on myself.*

"I knew the knife was missing," the girl said. "And I guessed what you would do with it. So, I waited. The pig raped me many times."

"What's your name?"

"Nina."

"My name is Hala."

"I know. You are famous. Come, you will shower. I have clothes for you."

Nina led Hala down to the second floor where Chalibi's quarters were. "No one is allowed on this floor without Commander Chalibi's permission," Nina explained. "That means you are safe for the moment. But I have no way to know if meetings were scheduled. And, when Ferran Mostafa finds out what happened, he will be furious. So, hurry."

The bathroom and shower were modern by Syrian standards. And the hot water turned pink as it pummeled Hala, ran down her legs, and swirled around her feet. Hala felt no guilt, and no sorrow regarding what she'd done. Just a profound sense of satisfaction.

Hala hurried to finish, dry herself with a towel last used by Chalibi, and exit. Nina was waiting. "You will dress as an old woman," the girl instructed. "And I will be your daughter. We must wear the *niqab* over our faces, the *abaya* over our bodies, and the black mesh over our eyes. Yes, and gloves too... And socks."

Hala was used to the ISIS imposed restrictions by then, and hastened to put the clothing on. "You must use *this*," Nina said, handing Hala a cane. "And limp. I will hold your arm as if giving support. Your name is Farida Obaid, and you are here to visit your sister Saba. Do you understand?"

Nina had clearly been planning the escape for days and Hala was impressed. "Yes, I understand. Let's hope that no one questions us. Where will we go?"

"To the Women's Place," Nina answered without hesitation. "I took Commander Chalibi's money. So, once we are clear of Sur-Na, we will travel by bus. I have a map."

Hala had heard of the village. It was called "Almakan Alaman," the Safe Place, and had been established in 2016 during the Syrian Civil War. It was inspired by the women's village in Kenya, and based on the principle of self-sustainability.

"You are wise beyond your years," Hala said. "Your mother would be proud."

Tears began to flow, and Hala realized her mistake. It seemed natural to reach out and embrace Nina's stick-like body. "I'm sorry," Hala said. "So sorry. That was stupid of me."

Nina sniffed. "Thank you. We must go. Don't forget your cane."

Which one of us is the adult? Hala wondered. *So much has been taken from Nina. Including her childhood.*

The rest of the servants were on the first floor, some resting, some on call. Nina checked to ensure that the back entrance was clear, motioned for Hala to follow, and led her out into the cool night air. "Now," the girl whispered. "Use your cane and limp. We will walk north."

There were no streetlights and traffic was sparse. Houses were marked by rectangles of yellow light. A dog barked in the distance.

That was when Hala saw the two-man patrol ahead. The ISIS fighters were walking towards her, rifles slung, looking for any villager stupid enough to violate strict Sharia law. Would they stop the women? And interrogate them? Or allow them to pass?

Hala's pulse was pounding as the distance closed. "*Masa' alkhayr ya jadati,*" one of the men said. (Good evening grandmother.)

"*Shkran lika. Qad yakun allah maeki.*" (Thank you. May Allah be with you.)

And that was it. The two parties went their separate ways.

"We will leave the road and make our way to an abandoned house," Nina announced. "I have food and water stored there. Then we will wait three days before walking to the village of Baka. The search should be over by then."

"If Allah wills it," Hala said automatically.

"Allah cares nothing for us," Nina replied. "We are women."

***

Superbase Tabqa, Syria

Two days had passed since the rescue flight. And the *Double Deuce's* crew was on hand as thirty-seven bodies, in thirty-seven transfer cases, were loaded onto a C-17 bound for Dover Air Force Base in the United States.

Lieutenant Jonny Lee's body was in one of the flag draped caskets, but Soto didn't know which one.

Alvarez shouted, "Atten-shun!" And when Soto saluted, the rest of them did as well. The *Double Deuce's* crew were the only mourners because the dead soldiers, marines, and airmen were from units all over Syria. They held their salutes until the last transfer case disappeared into the C-17.

Then, when Alvarez said, "At ease!" the crew looked at Soto. "Jonny was one helluva pilot," Soto said awkwardly. "And a nice guy. Please join me at the club. I'm buying."

Allied service men and women weren't allowed to drink off base out of respect for the mores of the local community. But for the sake of morale, officers and enlisted alike could frequent the huge "club," which was open 24 hours a day.

There were occupation specific rules—like those that applied to air crews who weren't supposed to fly within eight hours of consuming alcohol. But that wasn't a problem since Soto and her crew weren't scheduled to fly until the next day. And they weren't on standby.

Once in the club, with drinks in front of the crew, conversation centered around Lee. Soto had heard most of the stories before, but not all, like the time Lee "borrowed" an Italian observation plane and went for a joy ride. All in all, the session was good for morale, even if there were tears.

The following morning Soto went to the DFAC for breakfast, and was sitting at her usual table, when a tall, gangly second lieutenant appeared in front of her. "Excuse me, ma'am. My name is Ziggy Jones. I was told that I might find you here. May I join you?"

Soto eyed the wings on the lieutenant's jacket. They were very shiny. A newbie for sure. "Of course. Do you want to get some food first?"

"No, ma'am. But thank you."

"All right, what's up?"

"I'm your new copilot."

Soto frowned. "That seems unlikely. You have a five-pointed star tattooed on your forehead."

Jones feigned surprise. "I do?"

"Yes, you do. And facial tattoos aren't allowed in the army."

Jones nodded. "Yes, ma'am. That's what I thought. So, I got one. Then they changed the rules and drafted me anyway. It seems they're desperate."

That *was* a sign of desperation if true. An indication of how many casualties the United States had suffered. But the story caused Soto to grin nevertheless. "That sucks. So, how did you wind up as a pilot?"

"I wanted to be a GS-04," Jones told her.

"Which is?"

"A clerk," Jones replied. "I figured that would be relatively safe."

"And?"

"And they gave me a whole bunch of tests, told me that I would make an excellent pilot, and sent me to flight school."

"*Are* you an excellent pilot?" Soto inquired.

Jones shook his head. "No. I'm average at best. But I hope to get better."

Soto sipped her coffee. "Well, you're honest. And I like that. Tell me about 'Ziggy.' Is that a nickname?"

"No, ma'am. It's my name *and* my callsign. It means 'victory.'"

"You're shitting me."

"No, ma'am. That's straight up."

Soto stared at him. "We have a mission scheduled for 1300."

"Yes, ma'am. That's why I came looking for you."

"Okay, Ziggy, welcome aboard. We're slated for a supply run to FOB Smiley. It's right in the middle of tango territory. So, by this time tomorrow, you'll be a combat veteran."

Jones followed Soto around like a puppy dog, echoed the things she told him, and clearly knew his way around a Chinook. It soon became clear, however, that Jones had trained on newer CH-47F aircraft, rather than Ds, which had less horsepower and less sophisticated avionics.

As for the facial tattoo, the gunners were particularly impressed and thought the tat was cool.

Not Alvarez though, who was noticeably silent when the subject came up.

There was a difficult moment for Soto when Jones entered the cockpit and took a look around. All indications of Lee's death were gone. The window with a bullet hole through it had been replaced. And what little bit of blood there was had been removed.

"So, what happened to my predecessor?" Jones wanted to know. "Was he promoted?"

"No," Soto replied somberly. "He was killed."

Jones made a face. "Sorry."

"We all are," Soto said. "Let's run the check lists."

Once the checks were complete, and the rotors were turning, Soto took off.

Ziggy's interchange with air traffic control was a bit uncertain, but the trip to Helipad 1 went smoothly, as did the subsequent takeoff. There was nothing flashy about Jones. He had good hands and good feet. In fact, he was, if anything, a bit better than average.

Had Jones been sand bagging? Or was he having a good day? Time would tell.

Soto intended to let Jones fly all the way to FOB Smiley, where she would take the controls, and land.

However, at a point well past the halfway marker, the port engine shut down, and the Chinook began to lose altitude. "I have it," Soto said, as she took control.

"You have it," Jones replied.

There were all sorts of problems that could trigger a shutdown, including a clogged fuel filter, a blocked oil filter, an overheated transmission, an engine chip light and, as always, the possibility of a golden BB. Because hajis took pot shots at helicopters all the time.

But regardless of the reason for the shutdown, Soto knew that flying with one engine was risky. Should she put down right away? Or keep going, and land at FOB Smiley, where both the crew and the helicopter would be more secure?

That, Soto decided, was a no-brainer. "Radio Bravo-One-Two at FOB Smiley, and tell him that we're twenty out, and coming in on one engine.

"The likelihood of a fire is low, but it would make sense to break out the extinguishers, and to clear all personnel from the area around the helipad. Got it?"

"Got it," Jones replied. He made the call seconds later, received an acknowledgement, and began to run the appropriate checklists. Not bad for a dude with a star tattooed on his face.

When the FOB appeared in the distance, the *Double Deuce* was flying at 600 feet, and vulnerable to ground fire. A common occurrence while arriving at, or departing from, FOB Smiley. The crew already knew about the shutdown but Soto told them anyway. "We're going to land on one engine. Other than that, everything is hunky dory."

As the Chinook's shadow floated in over the FOB, Soto concentrated on bringing the ship down in between the red flares. "Clear right, and clear left," Alvarez said. The gunners agreed.

Soto felt the gear touch down, applied the brakes, and came to a stop. Then, with help from Jones, she ran through the lists.

"Hey Wiz," a male voice said over the radio. "This is One-Two. You're looking good. Welcome back. Over."

The emergency was over, but the work was just beginning. Most of the possible problems could be handled by Alvarez with help from her gunners. The chief was breaking out her tools as Soto entered the cargo area. "My money is on a clogged fuel filter," Soto announced.

"And mine is on contaminated fuel," Alvarez replied. "Ten smackers?"

"You're on," Soto replied. "I'm going to check in with Hickok. He'll want to take his cargo off."

Soto left via the rear ramp. Bravo-One-Two, aka Captain Hickok, was there waiting for her. "Nice job, Marie… Welcome back to your home away from home. Can we unload?"

They could, and they did. The beer came off last, and just in time for a mini celebration. Two cans a piece. And thanks to some coolers, the beers were cold.

Soto was chatting with Hickok's XO when Alvarez appeared. There was a grease smear on her face. "You owe me ten bucks," the crew chief said, as she plopped down. "We found contaminated fuel. Only one tank though."

"How long to fix it?"

"A couple of hours."

Soto looked at the sky. It was getting dark and they weren't going anywhere on one engine. So, they would have to stay. The crew was tired, especially Alvarez. And the chief would be toast by the time the repair was complete. Besides, if additional problems surfaced, Soto wanted to deal with them during daylight hours.

Dinner consisted of whatever MRE a person could grab, steal, or trade for. Soto ate hers with Hickok. "Chili and Mac," Hickok exclaimed. "My fav. What have you got?"

"Beef Ravioli," Soto answered. "That's my guess."

Hickok laughed. "The DFAC looks pretty good from here, doesn't it?"

"It does," Soto agreed, as she sipped water from a bottle. "So, we can expect a good night's sleep? Or will the hajis attack?"

"Your guess is as good as mine," Hickok replied. "Your bird is an inviting target. But, if they come, we'll be waiting."

Soto and her crew slept in the back of the helicopter. There was more than enough room, and all of them had sleeping bags, which they stored onboard.

Soto kept her weapons close by just in case. But there was no need. The night passed peacefully. Not a single shot was fired.

Soto awoke tired and sore. An air mattress. She needed an air mattress.

After getting up, and swinging by "the lady's room," Soto went looking for Jones, and found him eating breakfast. He appeared fresh as a daisy. "Good morning, ma'am. The doughnuts are good. We brought them in."

"Marie is fine most of the time," Soto told him. "Should I go with sprinkles? Or plain?"

"Plain," Jones replied. "Sprinkles are for fighter pilots."

Soto laughed. Jones was growing on her.

That was when a shell hit the pinnacle that towered above the base, exploded, and sent an avalanche of rock *rattling* down. The Conex serving as the FOB's armory took a direct hit, and produced a loud *clang*.

Jones stood. "What the hell was *that*?"

"That was a shell of some sort," Soto replied. "Let's find Hickok."

The FOB's CO was right where Soto thought he would be— which was in the command bunker. He saw the pilots enter. "Come take a look... We're being shelled by a Russian T-72 tank. Who knows where they got it. From the Iranians most likely."

Hickok's statement was punctuated by a cracking sound as another shell struck the pinnacle, and *more* rocks clattered down.

The base had a number of drones, one of which was circling over a tank that was traveling with two transports and three gun trucks. "They're trying to bring the pinnacle down on top of us," Hickok observed. "Somebody has a brain."

"Can you reach the tank with your mortars?" Soto inquired.

"Nope," Hickok answered. "It's out of range. All we can do is hope for the best. If their plan succeeds the base will fall. I put in a call for air support, but nothing is available at the moment."

"How 'bout we drop a barrel bomb on the mother fuckers?" Jones inquired.

Soto turned to look at her copilot. "You're too young to know about barrel bombs."

Jones offered a crooked smile. "I know about Elvis Presley, Ben Franklin, *and* Julius Caesar. I have a degree in Global History."

"Shit," Hickok said. "That could work! If we assemble the bomb, will you drop it?"

Using the *Double Deuce* as a bomber was a dangerous proposition. The hajis would have machine guns, and quite possibly shoulder launched missiles as well. But, with the whole base at risk, Soto couldn't say "no."

"Yes, we'll do it. But let's hurry! If one of those shells falls short, it could hit our bird."

Orders were given, people ran every which way, and the shells continued to score hits on the pinnacle. One of them struck the peak and destroyed the flag pole. That caused the American flag to flutter and fall onto the steep slope below.

But the men and women of FOB Smiley were too busy to notice, and the helicopter crew was preparing to take off. There were two ways they could deliver the bomb—by rolling it off the rear ramp, or as a sling load.

After discussing the matter with Alvarez, Soto settled on the second option, because it offered a better chance of putting the bomb on the target.

The bomb consisted of a 50-gallon oil drum packed with all sorts of boom-booms plus a big chunk of C-4 plastic explosive for a trigger. A forklift brought the bomb out to where Soto and the others were standing. She could see that the words "Fuck You!" had been spray painted on the cylinder.

"Okay, this is how it's gonna work," the FOB's bespectacled EOD (Explosive Ordinance Disposal) specialist told them. "This is a wireless detonator. It's no good beyond 500 feet. So, watch your altitude."

Oh, great, Soto thought. *Why not 50 feet so they can fire pistols at us?*

But what she said was, "Got it. Give the detonator to the chief here. Jones and I will have other things to do."

The crew boarded the Chinook, the pilots ran their lists, and took off. The downdraft from the Chinook's rotors caused a miniature dust storm as Soto eyed her instruments. Everything looked good. "Okay, Chief... We're ready."

Alvarez was lying on the cargo floor looking down through the hook bay at a soldier on the ground. Ideally a rigger would handle the hookup, but there weren't any riggers at FOB Smiley, so a corporal was standing in.

As Alvarez called instructions, Soto moved the helo left and right, until the cargo hook was in the right spot. That was the corporal's cue to dash in and attach the sling eye from the barrel bomb's makeshift harness to the hook.

After receiving the all-clear Soto took the *Double Deuce* up to an altitude of 400 feet, and aimed the Chinook at the distant tank.

By charging the T-47 head on, Soto planned to catch the enemy by surprise, and reduce the amount of time the hajis had to prep their weapons.

Furthermore, Soto hoped that once the tangos realized what was coming their way, the fighters would assume that the Chinook was loaded with soldiers, and waste time getting ready for that. And, at 400 feet, the chances of a clean hit were better.

Wind pressure pushed the barrel back, and as the helo slowed to a hover, it was going to swing back and forth. *Shit,* Soto thought. *Why didn't I think of that earlier? Will Alvarez take that into account?*

Then the group of vehicles appeared up ahead, the time for second thoughts was over, and all Soto could do was fly.

The gunners had orders to ignore the tank and concentrate on the people who were scurrying around. They opened fire the moment their weapons came to bear. Geysers of dirt shot up into the air as streams of bullets chased the fighters down and slaughtered them.

Soto knew she had to slow down in order to hover over the tank, and began to reduce power long before the *Deuce* arrived, in hopes of reducing the barrel bomb's arc. "Watch the swing Chief! I'll drop the barrel on your command."

Meanwhile Soto could hear the all too familiar sound of bullets pinging the hull as the onboard Common Missile Warning System began to fire chaff and flares.

"Get ready," Alvarez said. "On three… One, two, three!"

Sling loads were released by the pilot. In order to drop the bomb Soto had to press two buttons on the cyclic at the same time. That caused the hook jaw to open, which released the sling eye and the load. Then it was up to Alvarez to detonate the bomb.

Soto couldn't take the time required to watch what happened next. But she *felt* it, as the pressure wave created by the explosion nudged the helicopter from below, even as she sought to gain altitude as quickly as possible.

The *Double Deuce* couldn't out-climb all of the shrapnel however. One piece punched its way up through the deck in the cargo area, and miraculously hit an overhead cross member, rather than traveling up through the fuselage and possibly striking a rotor.

"We nailed it!" a gunner exclaimed. "The turret is gone!"

That meant the cannon was gone as well. Soto felt a tremendous sense of relief. Somehow, in spite of the odds, the *Deuce* was still in the air.

"Wizard, this is Bravo-One-Two. We watched the whole thing via the drone! What you accomplished was nothing less than Wizardly. Thank you. Over."

Jones glanced her way. "This run is the exception, rather than the rule. Right?"

"Right," Soto replied. "We're truck drivers, and FOB Smiley is a stop on our route."

CHAPTER SIX

Moscow, Russia

Major Sergei Voronin peered out the window of the Ka-62 helicopter. The sky was gray, snowflakes whipped past, and it appeared as though a white shroud had been laid over Moscow. Viewed from above the capital city was a serpentine maze of streetlamps, headlights, and traffic signals.

Yes, WWIII was being fought to the east, but there was no sign of that in the capital. Not from hundreds of feet up in the air anyway. But, down on the ground, there were shortages of everything other than potatoes. Fortunately, Voronin liked potatoes.

What he *didn't* like was anything connected to politics. That was because politics were complicated, often lethal, and made his brain hurt.

Yet there Voronin was, on his way to a personal audience with Russian President Toplin, to discuss what General Garin described as a "personal matter."

A fucking "personal matter." Nothing could be more dangerous to a man like Voronin. It had taken sixteen long, hard years to advance from private to major without benefit of a college education, political influence, or the use of bribes.

And now Voronin was about to enter the exalted world of presidential politics where one misstep could cost him his career.

On the other hand, Voronin mused, *a success could result in a promotion. Podpolkovnik* (Lieutenant Colonel) *Voronin. I like the sound of that.*

"We're passing over Rublyovka now," the pilot announced. "We're almost there."

Rublyovka was a paramecium-shaped district located west of Moscow, and home to hundreds of Kremliads (Kremlin whores), oligarchs, and criminals. There being very little difference between them.

Voronin heard the pilot speaking with someone on the radio. Security? Of course. The pilot needed permission to land.

"That's the president's estate off to the right," the pilot said, as he put the helicopter into a turn. "He owns 37 acres, according to what I was told."

Voronin stared at the mansion as the helicopter landed. The three-story structure was made of stone pierced with tall windows, all set off by a tower with an onion-shaped top. It was painted gold. The color that oligarchs preferred for turrets and toilets.

Voronin could see half a dozen men in dark overcoats waiting beside the helipad, and felt sure that more were on call. One of them rolled steps into place. Another opened the door. He was very polite. "Welcome to the presidential estate, Major. Please follow me to the magnetometer. I'm sure you understand."

Voronin wasn't surprised. And had nothing to worry about since he'd left his pistol and knife at the hotel. He nodded. "Yes, of course."

After clearing security Voronin was led into the mansion via a side entrance, and from there to a massive hall hung with portraits of Russian heroes. Field Marshal Generalissimo Suvorov was there, as was Vladmir Lenin, and President Toplin. Ego—the enemy of men great and small.

Double doors opened onto a reception area where a severe looking woman waited to greet him. "Good morning, Major. I am Mischa Durov, the president's executive assistant. Can I send for coffee or tea?"

Tea was still widely available in Moscow. But coffee was hard to find. "A cup of coffee would be welcome," Voronin replied. "Thank you."

"Wonderful," Durov responded, as if Voronin was doing her a favor. "Please follow me. The president is in his office."

Voronin allowed himself to be led into a large, ornately decorated room complete with high arched windows, a massive desk, and two guest chairs. Toplin was a large man, thus his nickname: "*Medved.*" The Bear.

And that was strikingly apparent as Toplin stood, circled the desk, and offered his hand. "Major Voronin... This is an honor. Stories of your exploits precede you. Is it true that you single-handedly captured an American bunker, armed with only a knife?"

"Of course not," Voronin answered. "I was armed with a submachine gun, a pistol, and a knife."

Toplin laughed and slapped Voronin on the back. "Well said, Major... We will get along you and I. Please have a seat."

A servant arrived moments later, placed a silver tray on Toplin's desk, and left. "Ah, coffee!" Toplin said. "I drink far too much of it. Please help yourself."

Voronin poured steaming hot coffee into a beautifully decorated cup, retreated to his chair, and wished he could dispense with the saucer. But the flavor was excellent. Brazilian perhaps. A nonaligned country that continued to trade with Russia.

"So," Toplin said, "let's get down to business. You are a soldier, and I have a mission for you. Simply put, the task is to fly to Syria, find a woman named Hala Omar, and bring her back. She's special to me. So, I want her alive if at all possible. But failing that, you must find a way to preserve her body, and bring it back.

"Thanks to our friends at the Foreign Intelligence Service, we know where Hala's parents live, and that seems like a good place to start.

"You will have special powers for this mission Major, and that includes the authority to commandeer boats and aircraft. Do you have any questions?"

Voronin had lots of questions. Who the hell was Hala Omar? Why had she gone to Syria? And, why did Toplin want her back? Preferably, alive.

But Voronin sensed that he shouldn't ask those questions so he didn't. "No, sir. I'll do my best."

Toplin stood. A sure sign that the meeting was over. Voronin did likewise.

Durov escorted the soldier to the side door where she paused. "Would you like a word of advice?"

"*Da*," Voronin said. "*Pozhaluysta.*" (Please.)

Durov stared into Veronin's eyes. "Do not fail."

***

Superbase Tabqa, Syria

Master Sergeant Felix Bone left the base with a three-day pass, a pistol, and a plan. The goal was to steal all nine million dollars' worth of gold coins out from under Polat's nose, and leave the Turk to suck it.

Bone had spent many hours of research using an online translator and Google Earth to make sense of the material captured in the ISIS safehouse. But the effort would be worth it if he managed to snatch all the loot.

The checkout process was easy. All Bone had to do was show his ID, along with his pass, and logout. "So, what's the plan, Sarge?" a private inquired, as he entered the information into his terminal. "Visit some museums?"

It was an old joke, and one the soldier had employed a thousand times. "That's right," Bone replied with a wink. "I'm all about museums."

Both men laughed and Bone passed through the gate into the chaos that was Mud Town. According to legend the name "Mud Town" stemmed from the way the streets turned into a nearly impassable sea of mud each time it rained. Hence the elevated walkways made from anything the townspeople could find in the airbase's dump, including wooden cargo pallets, scrap metal, and fiberglass panels.

Most, if not all, of the citizens of Mud Town were employed by the base in one way or another. Soldiers like Bone were allowed to visit the community between the hours of 0800 and 1800, weren't allowed to drink there, and were subject to random breathalyzer tests by roaming MPs.

It was possible to stay in one of the B&Bs (Bugs & Beds) but very few people elected to do so. That however was what Bone would claim he'd been doing, if asked where he'd been for three days.

His real destination was the home of a civilian scout named Aboo Hassan. A man Bone knew he could depend on.

Thanks to his work for the Allies, Hassan lived in a two-story house, and owned a beat-up Toyota Land Cruiser. A rugged vehicle that Bone hoped to rent.

One of Hassan's daughters was there to welcome Bone into the house and lead him to the sitting room where her father was sitting with his leg up on a table. It was wrapped with bandages. "Good morning, Aboo... What the hell happened?"

"I caught one three nights ago," Hassan said in heavily accented English. "But one of your doctors took care of me. A medic comes by once a day."

"I'm sorry," Bone replied. "But glad to hear that you're getting medical attention."

"So, what's on your mind?" Hassan inquired. "I'm not available for missions right now."

"No," Bone agreed. "Of course, you aren't. But your Land Cruiser is. And I'd like to rent it. How does a hundred dollars a day sound?"

"It sounds good," Hassan replied. "Real good. Unless I don't get it back."

"Well how about this," Bone said, as he removed his Rolex. "We'll trade watches. And, if I fail to return your ride, the Rolex is yours. My wife gave it to me." *And I'm still paying for it*, Bone thought darkly.

Hassan weighed the watch in his hand. He knew Rolexes were not only expensive, but some of them actually appreciated. Which meant he wasn't likely to lose money if the American were killed. Doing *what?* Hassan didn't want to know. His watch was a Casio. He gave it over. "Done. How long will you be gone?"

"Roughly 24 hours."

"May Allah protect you. And my Toyota."

After collecting the keys, and leaving the Hassan residence, Bone walked to the nearest clothing store where he purchased a checkered head scarf called a *keffiyeh.*

It wasn't much of a disguise. But something was better than nothing. And, at a glance, other motorists might mistake the American for a local.

The Landcruiser was fitted with a 25-gallon fuel tank, and according to the gauge, it was nearly empty. That meant Bone had to stop at the local gas station on his way out of town.

It consisted of a shack fronted by ranks of five-gallon gas cans, the contents of which could be his for a mere fifty dollars each. It took two hundred and fifty bucks to fill up.

That hurt. *But*, Bone told himself, *once I become a millionaire, two-fifty will amount to chump change.*

Bone's destination was a burned-out convoy located about fifty miles southeast, near the town of Zabad. According to the notes captured along with the crude map, the twelve-vehicle convoy had been traveling east, when it was attacked by what the author believed to be *two* Reaper drones.

An ISIS leader named Hafeez Badri was the target, or so the unnamed author assumed, and had been killed along with his second in command.

One of the vehicles was a flatbed truck. And what the *Kafirs* didn't realize was that nine-mil worth of freshly minted gold coins were hidden in a concealed storage compartment under the vehicle's cargo deck.

And because the vehicles burned, and the idolators didn't know about the gold, it was still there. Did some of the gold melt? Perhaps. But even if it had, gold is gold, regardless of the shape it takes.

The plan was simple. Open the secret compartment, load the gold into the Land Cruiser, and transport it to the remains of an old French Foreign Legion fort.

While studying the sand drifted ruins of the fort via Google Earth, Bone noticed that one of the corner towers was partially intact, and figured that it would be a good place to hide his stash. Eventually, when conditions allowed, he would return.

The route took Bone east to Jibrin, south through the abandoned town of As Safrah, and Umm' Amud beyond, before turning east toward Zabad. And it was there, just south of Syria's largest lake, that Bone found what he was looking for.

The burned-out wrecks had been pushed off the highway where the windblown sand was beginning to pile up against them.

There wasn't a lot of traffic on the two-lane highway, but there was some, and the last thing Bone wanted to do was attract attention.

After crossing a bridge Bone circled back, and down into the dry wash that passed under the span. It was shady there and his vehicle was out of sight. *I'll move the Toyota up next to the flatbed truck after dark*, Bone decided. *I sure as hell don't want to hump 500 pounds worth of gold all the way down here.*

After grabbing a bottle of water, Bone locked the SUV, and made his way up a gentle incline to the sunbaked landscape above. There was very little cover, but Bone took advantage of what there was as vehicles approached.

Then, after reaching the wrecks, Bone was careful to keep them between himself and the road. The flatbed was the only vehicle of its kind and therefore easy to spot.

Bone felt his heart start to beat faster. Every fucking thing was about to change for the better. Yeah, Polat would be pissed. But what was the asshole going to do? File a report confessing his own guilt? Bone didn't think so. As for the possibility of physical violence, the Ranger was an expert at that.

All that remained of the crates originally loaded on top of the cargo bed was charred wood. Bone made use of his penlight to examine the underside of the truck.

That was when he spotted the vertical bolts that ran all the way down through the frame, and went to work with an adjustable crescent wrench. The nuts were tight, but soon came loose, thus freeing the bolts, which Bone had to remove from above.

The Ranger was short of breath by then, and giddy with anticipation, as he slipped a large screw driver into the crack that separated two folding doors and pried.

There was a *groan*, followed by a *clang*, as one of the hinged panels fell on the other. Bone's penlight probed the interior of the box. No gold. Nothing other than a sheet of paper.

Bone's hopes sank beneath an ocean of despair. Gone, all gone. Bone wanted to cry as he read the handwritten note:

Dear Sergeant,

Like you, I came here planning to take the stuff for myself.

You'll be happy to learn I didn't find it.

What I <u>did</u> find was more information about where it is.

And I won't be able to get it without your help.

So, we are as you put it, still "partners in crime."

Let's talk.

Sincerely,
Oscar

***

Almakan Alaman, (the Safe Place), Northwestern Syria

The Women's Place had been constructed on what had been a British airstrip during World War II. Old barracks buildings had been repaired, tents had been added, and the badly cracked runway served as a main street with metal hangars to either side of it.

The sun was an orange ball in the sky, there was very little shade, and the air was hot. Oppressively so. But Hala felt reasonably safe here. Many of the women were armed, lookouts were stationed in the old control tower, and conditions were generally peaceful in northwestern Syria.

Hala and Nina had been welcomed with open arms, especially by the Yazidi women there, who rushed to make the newcomers comfortable.

Hala tried to use a pseudonym, but the effort failed when one of the residents recognized her, and word spread. So, when she entered the hangar marked "Medical," she was greeted with her own name. "Good morning, Hala," the woman at the reception table said. "What can we do for you?"

"I would like to see the doctor."

"Is this an emergency?"

"No."

"Would a 3:00 PM appointment be okay?"

"Yes."

"I'll put you down."

Hala thanked the woman and left.

All of those who could work did so. And Hala had volunteered to help in the kitchen. Not as a cook, she didn't have the skills for that, but as an assistant.

Sometimes she was assigned to chop vegetables. But most of Hala's duties involved cleaning tables in between meals, serving food, and washing the mismatched dishes.

In keeping with Almakan Alaman's purpose, the resident imam was a woman, one of only a handful in Syria. And the sound of a female voice calling the faithful to the afternoon Dhuhr prayer sent a chill down Hala's spine, as she made her way to the wood framed mosque.

The structure had been a Christian church during World War II, and now stripped of pews, it served a different faith. One that Nina no longer believed in.

Hala had her doubts. But she still found comfort in the rituals. And, according to the tenets of the Muslim faith, men and women were equal in the eyes of God. Even if many men didn't agree, and hewed to the old ways. *Why?* To control women, that's why.

Hala arrived at the medical hangar on time, and after a short wait, was sent back to a screened area to see Doctor Essam.

Judging from appearances Essam was sixty something. She wore her hair pulled back, a pair of wire rimmed glasses were perched on her nose, and she was wearing a defiant slash of red lipstick. "Have a seat my dear… What a pleasure. I never expected to meet a world-famous gymnast here."

"I'm not world famous," Hala responded. "But thank you."

"You're welcome. What can I do for you?"

"I think I'm pregnant."

Essam's eyebrows rose slightly. "What makes you think so?"

"I missed a period. My breasts are swollen, I feel sick in the morning, and I urinate a lot."

Doctor Essam nodded. "Those are indications all right. But we'll run a test to be sure. Assuming that you're correct, what support, if any can you expect from the father?"

"None," Hala replied. "He's in Russia. And we're estranged."

"Well don't worry," Essam said. "We will take good care of you. Fatma! Please join us."

Hala had been introduced to Fatma at the dining hall, and knew her to be a nurse.

The speed with which Fatma responded suggested that she'd been close by. Eavesdropping? Yes, Hala thought so. That likelihood made Hala angry, but there was nothing she could do about it.

Fatma led Hala to a bathroom, gave her a kit, and explained how to use it.

Hala was hoping for a negative result, but was in no way surprised when the test was positive. The fear had been there all along, waiting to claim her, and now it did. Fear of being a mother, fear of what her parents would think, and fear of Toplin. Would he want the baby? No, of course he wouldn't. And that was equivalent to a death sentence for both Hala and her child.

Hala began to cry. And was still crying when Fatma called out to her. "Hala? Are you alright?"

"Yes," Hala replied. But that was a lie.

***

Superbase Tabqa, Syria

Clang! Clang! Clang! "Marie! It's Ziggy… Get up! We have a mission."

Soto groaned, turned to look at her bedside clock, and saw that it was 0214. *What the fuck?*

Soto swung her feet over onto the steel floor. "Hold on! I'm coming."

The lock clicked, the door opened, and there was Jones. He tossed a rock aside. "Sorry… But this one has hair all over it *and* it's on fire."

Soto was wearing a tee shirt and shorts. She shivered in the cold night air. "What's up?"

"The Secretary of State was headed for a conference in Mosul and someone shot her plane down. Somehow, some way, the pilot managed to belly flop and skid. A lot of passengers were killed, but some survived, and that includes the secretary. We have orders to pull them out."

"Shit. How far away is the crash site?"

"It's about 300 miles east of here."

Soto did the math. If she took an internal fuel tank, and left it behind in order to carry passengers, she figured that the *Double Deuce* could reach the site in two hours, give or take. "Did you notify Alvarez?"

"Yeah. She's going after the gunners. A medical team and a squad of Rangers will board shortly."

That was good and bad. The more people the *Deuce* carried, the slower she would be. But Soto couldn't see any way around it. "Good. Load an internal tank, and run the checks, but don't crank her up… We need to conserve fuel. I'll be there in fifteen."

Soto tried to imagine the scene as she got dressed. Flames? Maybe. Wreckage for sure. Dead and wounded all over the place. How many people were there? Dozens? Quite possibly. A mix of staff, press, and security personnel. All in a daze.

Soto stepped outside to discover that a gunner named Clarkson was waiting for her on a motor scooter. "Morning, ma'am… Hop on. I'll have you there in no time."

Clarkson wasn't kidding. Soto had to hang onto a grab bar as the private sped through nearly deserted streets to Revetment 7. The Chinook's nav lights were on, and the rotors were starting to turn. Alvarez was there to welcome them aboard.

Soto hurried past two doctors, half a dozen medics, and a squad of Rangers on her way to the cockpit. "Are we cleared to Heliport 2?"

"Yeah."

"You've got the aircraft. Let's go."

Soto was fastening her harness when she heard Albro's voice over the radio.

"Wizard, this is Charlie-Six. Do you read me? Over."

"We copy," Soto replied. "Over."

"You are cleared for an immediate takeoff. The situation at the crash site is deteriorating. According to the people at Central, an Iraqi Shia militia group shot the plane down using a missile that was probably sourced from Iran. And the assholes in Iraq are featuring the story on the news!

"So enemy fighters are moving in to capture or kill the secretary. Her staff, security personnel, and even reporters are fighting back. A-10s are on scene to provide ground support. Check in with them when you get close. Over."

"Roger that," Soto replied. "Over."

"Keep me advised," Albro added. "Over." A *click* signaled the end of the contact.

Jones felt a slight pressure on the flight controls and looked at Soto.

"I have the helicopter," Soto said.

"You have it," Jones agreed, as he relinquished control.

The runway lights disappeared behind them. Lights glowed in the distance, but not many, and darkness owned the land.

***

Just east of the Syria-Iraq border

United States Secretary of State Denise Howard didn't know how to fight, but she did know how to lead, and was making the rounds. Morale was critical. If the survivors could hold out long enough, a Chinook would pull them out.

Plane wreckage was spread all over the place, some of which was still smoldering. But a large section of the fuselage remained intact, and was being used as a headquarters of sorts.

It wasn't bulletproof however, far from it, and that made it necessary for the people sheltering inside to keep their heads down.

Howard crawled out over the stubby remnants of a wing, slid off, and landed on her feet. The landing gear was up, the port engine had been ripped off, and was resting on the ground near the tail. As for the other engine, that was lost in the surrounding darkness.

Approximately a dozen passengers, some wounded, had taken cover behind a rock outcropping, and were firing short bursts at targets Howard couldn't see, as she scuttled forward to join them. "Howard coming in!"

A reporter named Nick Adams was there to greet her. He was armed with a pistol and a six-shot 40mm grenade launcher. Weapons weren't a problem thanks to the small arsenal kept aboard Howard's plane. "*Semper Fi*, Madam Secretary... Once a jarhead always a jarhead."

Howard smiled in spite of herself. "I hope you're a better shot than a foreign correspondent, Nick. Your story on Israel sucked."

Adams laughed. "Sorry, Madam Secretary. But the truth hurts sometimes."

Someone yelled, "Tangos incoming! Nine o'clock."

Adams swiveled to the left, fired twice, and was rewarded with twin explosions. Someone screamed.

Howard scuttled to the left where a small fire marked another group of defenders. There were three of them, all members of the Diplomatic Security Service (DSS). Two were ex-military, all were good shots, and firing from cover.

Dick Newsom, the lead agent, turned to point an M4 at her. "Madam Secretary... What the hell are you doing here?"

"I'm supervising," Howard said with a smile. "Go ahead, shoot somebody."

"I damned near shot *you*," Newsom complained.

"I'm glad you didn't," Howard responded. "Keep up the good work. A Chinook is coming for us."

"It's going to get a hot reception," Newsom replied. "But I'm glad to hear it."

Howard's last stop was the remains of an adobe structure renamed "The Alamo."

Someone fired a flare, and an LMG rattled, as Howard called her name. She could see a pile of bodies in front of the Alamo where successive waves of enemy fighters had been cut down.

An aide named Adriana Sanchez was in charge there. Her business suit was torn, a makeshift bandage was wrapped around her head, and she was in no way surprised to see Howard. "Hi boss, how're we doing?"

"Extremely well, all things considered," Howard replied. "Just keep on, keeping on. Help is on the way. I see you're packing a shotgun. Do you know how to use it?"

"I'm learning," Sanchez replied. "They told me to point and shoot."

Howard laughed. "Give 'em hell! And be ready to pull back when the Chinook lands."

As Howard made her way back to the 757's fuselage she paused to look at the sky. "Hurry," she said. "Please hurry. Before they kill every single one of us."

***

Jones had the controls and the *Double Deuce* was fifteen minutes out when Soto made the call. "This is Wizard. We are a Chinook incoming from the west. Does anyone copy?"

"Hell yes, we copy," a familiar voice replied. "This is Boots, girl... Where you been? We are two A-10s. But we're low on fuel and ordinance. The ground party is using the callsign 'Sec-One.' Over."

"We're close, Boots. Break, break. Sec-One... This is Wizard. Do you read me? Over."

"We copy," a male voice replied. "Welcome to the party. We have a flat spot for you. We'll pop flares and call the color. Once you touch down, we'll pull back, and bring the wounded with us. Over."

"Roger that. We're less than ten out. Get ready. Over."

By that time Soto could see the sparkle of automatic fire, the occasional flash of light as a grenade exploded, and the eerie glow of a parachute flare as it descended over the crash site.

The Chinook's nav lights were off, but the enemy soldiers could hear the unmistakable sound of helicopter rotor blades, and were firing into the sky. Soto fired flares and chaff in an effort to lead shoulder launched missiles away.

That wouldn't work with RPGs however. All it would take was one lucky hit to bring *Double Deuce* down.

Soto tried to ignore that possibility as bullets *pinged* the fuselage, *snapped* through the cargo compartment, and cut a Ranger down. The medics went to work on him as Soto scanned the area ahead. "Wizard to Sec-One. Pop flares. Over."

Two yellow flares appeared. "I see two yellow flares. Over."

"Roger that, Wizard. Put down between them. Over."

The area around the flares was lit with a yellow glow. Jones watched the ground come up through the chin bubble as Alvarez dropped the ramp. Once the gear touched down the Rangers rushed out to establish a defensive perimeter around the helicopter.

A bullet hit the windscreen at an angle, caused a crack, and whizzed away. Then an explosion shook the ship. "That was a grenade," Alvarez announced. "The starboard engine took some shrapnel."

Jones was busy checking the damaged engine parameters in hopes of saving it.

Soto was worried about weight. How many people were boarding the ship anyway? And would the port engine be able to lift the *Double Deuce* off?

"Boots here… We're going to mow the lawn. And it will be tight. In from the south. Over."

Gatling guns roared, and tracers probed the ground east of the Chinook, as the "Hogs" made their final run. Soto was about to acknowledge the transmission when a voice with an Australian accent came over the radio.

"Wizard, Digger and Wallaby here… We are two F-35A Lightnings in from the west. Be advised that three Iranian MiG-29s are in bound at angels fifteen. No worries though… We have them surrounded. Over."

"Roger, and thank you," Soto replied, as Alvarez stuck her head into the cockpit. "The ramp is coming up."

The gunners called, "Clear left. Clear right."

Soto felt a sense of relief as Jones pulled up on the thrust level and both engines responded.

As the Chinook rose, the gear box located on the nose of the starboard engine produced a harsh *screeching* sound.

The gunners and the Rangers fired nonstop from the gunports, the aft ramp, and even the cargo hook hole as enemy fighters surged forward.

Jones went straight up as quickly as the engines would allow. Tracers followed. But the higher the Chinook got the less ground fire there was.

Then it was time to turn to the northwest. The question was whether to land and wait for help or to continue flying. "Push it up to the VNE (Velocity Never Exceeded)," Soto ordered.

"VNE," Jones confirmed. "Roger that."

After releasing her harness Soto turned to peer back into a scene straight from hell. The light was dim, a doctor was performing CPR on a man wearing the remnants of a business suit, and a medic was hanging an IV over a woman with a tourniquet around her right arm. The reason for that was obvious. Her right hand was missing.

And there, in the middle of the deck, was a dead body. A young woman was kneeling in a pool of blood and crying. "The secretary caught a bullet coming up the ramp," Alvarez explained. "At least three of the wounded are critical."

Soto turned around and refastened her harness. Her decision was made. They would make the trip on one engine if they had to. Jones looked at her. "How bad is it?"

"Really, really bad."

"Mind if I smoke?"

"You don't smoke."

"I do now."

Soto felt a brief moment of joy as Digger reported in. "Two enemy aircraft down, one on the run. Over."

But the sorrow returned after that. The trip to Superbase Tabqa seemed to take forever. All traffic was ordered to hold on the ground, or "go around," as the *Double Deuce* made her approach and landed on Helipad 2. Ambulances were lined up, lights flashing, waiting to accept the incoming casualties.

Getting there was a victory of sorts. But it didn't feel that way as the Secretary of State was carried off the aircraft. "It wasn't our fault," Jones said. "We did what we could."

"Yeah," Soto agreed. "We did what we could."

CHAPTER SEVEN

Tal Tamir, Syria

Major Sergei Voronin was a hunter. And, like all hunters, he understood the importance of patience. Even so, the long boring trip from Moscow to the Syrian town of Tal Tamir was a pain in the ass.

Because of wartime conditions it had been necessary to commandeer a patrol boat in the Russian port of Makhachkala, and make a highspeed run to Astara, Iran. From there the team had to travel overland to Tabriz, fly to Mosul in Iraq, and drive to the town of Tal Tamir.

According to Voronin's research, the city had originally been the administrative center of the Tell Tamer Subdistrict, which consisted of thirteen municipalities. That was before the civil war, and the arrival of the Islamic State militia in 2015.

The first thing ISIS fighters did was to target Christian Assyrians for killings and kidnappings. The Islamic State had been defeated since then, but not eliminated, and continued to be a factor throughout Syria.

None of that was central to Voronin's mission, but had to be taken into account, since an ISIS cell could spot Voronin's five-man team and decide to attack it.

One way to avoid that scenario was to keep a low profile by arriving in Tal Tamir at night, and going straight to the local Foreign Intelligence Service (SVR RF) safehouse. According to the briefing received before Voronin left Moscow, the safehouse was a tiny two-bedroom dwelling, owned by a parttime operative named Tahir Sayed.

"How can we be sure that Mr. Sayed is loyal to us?" Voronin had inquired.

"His brother lives here," the briefer replied, as if that was all Voronin needed to know. And it was, since the implication was clear: If Sayed made a mistake, his brother would die.

The Russians were packed into an ancient 1992 Land Rover Defender, and it was one of the few vehicles on the streets, as the "recovery" team entered town.

There were few streetlights, and most people were in bed, but a few squares of buttery yellow light could still be seen.

A stray dog chased the Land Rover for a block. But, other than that, none of the other residents took notice of the vehicle's presence. A number of twists and turns were required to approach the safehouse from behind.

Sayed was waiting and the six-foot-tall barrier seemed to swing open by magic. And, once the Defender was inside, the gate closed behind it.

Voronin was sitting on the passenger side and was the first to get out. Assuming the SVR RF briefer was correct, the Syrian spoke English. Voronin addressed him in that language. "Mr. Sayed? My name is Major Yenin," Voronin lied. "Thank you for letting us in so promptly."

Rather than the gown-like jellabiya that most men in the area favored, Sayed was wearing a carefully pressed suit with tie. The mark of the bureaucrat that he was. "You are most welcome," Sayed replied. "Please join me in the house. Refreshments are waiting, as are the photographs that I was instructed to prepare for you."

The Russians filled the tiny sitting area to overflowing, so Starshina (First Sergeant) Gregov ordered three of them to go outside and stand watch. "You will be relieved in two hours," Gregov promised. "No talking. Sound travels at night. And if the neighbors hear you speak Russian the word will spread."

A mousy woman served refreshments as Sayed opened a laptop and began to scroll through photos. "This is the Omar residence," Sayed told Voronin, as a picture of a house appeared. "It's two stories tall, has a central courtyard, and is the finest residence in Tal Tamir. I know because I am the local tax collector."

It was a beautiful house, and Voronin knew why. Subsequent to his meeting with the president, the special operator had been briefed regarding the "special" relationship Toplin had with Hala Omar.

Had Toplin's mistress been funneling money to her parents? Of course, she had. And they in turn invested the money in real estate which, during turbulent times, was more likely to retain its value than money in a bank.

"Do the Omars have any staff?"

"No," Sayed replied. "The Omars are modest people and take care of themselves."

"How about dogs?" Gregov inquired. "I don't like dogs."

"Yes," Sayed answered. "A dog roams the property at night."

"That's good to know," Voronin said. "How about access?"

Another photo appeared. It showed an elderly couple approaching a mosque. "The Omars attend the *Dhuhr* prayer at roughly 1:15 every afternoon," Sayed responded.

"Good," Voronin said. "That's when we'll enter. And you will come with us."

"*Me*?" Sayed demanded. "Why me?"

"Because we need a translator."

"But the Omars know me," Sayed objected, his eyes darting from face-to-face.

"Trust me," Voronin replied. "That won't be a problem."

The team rotated through two-hour watches until dawn, when it was necessary to withdraw into the house lest they be spotted by Sayed's neighbors. There was very little to do other than tweak gear, and play a card game called Durak.

Sayed and his wife made themselves scarce during the morning hours by keeping to their bedroom.

Finally, after what seemed like an eternity of waiting, twelve o'clock rolled around, and it was time to pack up and load everything into the Rover.

At one o'clock the entire party crowded into the SUV and Gregov drove them to the neighborhood where the Omars lived, turned into an alley, and stopped behind what Sayed assured them was the correct house. It took less than a minute to jimmy the gate and back the vehicle in.

The family dog was barking by then, leaping into the air, and clearly a threat. Voronin drew a suppressed pistol and shot the animal before getting out of the SUV. Gregov hurried to close the gate.

So far, so good. But, when the Russians tried to enter through the back of the house, they were confronted by a steel door and a high-quality lock.

That made sense, because haves always try to protect themselves from have-nots, and the Omars were haves.

Explosives were out of the question since the noise would attract attention from the neighbors, the police, and possibly ISIS as well.

As a result, Private First Class Zonov had to drill the lock out. A process that involved drilling a hole just above the keyhole to defeat the pins inside.

Unfortunately, the Omar's lock was made of high-quality steel, and the better part of ten minutes were consumed penetrating the casing, and intercepting the pins.

But after a good deal of swearing by Zonov the task was complete, the lock turned, and they were in. The first thing Voronov noticed was the smell of cooking, a garlicy odor in particular, which suffused the kitchen.

The rooms beyond were spotlessly clean, and the entire house was decorated with photos of Hala Omar. Hala the little girl, Hala the student, Hala the gymnast, Hala the reporter—and finally—Hala posing on a beautiful beach. The Black Sea perhaps? Voronin thought so.

Had Toplin been there too? If so, the photographer had been careful to exclude the politician from the shot.

Another wait began, but a brief one this time, and the Russians were ready when a key turned and the front door opened. It was a simple matter to take control of the elderly couple, march them into the sitting room, and order them to sit.

Mr. Omar was wearing a *keffiyeh* headdress, and sporting a white beard. He was clearly terrified. "Mr. Sayed... Who are these men? What do they want?"

Voronin waited for the translation. "Explain that we're looking for his daughter. And assure him that we won't harm her."

"But *why?*" Mr. Omar demanded.

"Tell him that an important individual in Russia wants Hala to return there. That's all I can share. Now, where is she?"

"I d-d-don't know," Mr. Omar replied. "Please! You must believe me!"

Voronin drew his pistol, took aim, and shot Mrs. Omar in her right thigh. She jerked, uttered a cry of pain, and clutched the wound.

Voronin turned to Mr. Omar. "Now, where is Hala?"

The Syrian's head was bowed. His voice was a barely heard whisper. "The Women's Village. Almakan Alaman."

Voronin turned to Sayed. The operative's face was pale and his hands were shaking. "Have you heard of it?"

"Yes," Sayed replied. "It makes sense. Miss Omar knew it would be dangerous to come here."

Voronin nodded. "Good." Then, with two perfectly aimed shots, Voronin shot each Omar in the head. The bodies slid down onto the floor, where their blood seeped into the Persian rug.

"Trash the house," Voronin ordered. "I want it to look as if thieves broke in, took what they wanted, and killed the Omars."

It took twenty minutes to open closets, rifle through dressers, and scatter things all about. Then, once the job was done, Sayed waited to be shot. It didn't happen.

"You did a good job," Voronin told the Syrian. "I will tell your handler. A bonus will come your way. *Russkiye nikogda ne zabyvayut.* Russians never forget."

***

Mud City, Syria

Two days had passed since Bone's discovery of Polat's message:

Dear Sergeant,

Like you, I came here planning to take the stuff for myself.

You'll be happy to learn I didn't find it.

What I <u>did</u> find was more information about where it is.

And I won't be able to get it without your help.

So, we are as you put it, still "partners in crime."

Let's talk.

Sincerely,
Oscar

Now, after a guarded phone conversation, the two men were about to meet. Not on base, where prying eyes were all around, but at the Turk's hootch in Mud Town.

Bone eyed a piece of paper, confirmed that he was on the correct street, and continued on his way. Store owners called out as the Ranger passed, urging the American to examine their "Class-A very good," merchandise.

A group of raggedy children were playing *Hajla*, a game similar to hopscotch, while two elderly men watched.

And there, up ahead, was the small dwelling where Bone and Polat were to meet. It was a one-story affair with gun slits instead of windows. That, plus the metal door, suggested that the owner had something to protect.

Bone stepped up onto a narrow porch and rapped on the door. He heard stirrings within, saw an eyeball through the quarter-sized peephole, followed by the click of a lock. "Good afternoon, Sergeant," Polat said. "No hard feelings, right?"

Bone forced a smile. "Right."

"Come on in."

Bone heard the door close behind him as he paused to look around. A generator was purring out back, and the interior was lit by table lamps.

The hootch was *what*? An office? A hideout? Some of each?

A map dominated one wall. A toilet crouched in a corner. Weapons were available here and there. But Bone didn't see a bed, suggesting that Polat slept elsewhere.

The Turk opened a tiny refrigerator. "It's never too early for a beer," Polat proclaimed, as he brought two bottles of *Efes Pilsen* to the table at the center of the room.

"Are you familiar with Turkish beer? No? Well, I think you'll like the coffee and chocolate aroma.

"Now," Polat said, as he sat down. "Let's talk business."

Bone took a swig. "According to your note you found more information. Tell me about that."

Polat nodded. "Americans are so direct. I love that. Well, after discovering the same thing you did, which was that the secret compartment was empty, I went forward to search the cab. It was a longshot, but that's what intelligence agents do, they chase longshots."

Bone felt stupid. The fucking cab. He should have thought of that, and hadn't. It wouldn't have made a difference, since the Turk had already been there, but the omission was an indication of sloppiness. The kind that could get him killed.

"Good thinking," Bone said, as he sipped his beer. "And what did you find?"

"*This*," Polat said, as he reached into a pocket and removed what looked like a chunky watch. He placed the device on the table. It was attached to a half-charred wristband.

Bone stared. A Garmin Foretrex GPS navigator! He didn't own one, but knew Rangers who did, and they spoke highly of the devices.

"So, it was just sitting there? That seems hard to believe."

"No," the Turk replied. "It was down on the floorboard, mixed in with bone fragments, and the remains of a charred seat cushion. That's why other people missed it."

"Good work," Bone said. "I assume its functional, or we wouldn't be having this conversation."

"You assume correctly," Polat replied. "Simply put, it's my opinion that the convoy wasn't carrying any gold, it was *headed* for the gold! Which ISIS fighters planned to place in the empty compartment."

Bone felt a rising sense of excitement. "You believe that, but you don't know."

"True," Polat conceded. "But consider this… The destination entered into this device is the Dead City of Abaz, located south and west of us.

"It's a huge ruin that includes some 700 sites. It's located in the Jebel Riha, about 50 miles southwest of Aleppo."

"Damn," Bone said. "What is that? An hour away?"

"It is," Polat replied. "But the gold could weigh as much five hundred pounds, the roads are dangerous, and lots of things could go wrong. That's why we'll fly in and out. In Captain Soto's Chinook."

Bone frowned. "Sorry, Omar, but I can't use a Chinook anytime I want."

"No, of course not," the Turk acknowledged. "But I will request a mission. And while we're out searching for Colonel Kaya, we'll instruct Captain Soto to make a detour to retrieve a top-secret cargo."

"What if she refuses?"

"She won't," Polat predicted. "But, if I'm wrong, we'll find a workaround.

"By the way, the Colonel Kaya thing is a cover for my *real* mission, which is to find a Syrian news reporter named Hala Omar."

Bone's eyebrows rose. "Whatever for?"

Polat shrugged. "That's above my pay grade, as you Americans would say. But I have a theory. Since Omar is, or was, President Toplin's mistress, chances are that my government plans to use her as leverage."

"To do what?"

"To help my country counter the Kurds. They want to subvert our government."

Bone knew that was complete bullshit. What the Kurds wanted was to control their ancestral homeland. But Polat believed it, or was pretending to believe it.

"Meanwhile my government continues to think that you're looking for Colonel Kaya," Bone put in.

"Correct."

Up until this point I haven't crossed the line, Bone mused. *But now, if I go along with Polat's plan, I'll be a traitor. So, what am I going to do? Turn Polat in? Which will get me in trouble, and cut off my access to the gold, or am I going to pay my bills?*

Polat was waiting. Bone raised his bottle. "To partners in crime."

***

Sur-Na, Syria

ISIS Cell Commander Ferran Mostafa was furious and for good reason. After seducing Group Commander Hatem Chalibi, the Syrian *eahira* (whore) stabbed him to death, then fled the village along with a Yazidi slave girl. Gun trucks had been dispatched to search the surrounding area, find Hala Omar and bring her in.

As for the girl named Nina, she would be gang raped, and shot. Then Mostafa would order his men to hang Nina's body in the main square as a warning to those who dared do violence to an ISIS leader. Or a fighter for that matter.

And that was why Mostafa had chosen to visit a girl named Aisha. She was the girl Nina shared a sleeping cubicle with prior to running away. Did they share confidences? Maybe, and maybe not. But Mostafa was determined to find out.

Aisha was trembling with fear when brought before Mostafa. He sought to calm her. "There's nothing to worry about, Aisha. You have nothing to fear so long as you answer my questions truthfully. Do you know where Nina is?"

Aisha shook her head.

"I believe you," Mostafa said. "Did Nina talk about running away? Remember, be honest."

Aisha stared at her feet. Her voice was so low that Mostafa could barely hear it. "Nina wanted to be free."

Mostafa nodded. "Did Nina dream of going to a particular place?"

"Almakan Alaman. The Women's Place."

Mostafa felt his heart leap with joy. "Why there?"

"Because women run it."

"Thank you, Aisha. You may go."

Thus freed, the girl turned and hurried away. Tears were streaming down her cheeks.

***

Almakan Alaman. The Women's Place, Syria

What appeared to be a water tank sat atop an otherwise bare hill up ahead. And, as Mostafa peered through the truck's filthy windshield, he could see a column of smoke rising from a point beyond it. He checked his map.

Yes, the old airfield was located beyond the rise. So, was a building on fire? Or was Almakan Alaman under attack? And if so, by whom?

The road curved south to circle the hill. But Mostafa wasn't about to lead his column into what might be a battle. He turned to the driver. "Leave the road. Climb the hill. Let's see what's going on."

The pickup veered to the left and the sudden motion caught the men in back by surprise. They managed to remain in place by grabbing onto the roll cage.

Mostafa spoke into his handheld radio. "Follow me."

The drivers of the other Toyotas did as they were told. An ancient track led upwards. It was a rough ride. And there were times when Mostafa wondered if his decision had been hasty.

But, when the truck topped the rise he saw that no, he'd been correct. Smoke boiled up out of what had once been an airplane hangar, and as Mostafa got out, he could hear the sound of gunfire. The binoculars had been Chalibi's. *Never fear, I'm going to find the whore who murdered you*, Mostafa thought, as he brought them up to survey the scene below.

It appeared to be a small-scale battle with no more than a dozen fighters on each side. But who were they? It soon became apparent that one group was comprised entirely of women. The defenders then.

And the others? They were light skinned males. Americans? No, that seemed unlikely. Americans would arrive in heavy vehicles or helicopters. And none were visible.

"Someone's speaking Russian," Mostafa's radio operator reported.

Aha, Mostafa thought. *Russian!* That explained the light skin, and suggested something else as well. Perhaps a team had been sent to recover Hala Omar. If so, Mostafa couldn't allow that. There was Chalibi's memory to consider, yes, but potential ransom money as well.

Mostafa brought the radio to his lips. "Snipers! Target the Europeans. No one else."

The team of sixteen fighters included three crack shots, all armed with Russian made OTs-03 SVU sniper rifles acquired on the black market. The ISIS fighters fired and a man fell.

***

Major Sergei Voronin swore as Private First Class Ivkin went down, quickly followed by Junior Sergeant Klokov. "They're on the hill!" Voronin shouted. "We have what we came for. Pull back to the vehicles!"

It was a good plan, but doomed to failure, as Toyota gun trucks bounced down off the hill. One of them turned toward the Russian SUVs, while two charged Voronin's men, causing them to dash for cover. The concrete bunker had been used to store bombs and ammo during WWII and was essentially bulletproof.

***

Starshina Gregov pushed Hala Omar inside and down a flight of stairs. She stumbled and fell. Her right knee hit the floor and the pain caused her to gasp.

"We're trapped," Voronin commented, as he peered out through a gun slit.

Hala struggled to stand. It all happened so quickly. A single Russian entered the village, claimed to have important news about her parents, and sent her the locket her mother habitually wore. A locket that contained a picture of Hala aged twelve.

But when Hala agreed to see him, he put a gun to her head, and more Russians appeared. The village security force attempted to intervene but were unsuccessful.

That was when the trucks arrived. Trucks that looked a lot like the vehicles she'd seen in the village of Sur Na. Not that it mattered who took Hala prisoner. All of them were enemies.

***

"We're here for Hala Omar," Mostafa shouted in English. "Send someone out. We'll talk."

The better part of a minute passed. "I'm coming out," a voice replied. "But understand this… If you shoot me, the woman dies."

Mostafa saw a man emerge from the bunker and went to meet him. The Russian was a full head taller than Mostafa and heavily armed. "Major Yenin."

"Commander Mostafa."

"So," Voronin said. "What can I do for you?"

"Give me the woman."

"In exchange for *what?*"

"Your lives."

***

Voronin didn't want to die for Toplin, especially since doing so wouldn't mean anything. And, so long as he remained alive, there was a possibility of getting Hala Omar back.

"Okay, that sounds like a deal. We'll take Omar to one of our vehicles, and drive her to the edge of town. That's where we'll release her."

Mostafa frowned. "What's to keep you from taking off?"

Voronin shrugged. "That would be stupid. You have more vehicles, and more men. You would run us down."

"Yes," Mostafa agreed. "I would."

***

Superbase Tabqa

The sprawling airbase was a complicated organism. But, by visiting the club, one could get a good idea of what was going on. Was it nearly empty? If so, a big operation was underway. Was it filled with army personnel? And very few pilots? Then an air op was in the offing.

At the moment Soto was sitting by herself waiting for Sergeant Bone. But why? Their relationship was strictly professional. And once a mission was over the Bone went his way and she went hers.

But for some reason the Ranger wanted to "Grab a beer, and shoot the shit," with her. Soto saw him enter and look around. She waved. He waved in return and pursued a zigzag course to her table. "Good afternoon, ma'am… Thanks for making time."

A civilian waiter appeared, took their orders, and left. "It's always good to see you, Sergeant. What's up?"

"Maybe you heard," Bone responded. "We're about to head out on another mission."

"To find Colonel Kaya?"

"Yeah. You have to give the Turks credit. They don't quit."

Their drinks arrived and Soto raised her bottle. "Confusion to the enemy."

"I'll second that," Bone said, as he did the same. He was wearing a short-sleeved sport shirt and his arms were covered by a wild tangle of tattoos.

Soto squinted. "'*Sua sponte.*' What does that mean?"

"'*Sua sponte*' is one of the 75th Ranger Regiment's mottos. It refers to a Ranger's ability to accomplish tasks with little or no prompting."

"A good plan implemented today, is better than a perfect plan implemented tomorrow," Soto replied. "Patton said that."

"Exactly," Bone agreed. "Look, I asked for this meeting to let you know that in addition to the search for Kaya, Polat and I have a secondary mission. One we aren't allowed to talk about. So, if that comes up during the next few days, don't be surprised."

"Thanks for the heads up," Soto replied. "But grok this… If you can't read me in, or produce written orders, there's a good chance that I'll say 'no.'"

Bone shrugged. "I get that. But, if it comes up, the side mission is likely to be a no-brainer."

"Okay," Soto said. "We'll see how things work out. Is there anything else?"

Bone shook his head. The meeting came to an end shortly thereafter.

Bone's prediction proved to be prophetic.

Soto received an encrypted text two hours later, and made her way to the Ops Center, where Bone and Polat were waiting with a briefer.

***

The woman is eminently fuckable, Polat thought. *And, if the situation was different, I would take a shot at her. But one should never mix business with pleasure. So, there won't be any of that.*

According to one of our operatives, Hala Omar is at the Women's Place, <u>and</u> she's pregnant. How will President Toplin view that? Polat wondered. *He'll want her, that's for sure. What he does with her, well, that's none of my business.*

***

The briefing was a predictable affair—complete with a good weather forecast, a low threat index, and a short list of emergency landing spots.

Once it was over Soto went to dinner, returned to her hootch, and hit the rack. She awoke three minutes before the alarm was set to go off, and made her way to the central showers, where she kept her pistol close at hand. Sexual assaults were rare, but they weren't unknown, and it was better to be safe than sorry.

Then Soto made her way back to her quarters, got dressed, and went to meet Jones at the DFAC. Her copilot was hunched over a heaping plate of ham, eggs, and waffles. His mouth was full, and his voice was muffled. "Good morning, Marie… Try the waffles. They're pretty good."

Soto *did* try the waffles, but without the ham and eggs, and they were good. "Listen Ziggy, there's something I need to share. Something iffy."

Jones continued to eat as Soto told him about her conversation with Sergeant Bone. "So," she concluded. "They may try to extend our mission to some sort of secondary objective. And if they do I may, or may not, agree to it."

"Copy that," Jones said, as he wiped his mouth with a napkin. "You can count on me."

"I do," Soto replied. And discovered that she meant it.

The Chinook's departure was a routine affair, just like hundreds of other takeoffs scheduled to take place at Tabqa that day, as planes and helicopters pursued the business of war.

The Women's Village was based at an old airfield located to the northeast, and was roughly an hour away, in an area which was classified as "Contested." A descriptor so vague it could mean the place was crawling with hajis, or subject to little more than a kidnapping or two.

Soto wasn't sure what to expect as the helicopter overflew the Industrial City of Sheikh Najjar and the arid looking farmland beyond.

Time passed and Polat came forward forty-five minutes into the flight. "I assume we're getting close."

"We're about ten out," Soto told him. "I plan to circle the village before landing."

"That makes sense," the Turk agreed. "It's a peaceful place by all accounts. But you never know." And with that Polat returned to the cargo area.

Soto eyed the old military base as it came into sight. A water tank sat perched on top of a hill. And, beyond that, Quonset style hangars lined both sides of the old runway, which served as the main street. One of them was scorched. As if it had been on fire.

And there, painted onto the street, was a white dove bearing an olive branch in its beak. The paint was fresh and the message was clear: "This is a place of peace."

As Soto circled the village she pushed the thrust lever down, thereby losing altitude, eyes searching for signs of trouble. There were none. Everything looked normal except for one thing. Lots of women were visible, and that made sense since the village was for women, but none of them were looking up at the Chinook. *Why?*

Chinooks are BIG, they're noisy, and something of a rarity in most locales. Still, that could be explained. The community was in a war zone, one or more had landed on the old runway before, and the women were busy.

"We're about to land," Soto announced over the intercom. "Everything looks good. But keep a sharp lookout."

The wash from the rotors kicked up a miniature dust storm as the *Double Deuce* touched down, and Soto was about to relax when Jones shouted. "A truck is coming straight at us! *Pull pitch!*"

Soto saw the oncoming vehicle roar out of a hangar and head at them. The semi was *huge*, large enough to destroy the Chinook, and the behemoth continued to gain speed as black smoke jetted up from vertical stacks.

Was the driver willing to trade his or her life for an Allied helicopter? There was no way to know, as Soto jerked the thrust lever up, and felt the engines respond.

Jones was yelling, "Shit, shit, shit!" as the truck bore down on them and automatic weapons opened fire from all around.

Bullets zinged, pinged, and zipped through the ship as it lumbered into the air and the big rig passed inches beneath it.

After passing under the cockpit the big diesel kept going. Alvarez was waiting for it. The crew chief was standing on the lowered aft ramp, M79 grenade launcher at the ready, a silhouette against the bright light outside.

Thanks to the fact that the target was huge, and traveling away from her, Alvarez had ample opportunity to nail it. And she did. The 40x46mm grenade struck the back of the cab and exploded. The driver was killed instantly, the big rig's fuel tanks erupted into flames, and the truck was consumed by an orange-red flower.

"Holy shit!" Clarkson exclaimed. "That was fucking awesome!"

In the meantime, Soto was doing her best to exit the bullet storm and gain altitude at the same time. By then it was obvious that the village was in the hands of hostile forces and Bone's team was too small to engage the enemy ground force. Once Soto filed her after action report a company strength unit would be sent to secure the village. Fortunately, there were no serious casualties as a result of the ambush attempt.

Polat came forward once the Chinook was a safe distance away from the village. "I have a secondary mission for you Captain... I'm not allowed to discuss the exact nature of the opportunity, but it's important."

Soto was in no mood for any additional spookery. "Do you have written orders for me?" she demanded. "Because that's what it'll take."

The Turk's anger was plain to see. "Your commanding officer will hear about this."

"Yes, he will," Soto replied. "From *me*. Who was the dumbass who classified that village as peaceful anyway? Somebody has some explaining to do."

"Whooee!" Jones exclaimed, once Polat was gone. "He's pissed."

"Fuck him," Soto grated. "And the general he rode in on."

CHAPTER EIGHT

Superbase Tabqa

Like a hundred and fifty of the other officers and senior noncoms, Soto and Jones had been ordered to attend what was described as "an operational briefing" at 0800, and to "bring your brain." That was how Major Albro put it, and Soto knew what he meant.

Most mega briefings were about security, comportment, and sexual hygiene. So Albro was trying to alert his company officers to the fact that something special was in the works.

Soto could tell that other people were aware of it too, because she could feel the tension in the air as the two of them followed some army officers into the auditorium. It was a cavernous space, located two stories underground, and theoretically safe from missile strikes.

The seats assigned to Charlie Company were toward the rear of the room, behind ranks of senior officers and civilians with ID cards dangling from their necks. Government officials? Spooks? Diplomats? All of the above most likely.

A full bird colonel served as master of ceremonies, urged people to find their seats, and looked nervous. Once the audience was settled in, he introduced himself. "My name is Colonel Watkins. And, for those of you don't know, I'm in charge of security here at Superbase Tabqa.

"And yes, I know about the infestation of jerboas (nocturnal rats). But, since they aren't aligned with the Axis, they're someone else's problem."

That got a laugh, since every person in the room had at least seen the pests, and most had been forced to deal with them.

"But we aren't here to talk about rats," Watkins said, as his expression darkened. "Not that kind anyway. Lieutenant General Alan Kelly will explain."

Soto had heard of "Machine Gun" Kelly, but had never seen the man before. He was tall, lanky, and possessed of "the thing." Meaning the kind of charisma that can fill a room, or an auditorium, and grab everyone's attention.

And sure enough, Kelly was packing his famous H&K MP7 in a thigh holster. "Good morning. And, welcome to the interdisciplinary, multinational initiative called 'Operation Scimitar.'

"What is it? Scimitar is a strategic plan to defend ourselves from a well-coordinated attack by a coalition of enemies that is about to come our way from the west, the south, and the east. Their goal is to inflict massive casualties on our forces and push us north into Turkey."

That produced all sorts of the responses—most of which were variations on "Holy shit," "What the fuck?" and "No way."

Kelly waited for the reactions to dissipate. Then he nodded. "Yes. For those of us who are paid to consider such things, I have to admit that a joint attack by hostile forces is an unexpected development, since the deep divisions in the Muslim world have been enough to prevent unified action in the past.

"But, even though six different factors are required to generate a tropical storm, they align occasionally, and the results can be devastating. And the same thing is true of war. So, here's the situation.

"As you know the Syrian Khalaf regime, which is based in Damascus, has a strategic relationship with Iran. In fact, Syria is often referred to as Iran's 'closest ally.' And both countries are part of the Axis dominated by Russia, China, and North Korea.

"As part of that relationship Iran has been supplying intelligence, weapons, and advisers to Syria.

"Okay, hold that thought," Kelly said, as a map appeared on the screen behind him. Soto saw that reciprocal arrows arched back and forth between numerous countries.

"The arrows symbolize the support that Iran provides to Hamas, the militant group currently in control of the Gaza strip, and to Hezbollah, which wields significant power in Lebanon. And by 'support' I mean intelligence, training, and arms.

"But as you know, nothing in this world is free. And that includes all the goodies that Iran provides to client organizations. So now, according to some solid intelligence, the Syrian government, Hamas and Hezbollah have orders to launch a synchronized assault.

"That means we're about to be attacked by tens of thousands of fighters surging north from Damascus, and entering Syria from Lebanon and the Palestinian territories. Meanwhile an Iranian backed Iraqi militia will strike from the east."

A new map replaced the previous one. Arrows arced in from the west, the south, and the east to converge on the city of Hama, Syria. A red dot appeared over the city. "*This*," Kelly told them, "is where the shit will hit the fan."

The map dissolved into a series of wide shots. Soto saw cell towers, minarets, and hundreds of mostly tan buildings. Her impression was that of a city which, judging from appearances, was peaceful and prosperous.

"Hama was founded in Neolithic times," Kelly added. "And has been ruled by the Assyrians, Persians, Ottomans and the French. But we don't have time to cover all that, so we'll stick to recent history.

"In the early eighties Hama was a major source of opposition to the Ba'ath government."

Photos of soldiers, tanks, and burning buildings appeared one after another, punctuated by a close-up of a toddler standing next to the body of a woman who might have been her mother. The baby was crying.

"The city was the site of a massacre in '81, and another in '82, when government forces used tanks and artillery to shell insurgent neighborhoods," Kelly told them.

"Government forces were accused of executing thousands of prisoners and civilians in the wake of the revolt, which became known as the Hama Massacre."

Kelly paused to scan the auditorium. "The Hama Massacre led to the military term 'Hama Rules.' Meaning the complete destruction of a military objective or target. Which, when you think about it, describes what Russia did to the Chechens, and to the Ukrainians in 2022."

"So," Kelly said. "Here's what you can expect. The attack is imminent. We will meet the enemy and engage them. We will hold Syria regardless of the cost. And finally, when the battle is over, we will emerge victorious.

"Remember, you are leaders, which means the men and women under your command will look to you to set an example. Don't disappoint them.

"Unit specific orders will flow down through the chain of command. God bless each and every one of you. That is all. Dismissed."

Soto turned to look at Jones. "What do you think?"

Jones made a face. "I want my mommy."

***

Master Sergeant Felix Bone was pissed. Officers and senior noncoms had been ordered to report to the auditorium for what was purported to be a BFD. And he was a senior noncom.

So, why had he been told to report to Hangar 12 for an interservice meeting? The oversight rankled. But, when he neared Hangar 12, and saw that two heavily armed Rangers were guarding a side door, Bone realized that something special was brewing.

"Good morning," a private said. "Could I see your ID please?"

Bone produced his card and watched the Ranger check his clipboard. "Thanks, Sarge. You're good to go."

Bone entered the hangar to find that it was occupied by an old observation helicopter and rows of folding chairs. Other people were filing in and taking seats with members of their particular species. Rangers with Rangers, pilots with pilots, civilians with civilians—plus a group of men with no insignia on their camos.

Bone went to sit with the Rangers, where he was greeted by people he knew. "Hey, Sarge, how's it hanging?"

"The Bone! Shit... This is getting real."

"Uh, oh, somebody's gonna get whacked."

Bone bowed and everyone laughed.

A major stepped up onto the makeshift stage and tapped a microphone. "Can everyone hear me? Good. My name is Chan, and I'm here to brief you on Operation Drop Kick.

"As we meet, plans are being laid to defend northern Syria from simultaneous attacks from the east, the south, and the west. The latter being the front that this group will focus on.

"Your task will be to carry out an airborne assault on a Hezbollah fortress located in southern Lebanon, where we will capture or kill a leader known as '*al'amrikiu*,' the American.

"His actual name is Malik Shammas. He's a second generation American who was radicalized while studying in the Middle East and is an influential cult figure.

"As of today, Shammas has survived *three* drone attacks. The most recent was carried out by a Hellfire R9X missile, often referred to as the 'Flying Ginsu,' a weapon which uses a combination of kinetic energy and metal blades to kill targets.

"Our experts credit good luck rather than magic for the fact that Shammas is alive. But his followers believe that Shammas is possessed by a powerful spirit called a *jinn*, which protects him in order to protect itself."

Chan paused to survey the faces in front of him. "That's complete bullshit needless to say. But thousands of people believe it, and since Shammas commands a small army, we need to take him off the battlefield.

"Your job will be to attack his fortress, capture Shammas or, failing that, kill the sonofabitch. And his *jinn*." The last comment provoked nervous laughter.

Chan smiled. "And you're the folks who can get the job done. Please allow me to introduce Seren (captain) Jabarin who, along with members of Israel's Sayeret Matkal, will lead the mission. Unit 262, as it is also known, is a field intelligence unit, and as such knows the target area well."

Bone had heard of the Sayeret Matkal, and knew the group was roughly analogous to the U.S. Army's Delta Force. Which meant they were the best Israel had to offer.

Despite this, Bone didn't trust them, or any foreign nationals, to lead Rangers. But what was, was.

"We are also fortunate enough to have a contingent of parachute qualified translators as part of our team," Chan said, as he gave a nod to the handful of civilians.

"And, last but not least, we have a handpicked company of Rangers who will provide Seren Jabarin with the lethal force required to deal with the target's household troops."

A Ranger raised his hand and Chan pointed to him. "Yes... What's your question?"

"How many fighters, sir?"

"About five hundred," Chan replied. "But only half of them will be on duty, and assuming all goes well, you'll have attack helicopters on your side."

"*Assuming all goes well,*" Bone thought. *How likely is that?*

***

Less than an hour after General Kelly's presentation, the *Double Deuce* received orders to transport a Forward Surgical Team (FST) to the tiny village of Fan al Wastani. A hamlet located north of Hama.

Central Command expected casualties, lots of them, and the FST's mission was to stabilize patients with life threatening wounds before sending them north to Tabqa.

According to the paperwork, the mobile surgical unit consisted of 20 staff members, which included 4 surgeons, 3 RNs, 2 nurse anesthetists, an administrative officer, a sergeant, 3 LPNs, 3 surgical techs and 3 medics.

All of the FST personnel were slated to go out, along with two of four HMMWVs (High Mobility Multipurpose Wheeled Vehicles), each with an M1101 trailer.

More Humvees, and more trailers, would be delivered in subsequent loads. Soto was checking the tie downs on a trailer when a major appeared. "Hello, I'm Doctor Casey Milo. I'm looking for a person called 'Wizard.'"

Milo had even features, a rumpled appearance, and was in need of a shave. "My call sign is 'Wizard,'" Soto told him. "I'm Captain Soto."

Milo extended his hand. "Your crew chief says you're the best Chinook pilot in Syria."

Soto smiled. "I appreciate her endorsement; but my CO wouldn't agree."

Milo laughed. "Can we talk? I have some concerns."

Soto nodded. "Yes, sir. What's on your mind?"

"The way I understand it at least three trips will be required to move my unit. I get that. A Chinook can only lift so much. But what about the timeline for trips two and three? We need *all* of our equipment in order to function. Can we requisition two additional helicopters?"

"You can try," Soto replied. "But Chinooks are in short supply as you can imagine. Perhaps one bird will do. We can make the round trip to Fan al Wastani in two and a half hours.

"The second load will arrive two and a half hours after the first, followed by the third trip, which will be one-way. So, in six or seven hours we can put your entire unit on the ground using a single Chinook."

Milo smiled. "That sounds good! You promise?"

"Yes," Soto said. "Barring mechanical problems."

Milo's team was boarding by then, and Soto noticed that they were armed. "Your people are carrying weapons. Is that typical?"

Milo made a face. "Yeah, it is. We operate close to the front-lines. And the enemy has been known to target aid stations."

"Well, that sucks," Soto replied. "Once we're airborne please feel free to come forward and sit in the observer's seat if you wish to."

Milo said, "Thanks," and turned away.

That was when Soto discovered that Jones was standing two feet away. "'Come forward? And sit in the observer's seat?' You never allow people to do that."

"I'm in a good mood," Soto replied. "Aren't you supposed to be doing something?"

Jones grinned. "Yes, ma'am. Right away ma'am."

Soto gave him the finger before turning to the cockpit.

There was always a high volume of traffic at Superbase Tabqa, but the tempo of activity had increased, causing long waits. Not for the *Double Deuce* however, which had a high priority.

Milo came forward soon after takeoff and peppered the pilots with questions. Could the Chinook fly on one engine? Could it autorotate? And could it refuel while in the air?

Then, after fifteen minutes or so, the doctor returned to the cargo area.

Fan al Wastani was 84 miles away from the superbase, and the *Double Deuce* was halfway there, when the initial reports of fighting started to filter in over the radio.

The lead elements of the Iraqi militia were speeding west on Highway 18, even as nationalist troops moved north on the M1, with armor out in front.

And, thanks to the self-propelled Pantsir missile systems provided to Syria by Russia, enemy vehicles were nearly impervious to attacks by Allied fighters and UAVs.

Soto knew the Pantsir systems were effective against helicopters too. So, now she had another threat to worry about. And that contributed to the queasy feeling in her stomach.

According to the most recent census, Fan al Wastani was a community of less than a thousand people. And, as Soto brought the *Double Deuce* in for a landing north of town, she couldn't see any military activity.

A farmer paused from plowing to shade his eyes and watch the huge helicopter as it landed. On one of his fields? If so, he'd be compensated. Although in all truth nothing could compensate the man for the possibility that his tiny patch of Syria was about to become a target.

Alvarez dropped the ramp and the work of unloading began. Humvees plus trailers backed out, followed by dozens of two-man storage boxes, and five-gallon water containers.

Doctor Milo worked as hard as the rest of them, and was a source of ongoing commentary. "What the hell is in this box Lieutenant? You're an anesthetist. What's so heavy?

"Hey, Lucas... What did I say about the Hawaiian shirts? You're not on Maui.

"This bottle is leaking, goddammit... Get the duct tape."

None of which seemed to faze the FST personnel, who appeared to be used to Milo's nonstop chatter, and grinned when he singled one of them out.

Soto was running a checklist when Milo stuck his head into the cockpit. "Thank you, Captain. I'll see you soon?"

"Yes," Soto promised. "You'll see me soon."

***

Milo watched the Chinook lift off. His thoughts turned to Soto. *God speed*, he thought. *Bad things are coming this way. I can feel it.*

***

Over southern Lebanon

Bone was falling out of the starlit sky. *Why?* Because Operation Drop Kick called for Captain Jabarin's hastily assembled team to neutralize "the American," before the bastard could leave his fortress.

The ground was coming up fast as Bone conducted a 360-degree check of his canopy, confirmed that his slider was fully extended, and compared his rate of decent to the jumpers around him. They looked green through his night vision goggles, and were falling at the same rate of speed he was. And that was a good thing.

Because the jump had taken place at 1,200 feet, the drop was almost over. The wind was blowing from the left. So, Bone reached up to grab the left set of risers, and pull them in towards his chest.

Then, as he faced the wind, Bone brought his feet together, and bent his knees slightly. His elbows were in tight against his sides and his eyes were open.

As an ex-instructor Bone knew the landing drill by heart: "Hit all five points of contact including balls of feet, calf, thigh, buttocks—and pull up muscle."

Bone hit, rolled, and hurried to activate both canopy release assemblies. Then it was time to shed his harness, free his weapons and prepare to fight. All the team members had orders to abandon their chutes and join their platoons as quickly as possible. Time was of the essence.

As the Ranger company's first sergeant, Bone was supposed to link up with Captain Eason who would assume command if something happened to Jabarin.

The sun was rising by then, which allowed Bone to stow his night vision goggles, as he jogged towards the fort. It resembled a misshapen wedding cake and, rather than being constructed, the monstrosity appeared to have been excavated from the flanks of a hill.

Then, according to Intel reports, mining machines had been used to create a system of tunnels, bunkers, and an internal reservoir. All of which meant the fort would be very difficult to conquer. Fortunately, the Rangers weren't expected to overwhelm the fort's considerable defenses. No, their role was to distract Shammas' fighters, and suck them down to the perimeter wall.

Meanwhile, assuming the Israeli special ops team managed to land on top of the fortress, they had orders to work their way down to the American's second level living quarters.

At that point the Israelis would capture or kill Shammas, and withdraw to the top level of the fortress where a helicopter would be waiting.

Forty mike-mike grenades exploded as Rangers fired them over the wall, and automatic weapons chattered, as the Hezbollah fighters returned fire.

Meanwhile unintelligible orders were issued over the fort's PA system, soon followed by a prerecorded war chant that Bone couldn't understand.

Each member of the Drop Kick team was wearing a headset with boom mike. And as Bone neared the rally point for HQ personnel, he heard Jarbarin's voice. "Dagger-Two, this is One. Five out of six. Over."

The message meant that five of the Israeli six-man team had successfully landed on top of the fort. The sixth man either overshot the landing zone or had been killed.

Eason's rally point was in the ruins of an old villa which offered reasonably good cover. The captain and his radio operator were crouched behind a rock wall. "There you are," Eason said, as if Bone was late for a class in high school. "Make the rounds. And be careful… The uglies are ten out."

Bone knew that the Apache pilots would try to stay off the Rangers, but accidents could happen, especially in the fog of war. He nodded. "Yes, sir. I'll be in touch."

The so-called "pop-up" company consisted of three platoons, two of which were facing the fort, while the third was positioned to protect the unit's rear flank against fighters surging in from the countryside.

Two-man OPs (outposts) were positioned to detect movements to the left and right. If required, the forward-facing platoons could swivel toward an attack.

Eason hadn't bothered to give Bone specific orders and didn't need to. Bone knew what his CO wanted, which was a firsthand assessment of combat readiness, and a sense of the company's morale. The fighting continued as Bone scuttled from one piece of cover to the next, and arrived behind the first platoon, where it was necessary to pause. "Thunder!"

The reply came a moment later. "Lightning."

That was Bone's signal to move forward. A corporal was there to greet him. "Hey, Sarge. If you're looking for the loot, he's about twenty yards to your right."

Bone thanked the soldier and elbowed his way toward the platoon's temporary HQ. He passed an LMG on the way. The gunner was firing short bursts with long pauses in between.

There was very little outgoing fire compared to the amount of incoming. And that was intentional. If the paratroopers weren't careful, they'd run out of ammo. So, their job was to keep the Hezbollah fighters engaged, using a minimal amount of force.

In fact, had trained officers been in command of the Hezbollah fighters, they might have wondered why the *Kaffirs* had made no attempt to breach the outer wall. But that wasn't the case. So, the hajis threw a lot of lead at the attackers with minimal results.

Bone could see the command position up ahead. And was almost there when the gunships arrived. "This is Tuxedo and Geezer in from the east with guns, rockets, and missiles. Over."

"Copy that," Eason said. "This is Dagger-Two. Stay off the top of the upper levels of the fort, and stay north of the red smoke. Welcome to the party. Over."

The uglies banked as they came in, weapons firing, while they circled the fort. Thirty-millimeter cannon rounds cut scores of defenders down, rockets obliterated machine gun positions, and Hellfire missiles struck the lower part of the fort.

Lieutenant Carrie Smith was in command of the 1st platoon. She yelled, "Hooah!" as the Apaches completed a circuit of the fort, and those close enough to hear echoed the famous battle cry.

Bone grinned. Morale? Check. "Thunder!"

A private said, "Lightning!" and Smith turned to see who had arrived. "Master Sergeant Bone... Did you bring coffee? I'm going into withdrawal."

"No, ma'am. Sorry. How's it going?"

Smith's expression turned serious. "Two KIAs, four wounded, none critical."

Bone winced. "I'm sorry."

Smith nodded. "Me too."

"I'll tell the captain," Bone promised. "We'll call for a medevac as soon as that's feasible."

Then it was time to visit the 2nd platoon, as the Apaches made another circuit, and most of the enemy fire shifted to them.

That was when Bone left cover. A section of bare ground lay ahead. All he could do was gather his strength, grit his teeth, and run. Somebody was waiting for that. Bullets kicked up geysers of soil all around the Ranger as he crossed open ground and made a dive for cover.

Bone's tac vest hit hard. He skidded, felt hands grab his harness, and jerk him into a hole.

A crash landing followed. Bone found himself at the bottom of a fighting position looking up. A grimy face peered down at him. Bone said, "Thunder."

The private laughed. "Lighting. Welcome to the 2nd. Follow the trench. The boss is about twenty feet that-a-way."

Bone did as he was told and found Lieutenant Dan Silva holed up behind a wrecked truck. A bloody bandage was wrapped around his right thigh. He looked pale. "Excuse me if I don't get up."

Bone was about to answer when Jabarin's voice was heard. "Dagger-Two, this is One. We have the package, we're on the roof, and are taking heavy fire from the stairways. We need a dust-off ASAP. Over."

No sooner had Jabarin spoken than a second transmission came through. "This is Scimitar-Six actual. Your ride is down. Another bird is on the way. ETA thirty minutes. Over."

That was followed by a long pause. Eason's voice sounded hollow. "Red-Dog-Nine... This is Dagger-Two. Take a squad, enter the fort, and join Dagger-One. You will exfil along with his team."

Bone clenched his jaw. "Copy that, Two. Tuxedo, do you copy?"

"I copy," the pilot replied.

"Destroy the front gate if you haven't done so already. I will be carrying an orange flare with a squad following behind me. Kill everyone else. Over."

"Your wish is our command," Tuxedo replied. "Over."

"Sergeant Deaver!" Silva said loudly. "You and your squad will follow Master Sergeant Bone! Rangers lead the way!"

***

Tabqa Superbase, Syria

After completing three round trips to Fan al Wastani, and delivering all of Doctor Milo's supplies, the *Double Deuce* had returned to Tabqa, where it was taken out of the rotation for twelve hours. For maintenance, and the sake of the crew, all of whom were exhausted.

Soto slept for a solid nine hours before getting up, heading to the showers, and making her way to the DFAC. And that's where she was when Alvarez appeared. The crew chief was visibly excited. "We have orders ma'am!"

Soto eyed the noncom over the edge of her coffee cup. "To do *what*?" she inquired suspiciously.

"We're going to fly General Kelly and his staff wherever they want to go. The CO wants to see you right away."

Soto sighed. "Okay, thanks. Does Jones know?"

"Not yet."

"Tell him. And warn the gunners. We might be gone for a while. So, they should pack an extra set of camos and their personals."

Albro. The last thing Soto wanted to do was take a meeting with Major Albro. But an order was an order.

Soto left the DFAC, and made her way to the command CONEX, where she was allowed to jump the line and enter Albro's office right away. There was no invitation to sit. And no pleasantries. "General Kelly needs a Chinook in order to move his headquarters staff and two vehicles from place to place. You are available, so the mission is yours."

The implication was obvious. Soto wasn't Albro's first choice. Had he been free to choose, the honor would have gone to Backwards Brody, or some other favorite. "Yes, sir."

"Don't fuck up."

"No, sir."

"Dismissed."

While checking in with Operations Soto learned that Kelly was scheduled to depart for a classified location at 1000 hours. *I hope the people on Kelly's staff are thinking about fuel*, Soto thought. *And where we can get more during the general's travels.*

Soto's concerns were put to rest when she met Major Haley Thomas, a bright-eyed sort, who was in charge of logistics. "No worries," Thomas said. "I know how much fuel you burn per hour, and I'll make sure more is available at our destination."

"Which is?"

"The village of Ithriya," Thomas answered. "Ithriya is located where the road that leads to Aleppo crosses Highway 18. A column of militia vehicles is westbound toward Hama.

"The General wants to stop them before they get anywhere near the city. So, he sent a tank company plus a mechanized infantry platoon to do the job. Now he plans to supervise."

"How many tanks is that?" Soto inquired.

"Fourteen," Thomas answered. "Plus support vehicles, and Bradleys for the infantry."

"Okay," Soto said. "Is there anything else I should know?"

"Yes," Thomas replied. "The General loves Hershey bars. So, if you leave one out, it's bound to disappear."

***

Southern Lebanon

"Move, shoot, and communicate." That's what the infantry was paid to do, and that was the essence of Bone's plan. He didn't know the seven men and two women in his squad, but knew what kind of training they had, and that was sufficient. The Rangers were crouched around him as the uglies began to fire on the main gate.

A civilian translator was present as well. He was armed with nothing more than a small bullhorn.

"*You*," Bone said, as he pointed at a private named Lang. "You will take point. Watch for IEDs. I'll be in the two slot."

"And *you*," Bone added, as he established eye contact with Sergeant Deaver. "You're second in command, and will walk drag. Watch our six."

Bone scanned the faces gathered around him. "We're going to travel fast. Shed anything that isn't a weapon, ammo, or water.

"We're going to fight our way up to the top floor of that fort, and reinforce the special ops people located there. It won't be easy, but what are we?"

"Rangers!" came the reply.

"Damn straight," Bone said, as he lit an orange flare. "Follow me."

With that Bone stood, vaulted over a waist high wall, and began to run. He was holding the flare high, like a runner at the

Olympics, but tilted slightly—so the hot stuff wouldn't fall on his hand.

The badly mangled gate was at least 500 yards away, and the fort another 500 beyond that. *I'm getting old*, Bone thought, as he struggled to suck oxygen. *I need to retire, to leave this shit behind. Is Polat on duty? Or loading the gold onto a truck?*

The question was left hanging, as Lang passed through the gate, and Bone followed. Thanks to the Apache gunships, scores of enemy fighters had been killed or wounded, and the rest were keeping their heads down. But not for long.

The hajis began to fire as a crazy Kaffir appeared, flare held high, legs pumping. Some of them even went so far as to stand. They paid a heavy price.

Tuxedo made a gun run to the left of the squad, just as Geezer did the same on the right, both risking RPG fire in order to do so.

Then, in a matter of seconds, the gunships had to turn in opposite directions, or slam into the fort. But thanks to the damage done, the squad was able to reach the fort untouched.

There a gaping hole marked the spot where the main door had been. Lang paused just short of it, tossed two grenades through the hole, and crouched.

Bone discovered that he was still holding the flare, and tossed it to one side.

The overlapping explosions produced a scream. Bone stepped into the cloud of dust, saw a muzzle flash, and fired his M4 at it. A half-seen body fell.

A flight of stairs led upwards, and Bone followed Lang, as the private hugged a wall. Lang's weapon was raised, and when he fired, a body tumbled down.

That was when a solid phalanx of fighters charged down the stairs screaming "*Allahu akbar!*" (God is most great.) A Ranger fell as those in front fired their weapons. Those to the rear couldn't fire without hitting the men in front of them.

A private named Tanaka stepped up, leveled his LMG and fired. The slugs from the M249 tore into the mob, killing at least half a dozen fighters and wounding others. Dead bodies tumbled down the stairs threatening to bowl Rangers over.

Bone jumped over a corpse, saw a wounded fighter raise his pistol, and shot him. He heard a voice via his headset. "Renner's dead."

"Take half of his tag," Bone replied, "and keep moving."

It's time to check in, Bone thought, as he stepped in a pool of blood. "Dagger-One, this is Red-Dog-Nine. We're on the first floor, approaching the second. Over."

"Copy that," Jabarin replied. "Be advised that Shammas fanatics occupy the third floor, and are still trying to reach the roof. Over."

Bone arrived on the second floor at that point. And there, blocking the way, were a dozen women—some with children clinging to their burkas. They were clearly terrified, and no wonder, since Shammas fighters stood behind them with weapons raised. One of them spoke English. "Surrender or die!"

That was when the squad's translator raised his bullhorn and gave an order in Arabic. The women were visibly confused, so he said it again. "Get down or be shot!"

Two women dropped to the floor soon followed by the rest of them.

That left the hajis exposed and Bone gave an order. "Shoot the bastards!"

The two sides opened up. Hundreds of bullets flew in both directions. Hajis went down and another Ranger fell. The interpreter hurried to give the man first aid.

"Cease firing!" Bone shouted, as the last defender fell. "Conserve your ammo! Carry the wounded... And follow me."

Lang yelled, "Grenade!" as a cannister fell from above, hit the stairs, and detonated. Smoke swirled as Bone charged up the stairs. He ran into what he knew must be a Shammas fighter and fired blindly. Bone heard a grunt, pushed the man away, and shot him again.

The rest of the squad had entered the fog by that time. Rangers grappled with Hezbollah fighters, knives slashed flesh, and pistols fired as the smoke began to thin out.

The defenders couldn't escape to the roof, and they couldn't descend the stairs. They were trapped. Fire lashed down from above and up from below.

The Shammas fanatics had a choice. They could surrender or die… And, with *Jannah* (paradise) waiting, most chose to die.

The Rangers had to step over bodies in order to climb the stairs. The walls were splattered with blood.

Surviving members of the Sayeret Matkal were waiting to welcome the Americans onto the body strewn roof. Malik Shammas had a hood over his head, was bound with paracord, and his legs were kicking. His voice was muffled. "You'll never make it out of here alive! You mother fuckers are going to pay!"

That was when a new voice was heard. "Dagger-One, this is Dancer. We are a Blackhawk inbound from the east. Pop smoke and clear the LZ. Over."

Bone could hear the *whop, whop, whop* of rotors by then, and sent a mental message to his wife. *Sorry, Yolanda… I'm still alive. So, there won't be any insurance money for you. Bitch.*

CHAPTER NINE

Near the village of Ithriya, Syria

General Kelly was sitting in the observer's seat as the *Double Deuce* neared the battlefield. And he was far from happy. Somehow, in spite of the armor sent to stop the Axis column, enemy units managed to sweep around Allied forces and attack them from the rear.

Munitions had been destroyed, Americans had been killed, and others taken prisoner. All because of a colonel who Kelly referred to as "Dumbass Duncan." The man who was in command of the blocking force.

Although not an expert regarding such matters, Soto had to agree as the Chinook overflew what looked like a parking lot full of burned-out supply trucks. Based on appearances, the mostly unarmed vehicles had laagered up without enough security to adequately protect them.

Did the tangos know that? Based on drone footage? Or did they luck out? Not that it made any difference.

"Goddammit!" Kelly exclaimed. "Look at that shit! Give me a three-sixty. I want to see the big picture before I hand Duncan his ass."

A "three-sixty" as Kelly called it would take the *Double Deuce* in a giant circle, passing over the tail end of the enemy column. Would the Iraqi soldiers be equipped with shoulder launched surface-to-air missiles (SAMs)? Most likely.

But an order was an order, and Soto understood the need. She spoke over the intercom. "Gunners will fire on targets of opportunity."

Soto turned to Jones. "You know the drill. Chaff and flares. Try to be judicious. We have a limited supply."

Jones nodded. "Roger that."

Soto put the Chinook into a gradual turn which carried them south, and then east, toward the far end of the enemy column. RPGs sailed up at them, small arms fire pinged the fuselage, and Jones called a near miss from a SAM.

Kelly's attention was elsewhere. "Look at that! A dump truck… A school bus… And tractor trailer rig. It's like a scene in a Mad Max movie."

Just then Soto saw something that didn't fit: A column of soldiers marching east. Not soldiers, prisoners! *American* prisoners.

"Look at that General," Soto said. "They're marching our people east… Should we try to pick them up?"

Kelly's eyes lit up. "Holy shit! A pilot with a pair of balls! Put down well beyond them. We'll back the Humvees off and go after the prisoners. Once we neutralize the guards, come get us."

The general's staff consisted of twelve people, most of whom were middle-aged senior officers. Could they fight? Soto was about to find out.

The Chinook passed over the column of POWs, some of whom waved. Others were limping along or being carried on makeshift stretchers. Guards fired at the helicopter.

"Hold your fire," Soto ordered. "The last thing we want to do is hit some of the prisoners."

"This looks good," Kelly said. "Put her down."

Dust flew as the *Double Deuce* landed in a storm of its own making.

Kelly's staff were ready by then, as was Alvarez, who put the ramp down. The first Humvee backed off, followed by the second, which was a boxy com truck.

Kelly hurried to board the lead vehicle which spewed gravel and roared away. The com truck followed at a more sedate pace.

"What if the bastards capture General Kelly?" Jones inquired.

Soto hadn't thought of that. Or the fact that such a disaster would be her fault since the rescue was her idea.

The Chinook broke contact with the ground as Soto pulled up on the collective. She could see Kelly's vehicles up ahead, bearing down on the column of prisoners, and skidding to a halt. "Pick your targets carefully," Soto ordered. "Don't fire unless you're certain."

The guards were putting up a fight. One went down quickly followed by another. A third opened fire on the prisoners. "Kill him!" Soto instructed. "Kill all of the guards."

By hovering directly above the column and moving west Soto delivered target after target to her gunners. And by that time some of the POWs had armed themselves with AKs and were taking part in the battle. It was over in a matter of minutes. But they were still in deep shit. "Vehicles inbound from the east *and* the west!" Jones announced.

"Damn it," Soto said, as she brought the Chinook down. "You have it. I'm going aft."

That was a no-no given the circumstances. Pilots were supposed to stay in the cockpit and let the crew chief sort things out. But Soto knew Alvarez would be outgunned and was determined to have her say.

"I have it," Jones said, as Soto left the cockpit. The ramp was down, thanks to Alvarez, and Kelly's people were preparing to load the Humvees.

It was extremely noisy, forcing Soto to shout. "Destroy the vehicles! There isn't enough room for them... Plus we don't have time to load them. Tangos are inbound from the east and west. That's an order."

Kelly materialized out of the swirling dust. "Who are you to order my staff around?"

"I'm the pilot of this aircraft," Soto exclaimed. "And what I say goes."

Their eyes were locked as Kelly considered her words. Then he grinned. "You're right Captain. My bad. Let's get these soldiers aboard."

Soto hurried back to the cockpit knowing that her crew would take care of the wounded soldiers. "Get us out of here, Ziggy... Fast."

Soto keyed the intercom. Then she turned to Alvarez. "Get busy with your grenade launcher, Chief... Destroy those vehicles. Start with the com truck."

The M79 was racked above the aft ramp control handle. Alvarez took the weapon down and fired from the ramp. Two members of Kelly's staff flanked her with ARs.

Jones had the engines at maximum power. And, as the *Double Deuce* accelerated away from the burning Humvees, Alvarez continued to fire her M79.

"Okay," Soto said, as enemy vehicles flooded into the area. "Haul ass!"

Jones looked her way. "It won't go any faster, boss."

Soto held her breath as Jones flew the *Double Deuce* north, passed over a hill, and dropped a hundred feet to hide the Chinook's heat signature. Then it was a simple matter of speeding over the desert until the hajis were no longer in range.

Kelly sat in the observer's seat. "Nice job Captain, and if anyone asks me, I'll tell them you really are a Wizard. Now, let's get the wounded to an aid station."

***

Superbase Tabqa

Aboo Osman rolled out of bed knowing that he was going to die and looking forward to it. Because, according to Muhammad, "The smallest reward for the people of Heaven is an abode where there are eighty thousand servants and seventy-two houri, over which stands a dome decorated with pearls, aquamarine, and ruby, as wide as the distance from al-Jabiyyah to San."

Even if the scholars were wrong, and Osman received only a fraction of that bounty, it would be vastly superior to his hand-to-mouth life in Mud Town, the mind killing job in the DEFAC, and the hopelessness he felt.

There was one bright spot in Osman's life however, and that was camaraderie he shared with his fellow *mujahideen* (those engaged in jihad), eleven of whom would join him in the attack.

Up to that point Osman and his brothers had been acting as spies, writing reports and sending them out via courier. Where did they go? Who read them? Were they valued? He would never know.

But now that the Syrian government, Hamas, and Hezbollah had launched a joint attack on the Alliance, orders had arrived. Orders instructing all members of Osman's cell to attack the airfield's com center.

The orders didn't say why because the answer was obvious. Superbase Tabqa was home to Alliance's regional command center, and would play a critical role in responding to the unified attack. But only if the center could communicate with units in the field.

Osman smiled as he started to dress. The necessary weapons and explosives had been smuggled into the base piece-by-piece over the last three months. Enough explosives to destroy the com center three times over.

Osman saw no reason to shower, or to eat breakfast, but it was important to shave. The Kafirs were automatically suspicious of anyone with a beard. So, like his comrades, Osman was clean shaven.

Osman viewed the world in a different way as he walked to the gate. Rather than a slum, Mud Town was a source of delightful smells, playful children, and wise elders.

The air was heavy with the tang of woodsmoke, the tinkle of pop music leaked out through a window, and his senses were fully awake. It was a wonderful moment, and one he would savor in *Jannah*.

The gate consisted of two passageways. One for vehicles, and one for pedestrians.

It was necessary to wait in line to get through the pedestrian gate. And, as Osman eyed the people ahead, he spotted Haadi. That was a good thing.

The widely spaced line moved slowly. Which was typical. The *Kaffirs* had every reason to be careful. And they were for the most part. There were scanners to pass through, plus blast traps and bomb sniffing dogs. But, at the end of the day the *Kaffirs* were human. Evil, but human.

That meant some of them came to recognize the civilian workers and remembered their names. And that's why Corporal Martin said, "Good morning, Aboo... I'll see you at the DFAC."

Osman nodded and smiled. *No, wajh qadhar* (shit face), *you won't*, he thought. *Because I'll be dead by lunchtime.*

After entering the base Osman made his way through a maze of streets to Building 42, the maintenance center where Haadi and Said began each day.

Haadi was waiting inside the side door. He opened it. "Come in. Said is here. We're waiting for the others. Make your way to the west side of the garage. That's where we will prepare."

Osman had to circle a dump truck in order to follow Haadi's instructions. And that's when he saw the body. The European contract worker was lying face down with a pickaxe embedded in his back.

And there were more bodies. A man with a garotte wound around his neck, eyes bulging, lay next to a worker who'd been killed with a fire axe.

Objective one, check.

A radio was tuned to the Tabqa's station. "Good morning, Tabqa!" a woman said enthusiastically. "And welcome to Radio Free Syria!"

Osman turned it off.

***

Once Shammas was captured, and shipped off to the United States, the pop-up company was disbanded—and Bone returned to Tabqa. His reward was a pat on the back and two days off. All he had to do was muster with his unit each morning.

Based on the content of the morning briefing it sounded as if things were getting worse rather than better.

It seemed that a colonel named Duncan had fucked up, allowed the hajis to attack him from the rear, and been relieved of duty by Machine Gun Kelly. So, the beat went on. And Bone knew he'd be back in the shit soon.

In the meantime, he had plans to check in with his lawyer stateside, track Polat down and have a couple of drinks at the club. Or, maybe he should tackle the list in reverse order.

That's what Bone was thinking when sirens began to bleat, and a male voice came over the base-wide PA system. "Condition Red. I repeat, Condition Red. This base is under attack! Military personnel will report to their units, and civilian personnel will enter the shelters."

Bone was about to turn back when a pickup truck screeched to a stop beside him. A lieutenant was at the wheel. "Grab a weapon out of the back, Sergeant... The bastards are inside the wire. We don't have time to muster. Get out there and kill some hajis."

Bone jumped up into the truck, surveyed the weapons available, and chose a M2020 Enhanced Sniper Rifle, plus a canvas bag loaded with extra magazines.

Though not a sniper, Bone was a marksman, and figured the long gun was a good choice for a sergeant without a squad.

He jumped to the ground, heard tires squeal, and pulled a quick three-sixty. The sounds of battle were all around him. He could hear automatic fire, explosions, and the steady stream of blah blah from the PA system. The base water tank caught his eye. The tank was something like five stories up off the ground, and equipped with a circular walkway.

That was the good news. The bad news was that there wasn't any cover. But, if all went well, the enemy wouldn't spot him. The sounds of fighting increased as Bone ran.

The rifle was equipped with a sling, thank God, because there was no way he could go up the blue ladder, and hold onto the weapon at the same time.

Bone removed four magazines from the bag, stuffed them into various pockets, and started to climb. Bone's breath was coming in short gasps by the time he arrived on the walkaround. His legs felt as if they were made of lead, and his hands were shaking as he readied the rifle.

It was chambered for .300 Winchester, equipped with a 24-inch barrel, and fitted with a five-round, detachable magazine. A quick check confirmed that the magazine was full up.

But that wasn't all. The highly adjustable weapon boasted a sound suppressor and muzzle brake designed to reduce recoil. What Bone's dad would have called, "All the fixings."

The shakes started to fade as Bone sat down, rested the weapon on a rail, and began to scan for targets. There were plenty to choose from. And the Leupold Mark 4 6.5-20x50mm ER/T scope brought them in close.

Binoculars would have been nice—for a good look at the overall situation—but Bone could still get a general idea by panning back and forth. From what he could see, at least a hundred enemy fighters were inside the wire. And, unlike what Bone expected, they had a plan.

The headquarters CONEX, the diesel-powered generators, and the control tower were all under attack. And that was when Bone noticed the dump truck.

***

Haadi was supposed to drive the truck, but Haadi had been killed. So, Osman was at the wheel. The plan was simple. Deliver the explosive charge to the Communications Center by crashing into the concrete structure and penetrating the lobby. Then all Osman had to do was press the remote, and *BOOM*, he'd find himself in heaven.

Osman was still marveling at the size and audacity of the plan. Now he realized that his cell was one of many, each unaware of the others' existence, until the moment when all of them took action simultaneously. It was a wonderful thing! It was…

And that was the moment when the .300 Winchester bullet shattered the window next to Osman and drilled a hole through his head.

***

Bone was almost certain that the man behind the wheel of the dump truck was a tango. A man determined to destroy the Com Center. But what if he was wrong?

Bone held his breath as the truck careened into a parked car and ground to a halt. Then a bright orange explosion destroyed most of the truck. A dead man's switch? Or a post mortem finger contraction? Bone was satisfied either way. Tango down.

But the overall situation could only be described as bad. Now, with a moment to survey his situation, Bone realized that planes had been taking off so quickly, that the sound of their engines was a nearly continuous roar.

Not so the helicopters. Two uglies were up, and using their considerable firepower to support base personnel. That was good.

But, because so many of Tabqa's personnel were elsewhere fighting, there were hundreds instead of thousands of Allied soldiers and airmen on base.

Was that luck? Or part of a plan? Bone felt sure it was the latter. His mind processed that even as his eyes searched the streets below looking for the right kind of target. Bone wanted to kill leaders if he could, but they were difficult to identify. All of the attackers wore similar clothing.

But leaders act like leaders. They point. They direct. And they move from person to person. Bone spotted one such individual among the group firing on the military police station. A tall man wearing a black and white *keffiyeh* (head scarf).

Bone waited for the man to pause, took the left to right breeze into account, and squeezed the trigger. The slug was four inches low and tore through the attacker's throat. Blood sprayed the person he'd been talking to. He was clutching his neck when he keeled over.

Is the sight out of whack? Bone wondered. *Bring it up next time.*

The next target was standing in a shadow, holding a sat phone up to his right ear. What the fuck? Who was he talking to? Someone up the chain of command? That seemed like a good guess.

Bone put the crosshairs over the man's chest this time, figuring that if the bullet hit lower, it would still put the bastard down. He squeezed, felt the recoil, and saw the target jerk.

A red stain blossomed on the target's white tunic, and he collapsed. *Right in the breadbasket*, Bone thought. *I'll shoot high from now on.*

A man with a satchel was kneeling next to a wounded haji. A medic? Yup.

Bone had a soft spot for medics, but couldn't let this one run around reviving enemy fighters. He fired, saw the medic fall on top of his patient, and felt a pang of regret.

That was when an RPG hit the water tank and exploded. Water gushed out to splash on the bone-dry ground below. Was the grenade directed at him?

Hell yes, Bone decided, as bullets pinged the tank. *I need to amscray.*

After slinging the rifle Bone hurried to the blue ladder. By braking with his hands, and placing his boots outside the side rails, Bone slid down. Bullets splattered the tank above him as he descended. Bone's worst fear was that instead of firing at where he'd *been*, some bright lad would aim at where he was *going*, and give Yolanda something to celebrate.

But it didn't happen. Bone lost control and fell the last six feet. That knocked the wind out of his lungs. *Gotta get up... Gotta run... Move, shoot, communicate.*

Bullets kicked up geysers of dirt as Bone rolled over, performed a pushup, and took off. He didn't have a plan, just a desperate need to find cover. And the best possibility was the metal dumpster directly ahead. Was the steel thick enough to shield him?

Bone hoped so as he ran straight at the garbage container, made the necessary jump, and fell inside. Bullets clanged as they hit the north side of the dumpster and failed to penetrate. Bone gave thanks as he sought to catch his breath. Now what? Could he exit over the south side of the container? And sprint to the police station? There was only one way to find out.

Bone mounted a pile of construction debris, vaulted over the side, and began to run. His back was exposed and he expected a bullet to strike him at any moment.

But the MPs, and other personnel holed up in the bunker-style structure, saw him coming and opened fire. Bone wanted to zigzag, but decided not to, fearing that one of the MPs might hit him.

The clatter of gunfire was nearly deafening as Bone neared the station and took a dive. Hands took hold of his uniform and dragged him in. "Hey, Sarge... Are you okay?"

Bone rolled onto his side. And there, looking down at him, was a dyed-in-the-wool Bonehead. "Don't just stand there Levy, give me a hand."

Levy pulled him up. "Glad you made it, Sarge. This is a good spot."

"For what?"

"Some Hogs are inbound," Levy told him. "Our strong-points are supposed to pop orange smoke... And God help any-one who doesn't have any. They'd better dig deep. It's gonna be brutal."

Levy's words proved to be prophetic. The A-10 pilots did everything they could to avoid hitting friendlies, but their orders were clear: "Sanitize Tabqa, no matter the cost."

Four Hogs made two passes each. Explosions shook the ground, cannon shells swept the streets, and scores of invaders fell. Those lucky enough to survive fled for the fences. And that's where the Apache gunships were waiting.

Enemy fighters died running, died trying to pass through the holes in the fence, and died running toward Mud Town. The attempt to take and occupy Tabqa Superbase had failed.

***

Fan al Wastani, Syria

The fighting was getting closer and closer to Dr. Casey Milo's Forward Surgical Team. What had previously been little more than a steady rumble was different now. Milo could hear the sharp crack of shells exploding nearby, mixed with the chatter of automatic weapons.

On three different occasions Milo had been ordered to pack up and pull out. And on three different occasions he had refused to obey. "Stop the flow of critically wounded soldiers and we'll leave," he promised. "Otherwise, what are you going to do? Let them bleed out?"

The colonel Milo was talking to had no answer for that. So, the FST was in a precarious position. But thanks to a lull in the fighting, the unit was going to relocate to a Forward Airfield (FA) that could accommodate C-130s plus rotary aircraft. And provide both with fuel.

That meant wounded soldiers could be medevacked to the airfield, stabilized there, and loaded onto a transport for the trip back to "the world."

But, before that could take place, Soto and her crew had to load the FST's gear onto the *Double Deuce*, fly to the FA, unload and go back for more. It was exhausting.

As the helicopter crew made their final trip back to FST's previous location, the situation suddenly got worse. "Wizard, this is Turtle. Turn back. We have hostiles inside the perimeter. Over."

"Turtle" was one of Milo's doctors, and Soto could hear the fear in her voice. Soto had a choice to make. She could do the rational thing, and turn back, or the stupid thing—and continue on. Soto chose the stupid thing.

"That's a negative, Turtle. Forget the gear. Lagger up. Fight back. And be ready to light a flare. We're fifteen out. Over."

Soto pushed the helo's speed right up to the red line and warned the crew. She glanced at Jones. "Sorry."

"Don't be," Jones replied. "You made the right call."

The fifteen minutes seemed to last forever. But finally, thanks to her night vision goggles, Soto saw muzzle flashes up ahead and knew that the medics were duking it out with the bad guys.

Jones was on the radio. "Turtle, this is Stargazer. We're incoming. Light a flare. I'll call the color. Our gunners will cover you. Prepare to board in a hurry. Over."

"Copy that, Stargazer," Turtle said above the rattle of gunfire. "Thank you. Over."

A red flare appeared, and as it did, enemy fire shifted from the medical team to the Chinook. That was understandable but stupid. "Turtle, I see a red flare," Jones said. "We're coming in."

Soto had calculated her approach to take advantage of the fact that while the Chinook had a machine gun on the port side, it had *two* on the starboard side, both of which fired at enemy muzzle flashes. Then, as the *Double Deuce* neared the FST, the third gun began to chatter as well.

Soto was painfully aware that a single RPG round could destroy the Chinook as she lowered the big bird to the ground. And that's where the ship sat, rotors turning, as Alvarez employed hand signals to urge people up the ramp.

The entire process consumed no more than three minutes during which bullets pinged the hull, the gunners fired nonstop, and a strange whining sound was heard. "What the hell *is* that?" Jones wondered out loud.

"I don't know," Soto replied. "But it sucks."

"All personnel are on board," Alvarez told them. "*Pull pitch!*"

Soto was ready. The hundred-foot-long aircraft practically jumped off the ground, the whining noise stopped, and Soto banked away from the worst of the incoming fire.

Then, as the Chinook turned north, they were able to put the shit show behind them.

Turtle's actual name was Brook Evans. She came forward to sit in the observation seat. "Thanks, you guys. I thought we were history."

"You were very brave," Jones said.

The blonde managed a smile. Her teeth were very white. "So were you."

Soto made a face. "*You were very brave.*" "*So were you.*" What a pickup artist.

Men, she thought. *They're predictable, if nothing else.*

***

Forward Airfield Victor

The *Double Deuce* and its crew were under orders to remain at Forward Airfield Victor, "Until basic services and full security can be restored at Superbase Tabqa."

Language which translated to, "The attack fucked everything up, and we need to plug the holes."

Meanwhile "Machine Gun" Kelly had been recalled to Washington D.C. where, according to the rumors, he was likely to take an ass kicking at the Pentagon, and be eviscerated by the media prior to being relegated to a desk.

Soto had no way to assess if the disaster at Tabqa was truly Kelly's fault, and felt sorry for him, since he might have been chosen to be the fall guy.

Ironically the colonel who Kelly referred to as "Dumb Ass Duncan," had been cleared of any wrong doing, and was still in command of the eastbound expeditionary force. Soto knew, because the *Double Deuce* had repeatedly been called upon to pick up casualties in Duncan's AO (area of operations).

"The Diner" consisted of a large tent with the side flaps rolled up. The stools were five- gallon buckets, the cuisine consisted of MREs, and the service was nonexistent. The DFAC was a five-star restaurant by comparison.

Soto had just spooned some lukewarm chili con carne into her mouth when Jones appeared. He waved a piece of paper at her. "We're slotted to take twelve stretcher cases and three ambulatory patients out at 1900."

Soto wiped her mouth on her sleeve. "Where to?"

"Aleppo International. That's where they'll be loaded onto a C-17 for the trip to Europe or the U.S."

Soto nodded. "Hmm... Perhaps we can overnight in Aleppo."

The expression on Jones's face brightened. "As in have a drink and eat a real dinner?"

"Exactly."

"I'm in."

"You're in anyway," Soto replied. "But I appreciate the enthusiasm."

By the time 1900 rolled around, the passenger manifest had increased to thirteen stretcher cases, plus a medic to care for them in flight. After completing her external walkaround and reentering the aircraft, Soto paused to chat with each patient before entering the cockpit.

All but one that is, since Private Al Pesko was only semi-conscious, and hooked up to an IV. "He took a round in his right thigh," the medic explained, "and suffered a head injury as well."

"Okay," Soto said, as she eyed Pesko's bloodstained head wrap. "We'll get everybody to Aleppo as quickly as we can."

There was a momentary wait for a plane to land, followed by an "All clear" from Air Traffic Control. Once at cruising altitude Soto announced, "You have it," knowing that Jones was always eager to rack up more hours.

"I have it," Jones acknowledged. "Aleppo, here we come."

Soto closed her eyes. Sleep was hard to come by, and even a fifteen-minute nap would be welcome. The dream was the same dream she had dreamt since the age of twelve.

She was standing on a bridge and, when she looked over the rail, she fell. Falling was scary, but the fear was ameliorated by the knowledge that she was dreaming, and would never hit the water.

Soto awoke to the sound of gunshots, screams, and Alvarez shouting. "Grab him! Get the gun!"

Soto awoke with a start, realized she wasn't dreaming anymore, and released her harness. "You have it."

"I have it," Jones responded, as Soto hurried out of the cockpit, and more shots were fired. The scene in the dimly lit cargo area was like something straight out of hell.

Pesko was on his feet with a pistol clutched in his right hand. The soldier's IV bag was laying on the deck, right next to the dead medic.

A gunner was holding his arm as blood leaked out between his fingers. Alvarez was pointing her sidearm at Pesko, while he pointed his at her.

Soto considering pulling her own weapon and decided not to. The last thing they needed was more bullets flying around. "You killed them!" Pesko shouted. "You killed my friends! Now it's your turn to die!"

Soto was behind the soldier. She threw herself into the air and landed on Pesko's back. The impact caused Pesko to release the pistol as he reached for Soto.

Pesko couldn't get his hands on Soto, so he shook her off in the same way that a dog might dislodge a flea.

The pilot fell sideways and landed on a stretcher patient. He screamed as Pesko charged Alvarez and hit her. The crew chief toppled over backwards.

A gunner, along with one of the ambulatory patients came to the noncom's rescue, and wrestled Pesko to the deck. "Kill me!" he insisted. "I want to be with my squad!"

Soto added her weight to the scrum, and by working together the three of them managed to wrestle Pesko onto his stretcher and tie him down. "How did he get the gun?" Soto demanded, as she stood.

Alvarez was breathing heavily. "I think it was in a hideout holster. We could search him. But I wouldn't recommend it.

"The whole thing started when he sat up, ripped the IV out, and pulled the pistol. Then he stood, bad leg and all. The medic tried to intervene and he shot her."

Soto looked at her. "So, we don't search patients?"

Alvarez shook her head. "We never have."

Soto sighed. "I think that's about to change."

CHAPTER TEN

Superbase Tabqa, Syria

Oscar Polat returned from Turkey to find that the situation at Tabqa was worse than the descriptions he'd read in the *Daily Sabah* newspaper.

But that wasn't surprising since the *Sabah* was widely considered to be the propaganda arm of the Turkish government. And Turkey was officially part of the Alliance, even though it had sub rosa ties to Russia, and was determined to suppress the Kurds.

Polat's arrival wasn't a minute too early, because in the aftermath of the "Holy" attack on the airbase, the Allies were about to level Mud City. Which was understandable given the number of enemy fighters who'd been living in the slum while they worked for the stupid Americans and spied on them.

Polat had to hurry to reach his small dwelling, rescue his belongings, and load them into a dusty taxi before a bulldozer destroyed it. "Take me to this address in Al-Nayrab," Polat said, as he gave the driver a slip of paper.

The cabbie produced a grunt of acknowledgement and they were off. The residents of Mud Town were loading their belongings into old cars, donkey-drawn carts, and even wheel barrows as they struggled to save what they could.

Children were roped together into lines so they couldn't stray, dogs barked at soldiers, interpreters bellowed through bullhorns, a drone patrolled the air overhead, and dust swirled everywhere.

Polat felt sorry for the residents of Mud Town—having been born in the notorious slum of Cincin—he knew what it was to be poor. *But soon*, Polat thought, *I will know what it is to be rich!*

Al-Nayrab had been a village once, prior to being absorbed into Aleppo, and Polat had orders to establish a safehouse there. Preliminary arrangements had been made by functionaries at MIT (Turkey's National Intelligence Organization) so Polat wasn't sure what to expect.

The drive took the better part of an hour, and when Polat arrived, he was pleased. The apartment, if that was the correct word, was located on the second floor above a busy garage.

Polat liked that because his "guests" were less likely to be noticed due to the frequent comings and goings.

A flight of stairs ran up the side of the building to a steel fire door. Just the thing for slowing intruders down. A key had been sent to him and turned smoothly in the lock.

The door opened into an open space which had previously been used to sew clothing, judging from the work tables and antique foot-operated sewing machines that sat atop them.

A sweat shop? Probably. And there, back in a corner, was a full-sized bed with neatly folded blankets, sheets, and towels piled on top of it.

But, before Polat could explore further, he had to go down and fetch his belongings. Six trips were required to bring everything up. Once that was accomplished Polat was free to explore the rest of the apartment.

Restrooms, one for men and one for women, were down a short hallway. The ladies' room was the larger of the two, and boasted a shower. It was clearly new, and therefore spotlessly clean. A pleasant surprise indeed.

That was when Polat noticed the steel ladder which ran up a wall to a hatch in the ceiling. He climbed up, pushed the hatch cover out of the way, and crawled onto the flat roof. It was the perfect place to make sat phone calls, and to do so without being observed, since the neighboring structures were one story tall. An unexpected bonus.

Polat removed his phone from an inner pocket, turned it on, and dialed a long string of numbers. The phone rang twice and was answered by an AI, which demanded an access code. After entering the required four digits Polat was routed to a *second* nexus which required him to state his code name: "Kyzaghan." The Turkish god of war.

That was followed by a click and three rings. Polat recognized the voice that answered as belonging to Major Rick Wells. A member of the U.S. army's intelligence staff at the superbase.

Hey, Oscar... I'm glad you called. I have something for you."

A lot of the chores the U.S. sent Polat's way amounted to scut work. But every now and then they handed him a gem. So, what did Wells have in store? A turd? Or a diamond?

"We're watching a new ISIS base," Wells said. "And we're monitoring two cell phones associated with that location. You'll be interested to know that one of them is being used to sell a hostage to a Russian. Who knows? Maybe the prisoner is Colonel Kaya."

Polat felt a rising sense of excitement. Colonel Kaya didn't exist. But Hala Omar did! And it was quite likely that the Russians wanted to retrieve her.

If Polat managed to abduct her, he'd be promoted, and would spend the rest of the war in a comfortable office!

"That's excellent news," Polat replied. "I'm eager to check it out. Can I borrow the usual team? And the helicopter?"

"We're short of everything due to the fighting down south," Wells replied. "Especially special ops personnel and helicopters. But we place a high priority on supporting our Turkish allies. I'll see what I can do."

Did Wells believe that the Turkish government was wholly committed to the Alliance? No, of course not. And Polat didn't either. But both men understood the need to promote that fiction. "I understand," Polat replied. "Thank you."

"Check back around 1800," Wells told him. "And I'll give you a status report."

The call came to an end. That was that for the moment at least. But what about Sergeant Bone? Would Wells be able to secure the Ranger's services? And what had the bastard been up to anyway? Stealing the gold?

Don't worry, Polat told himself. *The American knows that the gold is hidden in the Dead City of Serjilla. But the ruins cover a large area, and Sergeant Bone doesn't know where to look. Fortunately, I do.*

***

Tabqa Superbase, Syria

Soto had been ordered to visit Major Albro. For *what?* An ass chewing? Or one of the company commander's rare attagirls. *I'll know right away,* Soto decided. *If I'm in trouble Albro will make me stand. And, if he invites me to sit down, I'll be in the clear.*

Soto was cleared to enter Albro's office after a short wait in the reception area, and did so with all of the flourishes that her CO insisted on by coming to attention, and stating her name and rank. As if he didn't know who she was. "Reporting as ordered, *sir!*"

Albro returned the salute. "Welcome back Captain Soto. Have a seat. I'm sorry about what took place on the *Double Deuce.* We all are.

"You'll be happy to know that a full review is underway. I suspect that patients with a medical profile similar to Private Pesko's will be searched in the future. And a good thing too, even though that will add still another checkoff to the preflight, and consume more time.

"By the way, thanks to General Kelly, you're going to receive an Air Medal the next time the battalion musters. And your crewmembers were approved for Commendation Medals. Please let them know.

"That brings us to your next assignment. It seems that the search for Colonel Kaya continues, and the Turks want you and Sergeant Bone to raid an ISIS hideout.

"That isn't equivalent to a day off, but it might be better than a day spent down south. So, I said 'Yes.'"

Soto had doubts, but kept them to herself. "Yes, sir. Thank you."

Albro was pleased with himself. "You're welcome. I hope it's a no brainer."

It will be a no brainer if I get shot in the head, Soto thought as she stood.

The officers exchanged salutes and Soto left. A message was waiting for Soto at the reception desk. It was from Master Sergeant Bone. "Meet us at the Ops Center at 1300."

It was just after 0900, so that gave Soto some time to catch up with her email, wade through some paperwork, and eat lunch.

In the meantime, Jones was discussing minor repairs with Alvarez, checking to make sure that the helo was fueled properly, and calling around to find a new gunner. The gunner wounded by Private Pesko hadn't been cleared for a return to duty yet.

Soto arrived at the Ops Center to find that Bone and Polat were already present. The first five minutes were spent sketching in what each person had been up to for the last two weeks, marveling at the way the enemy had been able to breach Tabqa's defenses, and the manner in which Mud Town had been erased.

Then the briefer entered the room and the session started. She wore her hair in a bun, had the manner of a retro school marm, and a southern accent. Her name was Procter. As in "proctologist."

According to Proctor, the team's destination was the city of Afrin, Syria which, like Tell Abyad, was currently under Turkish control. "During the day anyway," Proctor said. "But not at night. That's when the Kurdish resistance battles Turkish troops, ISIS fighters search for heretics, and criminals steal whatever they can.

"The ISIS cell that may, or may not, be holding Colonel Kaya, is headquartered in what was a shoe factory. The building is large enough to land on if you want to."

Soto's mental alarm bells began to ring. "Why would I do that?" Soto demanded. "My Chinook would be a sitting duck. Besides, even if the roof is large enough, could it handle the weight? We're talking about 25,000 pounds."

"You would do it for the team," Proctor said patiently, as if to a child. "Otherwise, the operators will be forced to infiltrate from the south, and make their way through contested neighborhoods, which could result in a firefight.

"Then, after alerting the neighborhood to their presence, the operators would have to exfil through a hostile environment. But, you're the aircraft commander, so you decide."

Bone cleared his throat. "We could repel down. And you could winch us back up."

Soto sighed. "Okay, we'll do one or the other. Let me think about it."

Bone smiled and Polat gave her a thumbs up.

Proctor nodded. "Good."

"I have a question though," Bone added, as he turned to make eye contact with Polat. "If Turkey controls the city during the day, why can't your troops roll up, and do the job?"

It was an excellent question. All eyes were on Polat.

***

Polat had been hoping that the question wouldn't come up. Because, in all truth, he *could* ask a Turkish army unit to do the job. But if Hala Omar was in the old Shoe Factory, and Turkish ground forces managed to free her—a Lieutenant, Captain, or Major would get the credit. And he would lose out.

But that wasn't all. Hopefully, if they could get Soto to agree, they would carry out a *second* mission. That was to recover the gold. And do so without the pilot learning the true nature of the cargo.

Polat cleared his throat. "Yes, well, as much as it pains me to say it, the army unit in Afrin is somewhat unreliable. An investigation is underway. But, until that effort is complete, I don't know who I can trust."

***

I know who I can trust, Soto thought. *And your name isn't on the list.*

"All right," Proctor said, "Let's wrap this up."

The rest of the briefing included a weather report, a list of emergency landing spots along their route, and some bad news. "Unfortunately," Proctor said, as she closed her notebook. "Air support won't be available within the city limits of Afrin."

Bone groaned. "Give me a fucking break."

"No can do," Proctor replied matter-of-factly. "That's the agreement we have with Mr. Polat's government. Our aircraft aren't allowed to overfly so-called 'disputed territories' without permission. And the folks in Ankara said, 'No.'

"Now, if you'll excuse me, I have another briefing to give. Good luck."

***

Afrin. Syria

ISIS Cell Commander Ferran Mostafa was standing on the factory's roof, waiting for a sat call from a Russian army officer named Ivan Ludkov. If that was the man's actual name—which seemed unlikely.

But that didn't matter. What mattered was that Ludkov represented a "senior official" in the Russian government who was willing to pay for Hala Omar.

Haggling had been underway for more than a week. Mostafa, on behalf of ISIS, was demanding ten million U.S. dollars.

Ludkov's "best offer" was a tenth of that. A sum Mostafa rejected, forcing Ludkov to ask for additional time, so he could consult with "higher authorities."

That made the telephone conversation so important that Mostafa was willing to stand in the hot sun.

***

Manbij, Syria

Russian Major Sergei Voronin was positioned on a hill with an excellent view of Manbij. It was a sizeable city, with a population of one hundred thousand, some of whom were Europeans. That was the reason why Voronin, and the remaining members of his team, had chosen to use the town as a base. So long as the Russians remained in a neighborhood mostly occupied by foreign nationals, they could blend in.

Voronin eyed his watch. Two minutes to go. Would he be able to get Mostafa to bring the price down? That was critical. The orders from Toplin, as relayed to him via the president's executive assistant Mischa Durov, were to pay no more than a million.

"Otherwise," Durov said, "you are to recover the goods by force."

That was ridiculous. With only three men left Voronin would be hard pressed to fight a well-armed squad, never mind dozens of religious fanatics. Yet, it was what he'd be required to do. Either that or desert.

A pair of vultures circled high overhead as Voronin thumbed Mostafa's number into his phone. It rang only once before the ISIS commander answered.

Thanks to the fact that the call was being routed through a Russian satellite, it was encrypted. But it would be naïve to think the Allies couldn't defeat the encryption if they zeroed in on the call. So, both men were circumspect.

"This is Ferran."

"And this is Ivan," Voronin replied.

"So, my friend… Are you ready to pay ten?"

"No," Voronin answered. "But we will pay one. I was unable to secure the increase you asked for."

"That's unfortunate," Mostafa replied. "Because ten is the price."

"Everything is negotiable in this world," Voronin countered. "For example, I could pay you one, or destroy the building you're standing on. You decide."

The threat was a risk. A *big* risk since Voronin was bluffing. He did have one thing going for him however, and that was the fact that Russian intelligence knew where Mostafa was.

***

Mostafa eyed the sky. Was a Russian drone watching him? Were the Kafirs willing to kill Omar? Would anyone else want her? Those thoughts and more blipped through his mind. "There's no need for threats, Ivan. We are reasonable men. I hereby accept your offer."

***

Voronin heaved a sigh of relief. "Thank you, Ferran. Let's discuss the exchange."

***

Afrin. Syria

The fire proof vault had been built in another time, before computer-controlled machinery, and before the endless war. Dusty shelves lined three of the four walls, each supporting rows of the carefully coded, wooden shoe lasts (patterns) once used to produce bespoke footwear.

And there, at the center of the room, was a metal bucket. Hala Omar knelt before it. The vomit rose, filled her mouth, and shot into the bucket.

Fifteen weeks. That was Hala's best guess. And she was starting to show. Did Mostafa know? Hala didn't think to. The bulge was concealed by her loose-fitting clothing.

Another surge of vomit came spewing out.

Toplin's baby, she thought. What would the Russian president do when he found out? *He'll kill us*, she concluded. *I'm sorry alsaghir* (little one). *Our fate is sealed.*

Hala wiped her mouth with a rag and stood. *If only I were a brave person*, Hala mused, as she perched on the edge of her cot. *I would go to heaven and take little one with me. But I am a coward.*

***

Aboard the *Double Deuce*, over northern Syria

Soto could see lights up ahead. They were like diamonds scattered on black velvet. The city of Afrin was waiting. Soto spoke over the intercom. "We're five out. Prepare to disembark. Please check the area around your seat to make sure you have all of your belongings.

"I'd like to thank you for flying *Double Deuce Air*, and hope you enjoyed all the amenities the crew provided, which is to say some bottles of water.

"Please rest assured that the return flight will be equally luxurious." The announcement provoked guffaws and a lot of profanity.

The first problem was to correctly identify the shoe factory without benefit of a flare or other type of illumination. In order to do that Soto had to rely on military GPS coordinates which were typically more accurate than those provided for civilian use.

That was because civilian devices typically relied on a single GPS frequency, while military receivers used two, thus correcting signal distortions caused by the Earth's atmosphere.

Soto knew that, and had to trust in it, but would have preferred to locate the landing zone the old-fashioned way—with her own eyes.

Finally, after consulting with her crew, and a good deal of internal debate, Soto had settled on a landing, rather than a rope out. There were a number of reasons for her decision, including less time spent as a hovering target, a quick delivery, and a fast getaway. Possibly with wounded soldiers to load and care for.

But was the roof strong enough? After studying aerial photos of the factory Soto thought it was. But the structure had suffered battle damage over the years, and appearances could be deceiving.

What Soto saw through her night vision goggles matched what she expected to see. The Chinook descended and made contact with the roof. It held. For the moment anyway. Once the ramp was down Bone led the twelve-man team off. Polat followed.

Soto assumed that everyone in the area knew that a helicopter had landed. But there was no reason to give them additional noise to home in on. So, the pilots shut the engines down. The waiting began.

***

Two ISIS lookouts were posted on the roof. One of them managed to thumb his radio and report the incoming helo, before a gunner cut him down.

The other fired his AK at the huge aircraft, and paid the price. He fell next to his buddy.

***

Based on aerial photography, Bone knew there were two stairwells that provided access to the building's flat roof, both of which were topped by boxlike structures. Bone decided to enter via the nearest stairwell since he didn't have any information about the factory's internal layout. The steel door was locked. No surprise there.

Bone stepped out of the way and pointed at the door. Corporal Levy stepped forward, placed a charge near the lock, and backed away. "Fire in the hole!"

That was followed by a loud *bang*, and roiling smoke. Bone kicked the door open, threw a flashbang grenade in through the opening, and stood to one side. After the device exploded the noncom entered. There was no reception party. *We caught them with their pants down*, Bone decided. *But they know we're here now, and it's about to get ugly.*

The plan was simple: Kill everybody except Hala Omar. That was all the team *could* do, since they didn't know where the hostage was being held, assuming she was present.

With that in mind Bone hurried down the first flight of stairs, opened a fire door, and entered a huge room. Empty workstations and silent machines lurked in the gloom. "Prop the fire escape door open," Bone ordered. "Take cover and wait for my order. Over."

The Rangers didn't have to wait long. Voices were heard, a shaft of light shot through the open door, and ghostly green people appeared.

Once five of them were on the floor, Bone gave the necessary order. "Fire!"

Automatic weapons cut the ISIS fighters down in seconds and, because they were equipped with suppressors, made very little sound.

Bone waited to see if more tangos would enter, but none did, either because there weren't any, or because they had the good sense to retreat.

Now, the risk of an ambush shifted to the Rangers, as they descended the stairs. Someone fired up at them from below. Sergeant Olson dropped a grenade down through the gap that separated two flights of stairs. The confined space served to amplify the sound of the explosion and the shooting stopped.

"We need to check each floor," Bone said, as they arrived at a landing. "We're going in."

***

A helicopter was on the roof! That's all Mostafa knew. So, he sent men up to deal with the situation, and hadn't heard from them since.

Who was responsible? The Americans came to mind as did the Brits. But more likely in Mostafa's opinion was Ivan Ludkov. Why pay a million for something if you could steal it? That's the way the fucking Russian would see it.

But how did Ludkov know where Omar was? *Russia has satellites and drones*, Mostafa thought. *May Allah curse them.*

Mostafa and two of his men were in what had once been the manager's office. The PA system was old, but most of it still worked. Mostafa took hold of the ancient microphone and flipped a switch. "Ludkov, I know you're here. Prepare to die."

***

Bone paused. Ludkov? Who the hell was Ludkov? *It's a Russian name,* Bone reasoned. *And the ISIS guy was talking to a Russian via sat phone. So, it's logical to assume that the Ruskie is named Ludkov. That's interesting, but doesn't make a difference.*

Bone waved his men forward. They were on the second floor. And it, like the top floor, had high ceilings, and was inhabited by mysterious pieces of silent machinery. Judging from the scuff marks in the dust, candy wrappers on the floor, and the pieces of cast-off clothing that lay here and there—the space was being used as a dormitory.

"Okay," Bone said. "We're going down to the main floor. They know we're coming. So, keep your heads on a swivel."

Levy was on point with Bone in the two slot. The corporal eased his way down two flights of stairs, and paused in front of a steel door.

Bone pulled it open, yelled "Grenade!" and threw a flashbang into the murk. His eyes were closed as the device exploded. The resulting blast wave was Bone's signal to move out. He expected to receive fire. There wasn't any. "Spread out, but not too far… Be careful. We know the assholes are here. Over."

The Rangers crept forward, heads swiveling right and left. All except for Sergeant Olson that is, who looked right, left, and *up.* That was when he saw the green figures on the catwalks and yelled, "They're above us!" A hail of bullets cut him down.

***

Soto was on the roof, stretching her legs, when the first mortar landed. The explosion was so unexpected that it took a moment to analyze what had occurred, consider the danger that more mortar rounds would pose, and yell, "Get aboard! We're taking off!"

Alvarez and a gunner followed Soto as she thundered up the ramp and made for the cockpit. She could already hear the steadily increasing *whine* as Jones started the engines. The sound grew in intensity until it sounded like the rotors might fly off. They didn't.

The noise hit an even higher pitch as Soto slipped into her seat. "You have it."

"I have it," Jones agreed, as he continued to scan readouts and flip switches.

That was when a second round hit the roof. It was closer than the first round had been. Did that imply an observer? Or a drone? Maybe. Or maybe it was luck.

Jones pulled pitch, the wheels left the roof, and the Chinook was in the air. Soto adjusted her helmet. "Gunners! Watch for the next flash… We've got to locate that tube and kill it."

In order to make the search easier Jones put the *Double Deuce* into a three-sixty, and was about halfway through the circle, when a gunner named Hines spoke up. "There! A flash at nine o'clock!"

"I have it," Soto said. "You have it," Jones agreed, as Soto turned toward the target. "Gunners will stand by," Soto ordered.

She saw the next flash, and wondered how much damage the factory's roof was taking. Could she land there again? Was there a secondary nearby?

"There they are," Jones put in. "Straight ahead."

Red tracers arced up, revealing the presence of an enemy weapons emplacement. "Ready on the guns," Soto said, as she took the Chinook down. The closer the *Double Deuce* got the more likely hits were. That applied to the enemy gunners as well of course. But were they prepared for a treetop level attack?

Soto hoped they weren't as the Chinook came in low, and somewhat to the left of the target, so the starboard gunners could bring their weapons to bear. Then she slowed to a hover.

Soto knew how risky that was, but saw it as a tradeoff against the dangers inherent in multiple passes, and was rewarded with a series of explosions.

Had the mortar been destroyed? There was no way to be sure, but Soto thought so, as she applied power and turned back toward the factory.

***

Both sides took heavy casualties as the ISIS fighters fired down on the Rangers, and the Americans fired up. A body thumped to the floor in front of Bone even as a Ranger performed a pirouette and fell.

There was no place to hide, that was the worst of it, and the two groups of fighters might have annihilated each other had the battle lasted longer.

But one ISIS fighter ran, soon followed by another, leaving only a handful of men to support Mostafa. And, as the cell commander paused to reload, the truth was undeniable. What remained of the American force was blocking access to the vault and Hala Omar.

Yes, Americans, not Russians. Because orders were being given in English. "Break contact!" Mostafa ordered. "We will live to fight on another day!"

Mostafa's bodyguards were quick to back away, turn, and flee.

Bone took a quick look around. Should the team give chase? Fuck no. At least half of his twelve-man squad had been killed or wounded. And they needed to find the woman—assuming she was there. "Levy! Take a man and search the area! Over."

***

Upon hearing the muffled gunfire and shouting, Hala Omar lay flat on the floor. What was happening? Did the fighting have something to do with her? Or was it just another firefight between ISIS and one of the many groups that opposed it?

Fortunately, the vault was virtually bullet proof. And Hala took comfort from that as the battle raged, slowed, and finally stopped.

Hala faced a dilemma. She couldn't open the door herself. So, she needed help. But if she were to call out, who would respond? Mostafa? Or someone even worse?

There was another danger as well… What if all of the combatants had left? She could starve to death.

Finally, convinced that she should summon help, Hala began to shout. "Please! Open the door! I'm trapped."

Hala tried Arabic first, followed by Russian, and English. And that was the language that produced a response. "Back away from the door! Cover your ears! We're going to blow the lock."

An American! Hala felt a surge of hope as she put her back to some shelving. The explosion was anticlimactic. There was a *bang*, followed by a cloud of dust, and a thump as something heavy hit the door. A man entered. "Hala Omar? I'm Master Sergeant Bone, United States Army. Are you hurt?"

"No," Hala answered.

"Good. Please follow me, and stay close. We need to reach the roof before more ISIS reinforcements arrive."

Then, after switching his radio back on, Bone spoke into his boom mike. "Wizard… This is Red-Dog-Nine. We have the package and are heading for the roof. Prepare to receive walking wounded and a stretcher case. Over."

***

Alvarez had the presence of mind to toss a flare out through the hatch as the *Double Deuce* lifted off. And it was still burning. That gave Soto a target to aim at.

"Roger that, Red-Dog. We were forced to lift off due to mortar fire. We destroyed the mortar and are incoming. Be advised that we will hover above the roof rather than touch down on it. It's impossible to assess how strong it is. Over."

"Copy," Bone said. "Over."

The flare cast an eerie red glow over the roof, and as Soto took the Chinook down, she half expected to be fired on from the surrounding area.

There was risk involved in activating the aircraft's gyro-stabilized belly lights. But in order to bring the helo down close to the roof Soto needed to see it. So, she took the chance.

The white glare lit a wide area but Soto's eyes were on what she could see through the chin bubble. There was nothing to go on except experience.

When Soto "felt" that the helicopter's landing gear was about a foot off the roof, she made a minute adjustment to the collective, and that caused the Chinook to hover. "Load 'em," she ordered. "And make it quick."

The gunners went back to help pull people up onto the ramp. Hoisting the makeshift stretcher high enough for the crew to grab onto it was the most difficult part of the evolution.

Unfortunately, five of Bone's Rangers had been killed, and their bodies had been left behind. That troubled Bone greatly.

But not Polat, who was ebullient. "We have Omar!" the Turk exclaimed. "I'm going forward to provide Captain Soto with coordinates for package two."

"Good luck with that," Bone said cynically. "And by the way, if any of the wounded are in serious condition, we're going straight to Tabqa."

***

Polat knew that the American was serious. He also knew that one of the Rangers was badly wounded. He'd been shot multiple times, and was lying on the deck in a pool of blood. A medic was there, with her back momentarily turned, and Polat knew that was his chance.

The Russian made OTs-38 Stechkin revolver was a favorite with Turkish intelligence operatives, because it was compact and virtually silent. That, plus the roar of the Chinook's engines, guaranteed that the shot wouldn't be heard.

Polat shot the Ranger in the chest, confident that the medic would assume the wound had been received in battle, and that no autopsy would be performed. The impact caused the soldier to jerk. Polat smiled.

CHAPTER ELEVEN

Aboard the *Double Deuce* over Afrin, Syria.

"**M**edic!" Polat said. "Quick! This man is coughing up blood."

The Ranger turned away from the IV bag and hurried over. After a brief examination she shook her head. "He's gone."

"Damn it," Polat said. "How are the others?"

"Don't worry," she replied. "The rest of the wounded are stable."

"*Alhamdulillah.*" (Praise Allah.)

Now, Polat thought. *All I have to do is deal with the pilot bitch.*

***

Soto was still feeling the after effects of the attack on the mortar, and the subsequent extraction, when Polat sat in the observer's seat. "Captain Soto… I need to speak with you."

Soto glanced at Jones. "You have it."

"I have it," Jones acknowledged.

Then, to Polat, "What's up?"

"I'm very sorry to inform you that the Ranger on the stretcher passed away."

Soto made a face. "Damn it."

"Yes," Polat said sorrowfully. "I saw him fall. He fought bravely."

Soto nodded. "Is that all?"

"No," Polat replied. "Our medic indicates that all of the wounded are stable. That being the case, it's our duty to carry out a secondary mission."

Soto frowned. "Which is?"

"Which is to land at a certain location and retrieve a cargo that belongs to ISIS. They are after it as well. So, it's imperative that we arrive first."

***

"Okay," Soto replied. "I hear you. But, since this secondary mission wasn't in my briefing, I need written orders."

"And I have them," Polat said smoothly, as he produced an envelope.

Soto stared. "Why not tell me ahead of time?"

Polat shrugged. "You didn't have a need to know. Until now."

Soto accepted the envelope and ripped it open. The orders were brief and to the point. "You are, upon a request from Special Assistant Polat, to render all possible assistance in recovering materials belonging to ISIS."

The document was signed by Colonel Ayaz Aksoy, Commanding Officer, Allied Military Liaison Office, Alexandria, Egypt.

"As you know," Polat said gently, "in keeping with the Joint Services Agreement that Allied countries are party to, Colonel Aksoy has the necessary authority."

That was true. In fact, one of the Alliance's greatest strengths was its ability to mix and match military personnel and units. Which meant that Polat was standing on solid ground.

"Okay," Soto said, as she folded the order into a small square and slipped it into a pocket. "Where is the load of something?"

***

The order was a forgery. And Polat hoped to retrieve it if he could. Maybe Soto would take her jacket off at some point, giving him a chance to recover it.

"Here are the coordinates," Polat replied, as he gave a slip of paper to Soto. "They aren't exact. We don't think so anyway... But they're close."

"Thanks. Is Sergeant Bone aware of the secondary mission?"

"Yes."

"Please send him forward."

She's going to double check what I told her, Polat thought. *Just as I knew she would.*

"Of course," Polat said.

***

Bone was eating a candy bar when the Turk reappeared, made his way back, and sat down. "The captain wants to speak with you."

Bone took a swig of water. "How did it go?"

"Fine. You know what to say. And don't forget the com stuff."

"I won't," Bone said as he stood.

***

"You sent for me," Bone stated, as he sat on the observer's seat. "What's up?"

"Polat gave me written orders for an additional mission," Soto answered. "Are you and your people up for that?"

"Yes."

"Why didn't you tell me ahead of time?"

"Because our secondary mission is top secret," Bone replied. "And you didn't have a need to know. And that includes air traffic control at Tabqa. We'll check in as soon as we can."

Soto eyed him suspiciously. "What else did you hold back?"

Bone shrugged. "There is no Colonel Kaya. The person we came for is a woman named Hala Omar. She is, or was, President Toplin's mistress. He wants her back, and the Turks plan to use her for leverage. And the rest of the Allies are inclined to let the Turks roll. That was top secret as well."

Soto felt angry. *Very* angry. At the assholes who kept her in the dark, and at Bone, who could have taken her into his confidence. "You are dismissed. Return to the cargo area."

Bone opened his mouth, as if to say something, and closed it again. Then he left.

"Are we having fun yet?" Jones inquired.

"Hell no. Let's plug in the coordinates and see where we're going, and more importantly, whether we have enough fuel to get there."

The answer as it turned out was a place called the Dead City of Abaz, which according to the Michelin Guide that Jones kept in his flight bag, was only seventy miles away—and encompassed 700 archeological sites.

"According to this," Jones said, "Abaz was abandoned in the seventh century. That's when the Arabs conquered the area, and key trading routes were disrupted."

"We have enough fuel," Soto replied. "That's the main thing. We'll land, load whatever it is, and head home. We have a dead Ranger to take care of."

The orange-red glow signaled the fact that the sun was about to rise. Seen from 500 feet, the gentle light transformed Syria from a battle field into a fairytale landscape of farms, hills, and wandering rivers.

Off to the west a V shaped formation of pink flamingos could be seen, flying north as if to escape the fighting in the south, and eager to reach a welcoming marsh. It was the sort of moment that served to remind Soto of why she loved to fly.

It took less than half an hour to reach the Dead City of Abaz, and Soto was struck by how intact some of the ancient structures were, in spite of centuries of looting, vandalism, and war. They were the exceptions however, since most of the city's buildings had been reduced to piles of rock, a free-standing column, and the outline of a foundation.

Soto had been to the ancient cities of Ephesus and Pompeii prior to the war, both of which were sizeable, but to her untrained eye Abaz was larger. "We're coming up on the coordinates," Jones announced.

Soto cut the helicopter's speed and eyed the area ahead. And there, just west of a hill, was a flat spot with very little debris. An ancient plaza perhaps? Soto thought so.

Dust swirled as the Chinook descended into a storm of its own making, and the crew members called "Clear." The helo landed with a thump.

Bone, and those Rangers who could, jogged down the ramp and spread out.

But it soon became apparent that there were no hostiles waiting to ambush them. The top of the hill was the obvious place on which to establish a two-man overlook. "Take water," Bone instructed. "And something to provide shade."

Soto arrived in time to hear the orders. She raised a hand to shade her eyes, and made a show of looking around. "So, where's the cargo?"

"Somewhere nearby," Polat replied. "We can assume that the ISIS fighters who left the shipment here were in a hurry. Their column had been shot up, and Allied forces were looking for survivors. The obvious place to start is inside the cavern."

Soto had to agree. The cavern was flanked by columns and framed by a beautiful arch. From what she could see the cave was manmade rather than natural.

It was hard to make out any details however, because the sun was still rising, and it would be another hour or so before the first shaft of sunlight dispersed the darkness within.

Rangers were bringing crates out and placing them on the ground. "I took the liberty of bringing shovels, picks, and a metal detector," Polat said. "Just in case."

"'Metal detector?'" Soto inquired. "What are we looking for? Weapons?"

Polat and Bone exchanged a meaningful look. "I guess it's time to get specific," Polat said. "Agreed?"

***

Bone felt his dreams of wealth slipping away. Once the nature of the treasure hunt was revealed it would become nearly impossible to keep it.

And now, looking back, he realized that the plan had never been realistic. But, like Polat, he wanted to believe. He cleared his throat. "No, ma'am. What we're looking for is a shipment of ISIS gold."

"ISIS minted gold coins to be exact," Polat added. "We came across information regarding the shipment during the mission to the safehouse near Tell Abyad. After we passed the information to the Intel people, they slapped a top-secret classification on it."

That was a lie. *The bastard still believes that we can hijack the gold*, Bone thought. *Maybe there's a chance. Not to remain in the army, but to take the loot and run.*

The fact that he would even consider such a thing came as a shock. But there it was.

"That's correct," Bone said. "And that's why we couldn't tell you."

"So, let's get to it," Soto responded. "I want to sleep in my own bed tonight."

The team was too small to establish a true perimeter. But, by removing the machine guns from the *Double Deuce*, and positioning them to cover the approaches to the plaza, the defenders could delay attackers long enough for everyone to board the helo and flee. That was the hope.

Jones was aboard the Chinook and ready to fire the engines up, and Alvarez was sitting next to Hala Omar on the ramp, chatting about who knows what.

The lack of a truly adequate defense niggled at the back of Soto's mind as she followed Polat and Bone toward the cavern. There were no footprints to be seen at first. But as the group entered the cavern hundreds of impressions were visible. And that, Soto decided, was due to the fact that the wind couldn't reach inside the cave to scour them clean. As a result, it was likely that some of the prints were days, weeks or even months old.

The timing was such that a ray of sunshine found the entrance and lit a huge statue. Just the way it was intended to. The headless figure had been carved from limestone. And, thanks to the protection offered by the cavern, had suffered very little erosion. What remained of the statue was seated on an ornate chair next to a crouched lion.

Who was Soto looking at? A king? A queen? A prophet? And where was his or her head? Sitting in a foreign museum perhaps. Or blown into a thousand fragments by ISIS as part of that organization's misguided effort to eliminate *shirk* (polytheism). And that seemed likely given the stone shards scattered about.

Bone sent Rangers in every direction with instructions to look for "Any fucking thing that might hide some crates."

Soto was kneeling next to a half buried human skull, when she heard the shout. "I found something Sarge! Come take a look."

That was enough to bring Polat and Soto to a spot located between the statue and the rear wall of the cavern. The Ranger, a private named Franco, was digging with a shovel. The process didn't take long.

Once the dirt was removed, a tarp was revealed. And there, beneath it, was a cargo pallet. Polat aimed a flashlight down between the wooden slats. The beam disappeared into a vertical shaft. "This could be what we're looking for," the Turk observed.

"It could be," Bone allowed. "But I'd say this shaft has been here for a long, long time."

"Why so?" Polat wanted to know.

"If ISIS fighters dug it, then where is the material they removed?" Soto interjected. "Plus, according to your account, they were on the run. This sucker would take a month to excavate using hand tools."

"I agree," Bone said. "I'll go down and check it out."

It took the better part of twenty minutes to fetch a block and tackle, create a tripod using stretcher poles, and get Bone hooked up. He was wearing a head lamp which left his hands free to rappel. A handheld radio was attached to his tac vest.

"Okay, here goes nothing," Bone said, as he took a step back and disappeared.

By peering down into the hole, the onlookers could see the light from the noncom's head lamp shrink to a pinpoint, before blinking out.

"I'm on the bottom," Bone announced via his radio. "I'm in an open area. It looks as if this was a mine. A limestone mine. The same stuff the statue is made of. Wait a minute, *snakes*!"

A series of muted pistol shots followed, interspersed with swear words. "There," Bone said. "I think that's all of them. Damn, I hate snakes!"

"Yes, of course you do," Polat said soothingly. "Now, what can you see other than snakes?"

"A pile of crates," Bone replied. "Hold on... I'm going to check them out."

***

Bone felt a rising sense of excitement as he freed himself from the rope and hurried over to a haphazard pile of crates. The gold! What else *could* it be?

Bone drew his KA-BAR knife and attacked the box on top of the pile. After inserting the blade into a crack, the noncom began to pry. Nails *creaked* as they came loose. And there, like a scene from one of his daydreams, were loosely packed gold coins! Hundreds of them.

Bone chose a coin at random and bent his head to put some light on it. The circumference of the coin was decorated with Arabic script. A geometric design served to separate the lettering from the symbols at the center of the disc. One of them resembled a mishappen "Y," and the other was similar to an "O." Or "YO." He laughed. If only the bitch could see him now.

Bone didn't know what the script meant, and didn't care. The coin was heavy, the way gold is supposed to be heavy, and slick to touch.

Bone gave the coin a kiss, slipped it into a pocket, and took another one for show and tell. "I found it!" Bone announced, as he hooked himself to the rope. "Pull me up!"

***

"We have it!" Polat exclaimed, causing Soto to wonder. Why was the Turk so excited? Was there something proprietary about his demeanor? Or was that her imagination?

Once Bone was on the surface everyone gathered around to look at the gold coin and remark on it. Soto allowed them a couple of minutes to do so before cracking the whip. "Enough sightseeing. Let's get to work. Is our tripod strong enough to handle the crates?"

"No way," Bone replied. "But rather than try to lift the crates, we can use packs and duffle bags."

Soto looked around. "Okay, let's see what we can scrounge from the Chinook."

It took more than half an hour to retrieve a hodgepodge of containers from the helicopter, lower a two-man loading team down into the mine, and bring the first pack load of gold up.

Once on the surface the coins were dumped onto a tarp, where they glowed as if lit from within.

The plan was to bring the empty crates up last, put the gold in them, and hump the containers to the Chinook. "If ISIS did it, then you can do it," Bone assured his soldiers. "It'll be good for you."

Soto smiled. Noncoms. They never change.

***

A nameless roadside market in central Syria

Mathew Chako was in the back of the stolen bus, stretched out on the queen-sized bed, with two naked women to keep him company. Servicing two women in rapid succession was a demanding task, but an important one, lest his reputation for virility begin to fade.

As with any mercenary band there were other men who were hungry for power, and any sign of weakness, no matter how trivial, could provide one or more of them with an opening.

Chako had just finished having coitus with a girl named Serena, when Yusuf Hajar, Chako's second in command whipped the privacy curtain aside. "We have what could be a juicy target, Boss. So, put your clothes on, and let's liberate a helicopter."

Chako was pulling his pants on. The girls were making eyes at Hajar. Would he become the band's *Qayid* (leader) one day? It was important to plan ahead.

"A helicopter? What *kind* of helicopter?" Chako demanded, as he laced his boots.

"One of those big cigar shaped helicopters," Hajar replied. "The kind the *al'amrikiiyn* (Americans) use to move troops and vehicles."

Chako felt a surge of excitement. What would such an aircraft be worth on the open market? A million? *Five* million? Chako didn't know, but felt certain that he could sell it to the Syrian regime, the Iraqis, or the Iranians.

"Where is it?" Chako demanded. "And how did you learn about it?"

"While you were humping the ladies, we stopped at a roadside market to buy food for lunch," Hajar answered. "The proprietor said that the helicopter arrived from the north, passed overhead, and landed next to a hill in the Dead City of Abaz."

"*Landed? Next to a hill?* How could he know that?" Chako demanded. "Abaz is at least twenty miles to the southeast."

Hajar shrugged. "The desert has a thousand eyes. And people have two-way radios."

"Good work," Chako said. "Let's get the *qafila* (convoy) in gear."

The bus was the next to last vehicle in the column. And Chako's Land Rover was up front. So, to reach it, he had to walk the length of the convoy. Past a gun truck, past a heavily loaded flat bed, and past three 4x4s of various linages.

"Return to your vehicles!" Chako shouted. "Get your asses in gear! We'll be rich by dinnertime."

The ragtag *murtaziqa* (mercenaries) had heard such promises before, only to be disappointed every time.

But even though Chako had never been able to deliver the riches they hungered for, he had managed to keep the *junud* (soldiers) fed and, by virtue of his cleverness, been able to win a number of skirmishes.

Engines came to life, spewed blue-gray exhaust, and roared as the caravan got underway. Chako's Raiders were going to war.

***

The Dead City of Abaz

Darkness was falling and Soto had given up all hope of returning to Tabqa. The process of loading gold into containers was tedious. And hoisting them up the shaft was tiring.

Then a seam burst allowing a duffle bag load of coins to shower the two-man pit crew. Now they had to search for the coins, collect them, and load the gold into a backpack.

Soto suggested that they leave the remainder of the gold where it was, and send a platoon of Rangers to retrieve it, but Polat and Bone weren't having it.

"Time is of the essence," Polat insisted. "Who's to say that an ISIS team doesn't swoop in and take what remains while we organize the follow up? What will our superiors say then? More than half the gold is on the surface now. We'll finish the job tomorrow morning."

"Yeah," Bone added wearily. "What he said."

The long day was finally done.

***

Five miles east of the cavern

Chako's Raiders were pulled over onto the edge of the sand drifted road. It was dark, and the mercenaries didn't have night vision gear, so Chako thought it was best to attack in the morning.

The mercenary tossed and turned all night, dreamt about helicopters, and strange battles. He cried out at one point, causing Serena to wake him. Chako had difficulty getting back to sleep but eventually succeeded.

A dim light was visible beyond the curtains when the alarm went off and Chako scooted off the bed. After leaving the bus to pee, and spraying himself with deodorant, Chako ate a hurried breakfast. It consisted of cheese on pita bread, and a large mug of instant coffee. The rest of the mercenaries were preparing as well, each in his or her own way.

Chako's mind was on the task ahead. To his way of thinking the best way to capture the prize was to send a small team forward, kill whatever sentries had been posted, and hole up inside the helo.

At that point the Kafirs couldn't attack without running the risk of destroying the very thing they sought to protect. Meanwhile Chako would order the rest of the raiders forward and polish the *al'awghad* (bastards) off.

Chako knew there wouldn't be much cover. He also knew that anyone who arrived in a gun truck would immediately draw fire.

The answer was to use the bus. What could be less threatening than a ten-year-old bus? With a peace sign spray-painted on both flanks?

After a great deal of shouting, profanity, and gesticulating the raiders were aboard their vehicles and ready to depart. Chako was on the bus and at the wheel. Gamal, Farhat, Deeb, Matar, and Yazbek were in the back with the curtains closed.

The bus was well inside the ancient city when the hill appeared. "That's it! It has to be," Chako said. "Get ready to put on a show."

Chako waited for the hill to pass on the right, spotted the helicopter, and felt a rising sense of excitement. It was huge! *Maybe I'll charge by the pound*, Chako thought, as he swerved off the road and braked.

Then it was time to get out, kneel, and peer under the bus. A window was open above his head. Farhat spoke loudly enough for Chako to hear. "I see them. There are two lookouts. Right where you would expect them to be. On top of the hill."

"Good," Chako replied. "Can you hit them?"

"Of course," Farhat answered confidently. He was the group's best shot, and the proud owner of a Soviet era Dragunov SVD sniper rifle.

"Two shots will be required," Chako cautioned, as he opened a storage compartment. "And you must drop the second man quickly so he can't report in."

"Of course," Farhat replied. "That's a given."

"Then do it," Chako said, as he dragged a spare tire out into the open. Were the lookouts watching him? Without a doubt, they were.

***

Farhat was kneeling between two seats, with the barrel of his weapon angled upwards. Curtains hung on both sides. A suppressor made the rifle even longer.

The task would have been impossible if Farhat had been armed with a bolt action weapon. That was because the second lookout could have issued a warning during the time it took to work the rifle's bolt and adjust his aim.

But, thanks to the fact that the Dragunov was semi-automatic, Farhat was confident that he could drop the targets in quick succession. He placed the crosshairs slightly above the tiny figure to the left, made a final adjustment for windage, and fired.

The men were only a few feet apart. So only the slightest adjustment was required to fire again. The shots were so close together that the first lookout was still in the process of falling, when a blood mist halo appeared around the second man's head. "Targets down," Farhat reported.

"Excellent," Chako replied. "Send the girls out. And tell Hajar to bring everyone else forward."

The "girls" consisted of two men dressed in women's clothing. Deeb and Matar had been chosen because they were short and slender. The commodious dresses the fighters wore were more than adequate to conceal their weapons as they ambled toward the looming helicopter. Would the Kafirs see them as curious onlookers? That was the plan.

***

Lieutenant Ziggy Jones spotted the bus and its passengers right away. They were impossible to miss. And, as a pair of women approached the Chinook, he made use of the helo's external speakers to warn them off. "That's far enough! Don't come any closer."

But they kept coming. Did they understand English? Maybe not.

The women ran forward, dresses flapping, in a desperate attempt to board the helo. But before that could happen the female imposters had to run the one-hundred-foot length of the Chinook.

Jones started both engines, flipped a switch which brought the ramp up, and went aft. The pistol felt heavy in his hand.

The ramp was halfway up by then. One of the would-be hijackers had been left on the ground. The other had been able to grab the steadily rising ramp, pull himself up, and swing a leg over. He tumbled into the cargo area as Jones arrived.

The pilot was holding his nine mil in the approved two-handed grip. *Remember to aim*, Jones thought, as he began to jerk the trigger.

The first three shots went wide, struck metal surfaces, and *clanged*. Meanwhile the intruder was struggling to free a submachine gun from the folds of his dress.

Jones forced himself to pause and steady his aim. The other man had been able to clear his weapon by that time, and was about to unleash a hail of fire.

Jones felt a sense of desperation as he fired, fired, and fired again. One of the bullets struck the other man in the chest and threw him backwards.

Jones continued to jerk the trigger until he was out of ammo. The engines were roaring by then and the pilot hurried forward.

There was no way to know what was taking place outside. But one thing was for sure, the *Double Deuce* would be safer in the air than it was sitting on the ground.

Jones pulled pitch, felt the Chinook jump into the air, and watched the ground fall away.

***

The team was up and working, when Soto heard a burp of static from her radio, quickly followed by the sound of her crew chief's frantic voice. "Captain! We need help! A couple of tangos tried to capture the bird and the Loot took off. He's circling overhead. Meanwhile three or four vehicles have arrived."

Soto turned to the Rangers standing around the tripod. "We're under attack. Pull the pit crew up... Grab weapons and join the defensive line. That goes for you too Mr. Polat. Follow me."

The sounds of fighting increased as Soto and Polat jogged out to join the battle. Soto could see the enemy vehicles that formed a semicircle in front of the plaza. Two of them were armed with LMGs, and one of the trucks exploded as a well-aimed 40mm grenade landed on it.

Alvarez looked like a goddess of war as she strode from position to position, yelling encouragement, and firing her beloved M79.

Thanks to Bone, the Chinook's machine guns were perfectly situated to defend the approaches to the plaza, where the *Double Deuce* had been parked only ten minutes earlier.

That was the good news. The bad news was that the attackers had plenty of rubble to hide behind, and the spaces in between the defensive gun positions were largely undefended. "Fill the gaps!" Soto ordered. "Protect the machine guns!"

***

Chako felt a tremendous sense of disappointment as he eyed the circling helicopter. Though only a few hundred feet overhead, the Chinook might as well have been on the moon. Some of Chako's Raiders were wasting bullets on it, and that angered the mercenary even more. "Bol! Get your ass over here."

Bol was Sudanese. And, as an ex-member of the Sudanese army, Bol had been trained to fire shoulder launched missiles. That included the FIM-92 Stinger Chako had purchased on the black market. Bol left cover to scurry over. "Yes, sah."

"Shoot the helicopter down, Bol."

Bol frowned. "I thought we were going to sell it."

Chako sighed. "Don't try to think. Do what you're told. Shoot it down."

Bol nodded and the ritual began. Aim the weapon, listen for the lock on signal, and pull the trigger.

***

Jones felt frustrated as he circled the hill and the plaza beyond. His people were on the ground, fighting for their lives, and he was doing loops overhead. Sure, the *Deuce* was taking bullets that might otherwise be fired at his friends, but that was scant comfort.

The missile warning tone came as a complete surprise. *What the fuck? The yahoos had SAMs?*

Jones fired flares and chaff. The tone turned steady. A lock on. *Shit. Marie will be pissed*, Jones concluded. The thought was followed by a flash of light, the sensation of falling, and nothingness.

***

There was a sudden clap of thunder from above. Soto looked up just in time to see the *Double Deuce* explode. The shock of it stunned her. Jones. Gone. The Ranger on the stretcher. Gone.

Soto's relationship with Jones had been professional. Nothing more. Or so Soto thought until a wave of sorrow washed over her. The sounds of fighting fell off as fiery debris landed on attackers and defenders alike.

Soto's dreamlike reverie came to an abrupt end when a four-foot-long length of rotor blade plunged spear-like into the dirt two feet away, and a bullet snapped past her head.

Someone shouted, "Get down!" and Soto was about to obey, when she saw Polat shoot a Ranger in the back.

The murder took place as smoking wreckage continued to rain down and machine guns began to fire again. Had anyone else noticed? Soto didn't think so. She dropped to the ground, and elbowed her way forward.

What the fuck was going on? The answer seemed obvious. The Turk was planning to kill the team one by one, and keep the gold for himself!

Soto came up on the Turkish spy from behind and stopped next to him. She had to shout. "Do you believe in *Jahannam* (hell)?"

Polat turned to look at her. "What?"

"Do you believe in *Jahannam*?"

Polat frowned. "Yes."

"Then I'll see you there," Soto said, as she pulled the trigger. The pistol was concealed by her left armpit, and held in her right hand. The sound was lost in the surrounding cacophony.

Polat jerked as the bullet penetrated his body, his face registered a look of surprise, and he tried to speak. The words died with him.

***

Chako took pride in his ability to change objectives when necessary. Forget the helo, he told himself. *Why are the Kafirs here? What are they doing? Stealing art? If so, they're stealing my art... Because artifacts belong to Syria, and I am Syrian.* He waved the surviving Raiders forward. "Kill them! Kill them all!"

***

Hala Omar had been left on her own. And, when the battle started, she saw her chance. The Chinook was still on the ground at that point. So, it was easy to go aboard, and empty a Ranger's pack. Three bottles of water went into the rucksack, along with the dead Ranger's pistol, and an extra magazine. The dead man had a knife too, and a lighter.

There had been a Hala, a younger more innocent woman, who would have been reluctant to touch a dead body. *But I'm different now,* Hala thought. *I have the little one to care for. So, anything is possible.*

Hala left the Chinook just as a bus stopped on the adjacent road. Alvarez spotted Hala, and shouted "Stop!"

But the crew chief was distracted by the sight of two women charging the helo. She shot one of them.

Hala took the opportunity to hurry away. She tried to run, but found that her belly made that difficult to do, so she slowed to a walk. *I can trust no one*, Hala thought. *Not my people, not the Americans, and not God. But I will find a way.*

CHAPTER TWELVE

The Dead City of Abaz

Bone was underground when the battle started. That meant he had to spend the first four minutes of the conflict being winched up. The noncom heard the sharp *crack* of a grenade exploding as he left the cavern. Then he saw muzzle flashes on the west side of the plaza and realized that the Chinook was gone. *Jones flew it out*, Bone concluded. *Good boy.*

Bullets blew divots out of the ground in front of Bone, forcing him to drop and elbow his way forward. He could hear Soto giving orders as Alvarez fired her M79.

That was when Bone spotted the body. Polat was down! Bone felt a surge of joy. One problem solved! Additional obstacles remained, but he would tackle them one at a time.

The most pressing need was to win the battle in front of him. And that, Bone realized, could only be accomplished by pulling the machine guns back, and into a more defensible position. And to do so before the enemy surged through the gaps.

"Pull back!" Bone bellowed. "Drag the guns with you!"

Bone scuttled forward to help move the center weapon, and realized that one of the Chinook's gunners was dead beside it. *Jesus, how many people have we lost? And who are we fighting?*

A gunner was decapitated as another grenade went off. Blood spouted as the headless corpse jerked spastically.

With help from Levy, Bone was able to push and shove the M240 machine gun in behind some blocks of limestone. "Watch your ammo," Bone cautioned. "Aimed fire only. Three round bursts."

Levy nodded. "Got it Sarge."

These fuckers are winning, Bone realized. *Where's their leader? And how would they manage without him?*

Bone swore as a bullet whizzed past his head, sensed that it came from the left, and looked in that direction. A bus, a fucking bus! With a sniper hidden inside of it.

"Sniper at nine o'clock," Bone warned. "Keep your heads down. Over."

Then Bone was off and running a zigzag course toward the bus. Could the sniper see him? Fuck yes. But even the best marksmen can miss moving targets. Especially those that zig and zag.

Bone circled the remains of a pillar, approached the bus from behind, and spotted the ladder. It led to the roof where bundles were secured to side rails.

Bone knew the sniper could feel the motion as he climbed the ladder, spotted an open vent, and hurried forwards.

A bullet passed up through the roof and came within an inch of hitting his right foot. Bone aimed his M4 down and fired. A voice cried out causing the noncom to fire again. Silence.

Now Bone had what he needed. A stable platform from which to scope the battlefield. He dropped into the prone position. His M4 was equipped with an M150 Advanced Combat Optical Gun sight. And, thanks to the additional elevation provided by the bus, Bone could glass things his team couldn't. That included the asshole holding a radio to his mouth. Their leader? Hell yes!

Bone fired three shots. All of them struck their target. The man jerked spastically, appeared to throw the radio away, and collapsed.

It took less than thirty seconds for the dead leader's followers to cease fire, pull back, and run toward the surviving vehicles. That included the bus.

Suddenly Bone had five targets running straight at him. He fired, and put two tangos down, before the M4 ran dry. It was faster to pull the nine rather than reload the carbine. And the runners were a lot closer by then. So first come, first served.

The first man seemed to stumble, tried to recover, and collapsed.

The second fugitive took a bullet to his left shoulder, jerked, and kept coming. Bone shot him in the head.

The third runner took a dive, was rewarded with two bullets in the back, and lay still.

As Bone hurried to reload his weapons, he realized that the sound of firing had stopped. Motors roared to life as the surviving tangos hurried to escape, and Bone had every reason to let them go.

He tried to contact the two lookouts on the hill. Nothing. Dead? Probably. Damn, damn, damn.

As Bone returned to the plaza it soon became apparent that three Rangers, two Chinook gunners, and Polat had been killed. Eight people in all.

No, Bone thought, as he spotted the burned-out wreck on the north side of the plaza. *The helo was destroyed. Make that nine people KIA.*

Bone felt a stab of guilt. *They'd be alive had we returned to base. That's on me. And Polat.*

Soto appeared. "Good work, Sergeant. I saw what you did."

Bone shrugged. "Thanks. But it wasn't enough."

"Don't blame yourself," Soto replied. "You were down in the pit when the shit hit the fan."

With the gold, Bone thought. *Would it buy me some peace? No. But it would pay for everything else.* "We were about to lift the last pack of gold when they attacked," Bone told her. "Do we have a radio that can reach Tabqa?"

Soto shook her head. "Polat had a sat phone. But we don't have the access code."

"Okay, Bone said. "I suggest that we bring the last load up, and spread it around. We'll hike out."

Soto made a face. "Screw the gold."

The pilot was about to elaborate on that theme when Alvarez joined them.

"Hala's missing Captain. I saw her take off toward the southwest right after the bus arrived."

"Goddammit," Soto exclaimed. "Okay, make the rounds. Pull the bodies together. Take their tags. Photograph the location. And prepare to hike out. I'll chase Hala down."

***

Given what Hala Omar had been through, Soto didn't blame the young woman for taking off. It was a stupid thing to do however, because Hala would be vulnerable out on her own, and it seemed reasonable to assume that ISIS was searching for her.

As for what Soto's superiors would want, well, that was obvious. Hala could tell them all sorts of things about Toplin—including details about his personality, his health, and his associates. All of which would make the Intel nerds deliriously happy.

So, with nothing more than her M4, nine mil, and a bottle of water Soto took off.

The pilot wasn't an experienced tracker, far from it, and didn't need to be.

Hala's tracks were plain to see. A light breeze was blowing from the west however. And, when Soto paused to examine a footprint, she could see that windblown grains of sand were already starting to fill in the depression. Still another reason to hurry.

The terrain consisted of large areas of sand, interspersed with islands of hardpan, which refused to record footprints.

But, as soon as Soto arrived at the next sandy area, she was able to find the trail again. There were ruins to circumvent, along with natural obstacles, and the combination forced Hala to veer this way and that. Where was Hala going? Did she have a plan? Soto didn't think so.

The ruins of what might have been a Christian church blocked Soto's path. Hala's footprints angled to the right.

Rather than follow them Soto chose to climb a series of limestone blocks which delivered her to a flat overlook. Soto raised the M4, peered through the sight, and scanned the area ahead. And presto! There Hala was. A tiny figure in a huge landscape.

I need to catch up, Soto thought, as she jumped from block to block to land on the ground. *Who knows what's going on back at the cavern? Hala and I need to return as quickly as possible.*

The sun was high in the sky and the temperature was rising. Soto allowed herself a swig of water before returning the bottle to her knapsack. The she began to run.

Now that Soto knew where Hala was, it was no longer necessary to constantly scan for footprints, and the pilot was free to proceed at a steady jog. *I'm out of shape*, Soto decided. *Too much seat time. I need to work out.*

Soto tried to maintain situational awareness as she ran, but that was difficult to do. After ten minutes or so she spotted Hala in the distance. The pilot was short of breath, but the sighting was enough to reenergize her.

Hala turned to check her backtrail a minute later, spotted the oncoming figure, and attempted to run. But the baby slowed her down which allowed Soto to catch up. Her breath came in short gasps and made it difficult to speak. "Hala… Stop… Let's talk."

Hala was breathing heavily as well. She sat on a rock. "What do you want?"

"I want you to return with me. We'll protect you... And, after we make contact with Allied forces, they will take care of you and your baby."

Hala frowned. "In return for *what?* Information about President Toplin?"

"Yes," Soto replied. "I understand your reluctance. But consider this: Does Toplin care about your wellbeing?"

"No," Hala admitted. "He sent men to kidnap me from *Almakan Alaman.* (The Women's Place.) And it's possible that they killed my parents as well."

"I rest my case," Soto said. "My government can protect you from Toplin's killers. No one else can do that."

Hala was silent for a moment. Then she nodded. "I will go with you."

"Good," Soto replied. "Let's get going. It's getting late, and the sun will set in a few hours."

After establishing radio contact with Bone, and bringing the noncom up to date, Soto led Hala back to the cavern. Frequent rest stops were required. And the sun was just about to fall below the western horizon as they neared the cavern. "Red-Dog-Nine, this is Wizard. We're five out. Don't shoot us."

"Welcome back," Bone said. "Weapons tight."

As Soto led Hala onto the debris strewn plaza, and toward the flickering light of a fire, she saw that things had changed. The surviving machine guns had been repositioned just outside the cavern. The hollow-eyed survivors were armed with a mix of enemy and Allied weapons; some were asleep. A pile of packs stood waiting.

"We have seven people left," Bone said. "Not counting Hala. So, if each one of us carries thirty-five pounds of gold, we'll be able to take the coins with us."

Soto stared at him. "So that's what comes first? The gold?"

"No, of course not," Bone said defensively. "I thought you'd want to know, that's all."

In an obvious effort to change the subject, Bone said, "We pulled a mattress out of the bus. For Hala."

The bus, Soto thought. *I forgot about the bus. We have transportation.*

"That was thoughtful of you," Soto said. "Thanks. Do we have any food?"

"Not much," Bone replied. "The MREs were on the Chinook."

"And water?"

"We have some," Bone allowed. "That includes the bottles we took off the helo, and the supply we found on the bus."

"Who *were* those people?" Soto inquired. "And will they return?"

"They're bandits," Bone said. "Or mercenaries. They weren't carrying business cards, so it was hard to tell. As for coming back, no, I don't think so. I'm pretty sure I killed their leader. But, if they do, we're ready."

"Good," Soto said. "Let's give Hala some food, and grab some shuteye. Did you set a watch schedule?"

"Affirmative."

"Add me to it. And I have a suggestion if I may."

"Shoot."

"Bring the bus into the cavern."

Bone made a face. "Sorry, ma'am. My bad."

"No prob," Soto replied. "It's been a long, ugly day."

***

The Syrian Desert, southeastern Syria

Caliph Saleh ibn Tariq ibn Khalid al-Fulan was an ascetic. As such he liked to spend time in the desert, any desert, where modern conveniences were stripped away—and Allah's voice could be heard more clearly.

The fact that there was no cell service for the Allies to tap into, no hills for spies to watch from, and no rooftops for snipers to use were adjunct factors. And important ones.

Al-Fulan's encampment consisted of a large tent for his party, surrounded by smaller tents occupied by staff, and minor functionaries like Commander Ferran Mostafa.

It was al-Fulan's habit to work late into the night. So, when the summons came, it was well past 9 p.m.—and delivered by a teenage boy. "The Caliph will see you now."

Mostafa was sitting on a rug with legs crossed, reading *Men in the Sun*, on his Kindle. He closed the cover and stood. Mostafa felt a painful emptiness at the pit of his stomach.

Not because he lacked food, but because Hala Omar had been taken from him in the city of Afrin. A loss that al-Fulan was well aware of. As were members of the caliph's staff who treated Mostafa with open contempt. "I'm ready."

"Follow me," the boy instructed, and turned to go. There was no need for a guide. The caliph's tent was lit from within and shadows could be seen moving about inside.

No, the messenger was a formality, a part of the complex protocols that al-Fulan insisted on.

Glittering stars were scattered across the sky, the air was cold, and a generator purred somewhere nearby. A heavily armed guard searched Mostafa before he was allowed to enter the tent where a staff member was waiting. "*Assalamu alaikum.*" (Peace be upon you.)

"*Alaikum salaam.*" (And unto you, peace.)

The man waved Mostafa forward. "You may approach the Caliph."

Al-Fulan was seated at the center of the tent within a U-shaped assemblage of low tables. They were stacked high with piles of letters, binders full of organizational records, and hand-kept ledgers. None of which could be accessed by foreign governments via the internet.

Mostafa came to a stop in front of al-Fulan. "Greetings eminence."

The caliph was writing a letter. A minute passed before he signed it and looked up. "Tell me something, Ferran Mostafa. Twenty-six of our brave *ghazis* (warriors) died in the city of Afrin. Yet you are alive. *Why?*"

Mostafa struggled to maintain his composure. "I would like to believe that it was Allah's will."

"And why would Allah deign to protect a nothing such as yourself?" al-Fulan inquired.

Mostafa swallowed. "The woman Hala Omar was taken from me. I admit that. And I regret it. But, thanks to the electronic tracker hidden in her clothing, I know exactly where she is. With Allah's blessing, and with your permission, I will recapture her."

Al-Fulan suffered from back pain, and was sitting in a chair from which the legs had been removed. It creaked as the caliph allowed himself to lean back. His eyes were dark, like pools of ink, and Mostafa struggled to meet them.

Finally, after what seemed like an hour, but was only a minute or so—al-Fulan spoke. "You claim that you can recapture Hala Omar. Do so, and all will be forgiven. Fail, and you will be proclaimed as a *Takfir* (an apostate). Will a member of the faithful kill you? I don't know. That will be up to them. Now go."

Mostafa felt a surge of fear. If he succeeded then good. But if he failed every hand would be turned against him. "Thank you, Eminence," Mostafa said as he backed away. "I will find Hala Omar, contact the Russian, and sell her. I will bring the money to you."

Al-Fulan nodded. "May Allah guide and protect you."

***

The Dead City of Abaz

Corporal Levy turned the key. The engine coughed, caught, and died. He had better luck the second time. "Okay," Bone said. "All aboard! Let's get the fuck out of here."

Soto was fifty feet away, taking one last look at the temporary graves, while thinking about those who had been lost. Jones, Polat, a gunner named Hines and all the rest.

Tears trickled down Soto's cheeks, and she was careful to wipe them away, before heading for the bus. She was the last to board.

Finally, Soto thought, as she sat next to Hala. *The nightmare is over. All we have to do is head west, find a main highway, and stop an Allied vehicle. The rest will be easy.*

The seldom used dirt road had lots of potholes, and was anything but straight, but soon delivered the bus to the remains of a wooden bridge. Judging by appearances the structure had been destroyed by a seasonal flood and left unrepaired. And that was to be expected in a war-torn country.

Had they been traveling in something like an MRAP (Mine-Resistant Ambush Protected vehicle), it would have been possible to cross the dry wash. But that was impossible due to the bus's forty-foot-long wheelbase and lack of all-wheel drive.

That meant the passengers had two choices. They could get out and walk, or follow the gully to another bridge, and hope it was intact. Due to Hala's condition, and how heavy the gold was, it was an easy decision to make.

Bone thought the team should head north, and away from the heavy combat in the south, and Soto saw no reason to disagree.

So, Levy turned to the right. The terrain was mostly flat, which made it possible to proceed with rear wheel drive, but there were a lot of obstacles. Rocks for the most part, but ruins too, which forced Levy to swerve back and forth.

Then it appeared. An east-west dirt road that led across a steel frame bridge. Tires rumbled on wooden planks as the bus crossed to the west side of the river bed. The passengers cheered. Shortly thereafter the engine quit and refused to start.

Soto declared a bio break while Alvarez opened the engine compartment in hopes of making a repair. The crew chief delivered her report fifteen minutes later. "The starter is shot," she announced. "We'll have to walk."

That was when the argument began. Soto wanted to leave the gold. "It's heavy," Soto complained. "And not counting Hala, each of us would have to carry something like thirty-five pounds of coins plus weapons, ammo and water. That's absurd."

"No," Bone argued. "It's our duty to take the gold with us. Who knows what will happen to it if we leave it behind? This place is lousy with tangos, bandits, and scavengers.

"I'll tell you what," Bone added. "We'll *try* to take the gold out. And if that turns out to be impractical, we'll hide it. What do you say?"

Soto could have said, "No." She outranked the rest of the survivors, and could theoretically order them to bury the gold. But Soto feared that Bone's hold on the Rangers was so strong that they might rebel.

So, Soto agreed to the compromise, confident in the knowledge that the team would soon grow tired of carrying the gold, and agree to leave it behind.

"All right," Soto said. "But we'll do it my way. We'll walk until 1100 hours, find some shade, and take a break until 1600. Then we'll walk till 2000 hours."

Bone opened his mouth as if to object, appeared to reconsider, and closed it again.

It took an hour to divide the gold, water and ammo into seven packs, each weighing approximately fifty pounds. Perhaps the Rangers were used to carrying that kind of load, but Soto wasn't, and hoped the insanity would soon end.

Bone was on point as the trek began. Levy was walking drag, and the rest of the party was strung out in between. Bone set a brisk pace at first. But Hala couldn't keep up. So, the noncom found himself too far out in front.

Soto could tell that Bone wanted to complain, wanted to order Hala to walk faster, but couldn't. That forced the Ranger to reduce his speed accordingly.

But if Hala was slow, she was also steady, and the team was roughly two miles from the stalled bus when 1100 rolled around. A large outcropping of rock threw a deep shadow, and judging from the detritus scattered around, had been of use to other travelers as well.

Soto's shoulders were sore by then, her back hurt, and she wanted to drink an entire bottle of water all at once. Rather than do so she took three sips before making the rounds.

Levy and Alvarez had cleared rocks away to create a small clearing for Hala. The fugitive thanked them, promptly curled up into the fetal position, and went to sleep.

The heat grew more intense until early afternoon when it leveled out and eventually began to decrease. In the meantime, the team took naps, played cards, and told war stories.

At one point a Black Hawk helicopter clattered overhead on its way to a destination somewhere in the southeast. Levy ran out into the open and waved his arms. The helo continued on its way.

Time passed slowly. And by the time 1600 arrived, Soto was eager to depart. As was Bone. He took the point and the rest the party followed. The air had started to cool a bit, long shadows pointed east, and birds were flitting about.

The road had deteriorated into little more than a wide trail by that time, which followed the path of least resistance, as it wound its way through a maze of rocks.

And it was then, as an open area appeared in front of them, that a shot rang out. Bone collapsed in a heap. Soto shouted "Take cover!" She was quick to follow her own advice.

Was Bone dead? No, Soto saw him try to get up and fall back. What did that leave? Six effectives, not counting Hala.

"You have Hala Omar," a much-amplified male voice said. "Send her out. We will take her and leave. There's no need for you to die."

***

Thanks to the tracking device concealed in Hala's clothing, Mostafa and his men had been able to anticipate where the fugitive and her companions were headed, and set an ambush.

Maybe the Kafirs would send Hala out. That would be ideal. But, if they refused to comply, Mostafa would take what he wanted. His life depended on it.

***

A sniper fired and a gunner named Hendricks fell. *Shit!* Soto thought, as her eyes probed the surrounding rocks. *We're down to five.*

Levy fired and a tango toppled off a ledge. The body hit the ground with an audible thump. Dust rose to float over the body.

"Here I am," Hala said, as she stepped out into the open.

Soto shouted, "*No!*" Then she left cover, and was about to go after Hala, when an automatic weapon opened fire. Bullets kicked up geysers of dirt all around her.

Soto turned, took a dive, and skidded into cover.

"Good!" the much-amplified voice said. "Now walk to me."

"No," Hala replied, as she made her way toward Bone. "Shoot me if you want to."

***

Mostafa *didn't* want to. So, all he could do was watch as Hala knelt next to the wounded American and applied first aid.

The key, Mostafa decided, was to distract the Americans while snatching Hala. Mostafa dropped the bullhorn and thumbed his radio. "Prepare to attack! If you kill the woman, I will kill you. Ready, fire!"

Weapons fired from positions on the west side of the open area, and were answered by those to the east, as Mostafa began to run. That was when he saw Hala stand and turn his way. Her right hand came up, as if to point at him, and Mostafa saw what looked like a spark.

The bullet smashed into Mostafa's left shoulder and turned him around. He staggered, managed to regain his balance, and faced her again.

A gun! How could that be? Women didn't fight. Then Mostafa remembered Chalibi laying on the floor, his head surrounded by a halo of blood. He raised his hands to block the bullets.

Hala smiled as she fired again and again. The third slug blew the top of Mostafa's head off, just as Alvarez fired her M79 at an enemy LMG. The 40mm grenade was dead on. The resulting explosion killed three ISIS fighters and left a fourth grievously wounded.

Bone managed to grab an ankle, give it a jerk, and pull Hala off her feet.

Bullets ploughed past them as the crew chief fired again. The blast produced a scream.

Alvarez was reloading when a bullet hit her between the eyes. She swayed and fell.

Soto produced a primal scream as she charged past Hala and Bone. Corporal Levy followed, as did a Ranger named Riley.

Hajis came out to meet them. Soto shot anything that moved during the wild exchange of gunfire that followed. Dust swirled. Bodies fell. And a bullet creased her cheek.

Then, as suddenly as it had begun, the battle ended. Soto stood on trembling legs as she fed a magazine into the M4.

Levy was down, as was Riley. Soto bent to check each soldier. Both were dead. She began to cry.

Tears continued to flow down her cheeks as she made her way to the spot where Hala was kneeling next to Bone. His blood was everywhere, and already attracting flies.

"Thank you, Hala," Bone said, as Soto crouched beside him. "You did all that anyone could. The Captain and I need a moment."

Hala stood and walked away. When Bone coughed, blood trickled from the corner of his mouth. Soto wiped it away. Their eyes met. "Can I call you Marie?"

"Yes, of course."

"Good. Polat and I were going to steal the gold. You know that by now. A lot of people died as a result. So don't feel sorry for me. I don't deserve any sympathy.

"But maybe, just maybe, some good can come of it. Wait till Hala goes to sleep, and hide most of the gold. Not all of it though… Put some in a separate cache. Report the larger stash like the girl scout that you are. The army will send a team to recover it.

"Then later, when it makes sense, return for the rest. Split it fifty-fifty. Half for you, and half for my family. Not Yolanda though… Not a cent! Do you read me?"

Bone reached up to grab a handful of Soto's flight suit.

"I read you five-by-five."

"And you'll do it?"

"Yes," Soto lied.

Bone released his grip. "Thank you, Marie. Thank you. Take this," Bone said, as he pressed a gold coin into her hand. "And remember me."

Soto watched the light slowly vanish from Bone's eyes. Then, when it was gone, she said a silent prayer. The coin was still clutched in her hand.

***

Aboard a Russian Kamov Ka-26 over Syria

Major Sergei Voronin was scared, and had every reason to be, while riding in a Russian helo. Yes, they were flying low, well under Allied radars. But that wouldn't protect the Ka-26 from being spotted by an American F-18. Or an A-10.

But if Voronin was scared, he was also excited. Finally, after weeks of fruitless effort, he was about grab Hala Omar! And not a moment too soon, judging from the most recent message from Mischa Durov, Toplin's executive assistant.

"The Bear is unhappy. Too much time has passed. You have seventy-two hours in which to finish the project. Do not fail."

"The Bear" was Toplin's nickname which, according to the rumors, was a reference to the president's luxuriant body hair.

As for the words, "Do not fail," there was no way to ignore the implicit threat.

But there's no need to worry, Voronin assured himself. *You will succeed.*

***

The Dead City of Abaz

Soto felt a rising sense of panic. Were ISIS reinforcements on the way?

Calm down. First things first. Where's Hala? She ran once. She could do so again.

But no, Hala was sitting on a rock, her head in her hands. And that was when Soto had a moment in which to ask herself an important question. *How did the bad guys know where to set the ambush?*

Soto went to join Hala. "Nice job killing that bastard. Did you know him?"

Hala looked up. "Yes. He was the one who held me prisoner in the shoe factory. And before that as well."

"Strip naked," Soto told her. "All the way down."

Hala frowned. "Why?"

"Because the bastard planted a tracker in your clothes. Check the seams. Check everywhere. You have to find it. Otherwise, the scumbags will follow us wherever we go."

Hala was visibly frightened. She stood, and began to undress.

Okay, Soto thought. *Where am I?*

The answer was on Soto's wrist. Thanks to her watch, the pilot was able to check her GPS coordinates, and write them down in the notebook she carried.

Now for the gold. The first task was to move from body-to-body, collect dog tag tabs, and lug the gold-heavy packs to a central pile.

As she did so, Soto scanned the area, searching for a good hiding spot. It had to be large enough to accommodate the packs, and easy to conceal, because she wanted to clear the area quickly.

From what Soto could see the best possibility was a small U-shaped cove at the bottom of a slope, where scree had accumulated over the years, and could be used to cover the stash.

Soto turned to look at Hala, and saw that the other woman was still naked, and checking her clothes. Good. There was no reason for her to know the exact location of the gold.

Soto set to work moving the packs to the hide. The last was the lightest and weighed something on the order of ten pounds.

The cove was at full capacity by that time, so Soto carried the rucksack over to the point where rocks led in a stair-like way up to a narrow ledge and crevice. The rucksack fit perfectly, and was soon invisible behind a wall of stacked stones.

Soto jumped to the ground. *Now,* Soto told herself. *Grab what you need, and haul ass.* That was when a Russian Kamov Ka- 226 (Hoodlum) helicopter *clattered* overhead on its way east. A coincidence? Hell no.

Soto said, "Shit," as she ran toward Hala. The younger woman was fully dressed by then. "Did you find it?"

"Yes!" Hala exclaimed, as she opened her fist to reveal a small disk.

Soto took the device, dropped it onto the ground, and stomped on it.

The sound the helo made was dying away. "Don't tell me—let me guess," Soto said. "Toplin sent a team to bring you back."

Hala nodded. "Will they see the plaza? And the cavern?"

"Yes, they will," Soto replied. "It's only a couple of miles away, and would be hard to miss. Especially with a burned-out Chinook sitting off to one side. Why?"

"Because they will land," Hala predicted. "And that will give us more time to get away."

"Why are you so certain that they will land?"

"They have to," Hala answered simply. "In case my body is there."

Soto frowned. "To confirm that you're dead?"

"Yes, but more than that," Hala replied. "Do you know what a Blockchain Wallet is?"

"An account? To store bitcoin in?"

"Exactly," Hala answered. "And, to access your wallet you need a Wallet ID, which consists of random letters and numbers.

A lot of them. I don't know how much money Toplin has in his account, but some people say he's a billionaire."

"And?"

"And if you forget your ID, you can't access your account. As some people have learned the hard way. That's why Toplin ordered me to strip, and shave my pubic area. Then a tattoo artist arrived, and well, you can guess the rest."

"The number is tattooed above your vagina and hidden by your pubic hair," Soto replied. "And that's why they want you dead or alive."

Hala nodded and tears began to flow. "Yes. Toplin called me his, *nebol'shaya rezervnaya kopiya,* which means 'little backup.' He trusted me.'"

Soto's mind was racing. Could the U.S. steal Toplin's fortune? Yes, it could! Unless the Russians managed to snatch Hala. She took Hala's hand. "He trusted you. I get that. But now he wants to kill you. And the little one. Follow me. I have an idea."

CHAPTER THIRTEEN

The Dead City of Abaz

The sense of anticipation that Voronin experienced earlier had been replaced by fear. Repeated attempts to reach his ISIS contact by sat phone had failed. And now, after leaving the helicopter, Voronin and his five-man team were entering the wreckage strewn battlefield he'd seen from the air. Was this the right spot? Perhaps.

But Voronin had received a cryptic instant message from his contact, which consisted of new coordinates, and the word: "Update."

After overflying the new meeting place, and seeing nothing of interest, Voronin ordered the pilot to proceed to the first rendezvous. And because wreckage was visible there, not to mention the presence of numerous dead bodies, Voronin ordered the pilot to land.

What if one of the bodies belonged to Hala Omar? *Please, please, please make it so*, Voronin thought. *Then I can take it to Russia. No one will blame me, and who knows? Perhaps a reward of some sort will come my way.*

Flies buzzed, and two vultures flapped into the air, as the Russians approached the plaza. The stench was horrific. "Pay attention!" Voronin ordered. "Hostile forces could arrive at any moment. Check each body. Compare faces to the photos I gave you. If you get a match, tell me right away." The stomach-churning process began.

***

Soto paused for what? The twentieth time? So that Hala could catch up. Their goal was to return to the plaza. *Why?* Because that's where Hala believed the Russian capture party would be. And the Ruskies had something that Soto needed. *We're close,* Soto told herself. *Damned close. Keep your eyes peeled.*

Being a pilot herself Soto knew where she would land if the plaza wasn't available. And that was on the road that ran east and west next to the cavern. The same road that the bus had been parked on. And sure enough, as the women approached from the west, there it was! The same Kamov Ka-26 they'd seen earlier.

The challenge was to sneak up on the aircraft without being spotted by the pilots, both of whom were seated in the cockpit, with the side door open for ventilation.

The ruins provided some cover, as did the natural rock outcroppings, and the shadows they threw. Hala was crouched next to the pilot. "Keep your pistol handy," Soto advised. "You may need it."

Finally, when Soto judged that they were as close as they could get without being seen, there was no choice but to run straight at the Kamov Ka.

Soto was about to go for it when one of the pilots jumped to the ground. Geysers of dust shot up around his boots. Then he unzipped a pocket, removed a pack of cigarettes, and lit one. That was the moment when Soto ran towards him.

The Russian saw her, flipped the cigarette away, and was reaching for his shoulder holster as Soto skidded to a stop. It was her split-second opportunity to take aim and she did.

Two shots hit the pilot and dumped him on his can. He looked down, saw the blood, and slumped sideways.

The sound of gunfire brought the second pilot to the door with weapon drawn. Soto fired, as did Hala, and at least one bullet hit him. The Russian fell back into the cockpit.

Speed! Now everything was about speed. Soto had to enter the helo, pull the body out through the door, start the single engine, grok the controls without being able to read Russian labels, and master the co-axial main rotor arrangement. A setup in which one multi-blade rotor sat atop another, dispensing with the requirement for an anti-torque tail rotor.

That configuration was different from the tandem rotors on a Chinook. But Soto had flown an experimental model at an airshow, and figured she could do so again.

It took the combined strength of both women to pull the dead pilot out of the cockpit and dump him onto the ground.

Don't flip switches randomly, Soto cautioned herself. *Look at the way they're grouped. Consider where they're positioned. Close to hand? Or off in a corner of the panel? Think it through.* The guessing game began.

***

Voronin heard what sounded like pistol shots. To the south? He thought so. The helicopter! Was it under attack? Or were the pilots indulging in some target practice?

Voronin thumbed his radio. "Gromov? Yelchin? What's going on?"

Silence. Voronin felt something cold trickle into the pit of his stomach. Had he led the team into an ambush? Was ISIS planning to keep Hala Omar, and steal the ransom money? "Follow me!" Voronin shouted, as he began to run.

That was when the Russian heard a high-pitched whine, followed by the sound of two piston engines starting up.

He ran even faster, tripped, and fell down. Seconds were lost as Voronin jumped to his feet. Did ISIS have a helicopter pilot? That seemed unlikely. So, what the hell was going on?

The Kamov Ka-226 shimmered like a desert mirage as it rose up from behind some ruins to hover over the road. Voronin skidded to a halt. Should he order his men to fire on it? If they did, and if they brought the helo down, how would that improve their situation?

The answer was obvious. *We'll get the briefcase full of money back*, Voronin told himself. "Shoot it down!" Voronin shouted. Then he opened fire.

***

Soto saw the sparkle of gunfire as she looked out through the bubble-shaped windscreen. She wanted to haul ass. Hala had something different in mind. There were all sorts of things back in the cargo area, including water, rations, and a satchel of grenades. "Fly over them," Hala ordered, as she settled into the copilot's seat. "I will handle the rest."

"You know how to use grenades?"

"Of course," Hala replied. "They do it in movies. Pull the pin and throw it. Or, in this case, drop it."

"Okay," Soto agreed. "One pass. That's all you get."

***

Voronin watched the helo come straight at him. As it did, he saw what looked like black dots fly out of the machine, and fall. It wasn't until the first one exploded that Voronin realized what the dots were. Grenades! He turned to run.

***

The helicopter's slipstream buffeted Hala's face and tugged at her loose clothing as she threw one grenade after another. There was no way to aim. All Hala could do was pull, toss, and reach for another bomb. She could hear the sound of muted explosions and heard herself screaming. "Die pigs!"

***

Voronin was running. But he couldn't outrun a helicopter. The Russian heard the helo's twin engines as the machine approached him from behind, felt the propwash as the Kamov Ka passed overhead, and saw a grenade hit the ground fifteen feet in front of him. It took a bounce and seemed to hang as if suspended in the air. *No!* Voronin thought, as his pounding feet carried him forward. *This isn't fair!*

What looked like a flashbulb went off, and a warm wind carried Voronin away.

***

Soto felt a deep sense of sorrow as she aimed the helo at the Tabqa Superbase. Sorrow for all of those who had died, and that included Bone who, in spite of his deceit, was an honorable soldier.

Fueled by adrenaline, Soto felt a sense of exhilaration too, thanks to the narrow escape. But that emotion was held in check by a healthy serving of fear. And no wonder. She was flying a Russian bird over mostly Allied territory and would be easy pickings for a Cobra gunship or a fighter plane.

With that in mind Soto selected a frequency which, though in the clear, was monitored by Allied forces. "Tabqa Tower, this is Wizard-Two-Two, incoming from the southeast.

"Be advised that I am flying a Russian Kamov Ka-226 helicopter with a high value civilian on board. Please don't shoot us down. Over."

There was a long pause. Because nobody was monitoring the unsecured channel? Or because an air traffic controller was bucking the message up the chain of command?

Finally, after what seemed like an eternity, Soto heard a male voice. "Wizard, this is Tabqa Tower. What are the last four digits of your DoD ID number? Over."

"Six-Eight-Four-One. Over."

"And the last five of your Chinook's tail number? Over."

"Zero-Two-Zero-Two-Two. Over."

"And the first name of your next of kin? Over."

"Samuel. Over."

"Climb to five thousand and stay on your present course," the controller said. "Over."

That was followed by an even longer pause before a female voice came over the radio. "Wizard, this is Tabqa Tower. Two uglies are headed your way and will escort you in. Rest assured that all fighter aircraft have been notified, and will stay off you. Over."

Soto was well aware that, while the Apache gunships would serve as escorts, they would also be ready to blow her ass out of the air, should they notice something suspicious.

Still, the uglies were a welcome sight when they appeared, and took up stations on either side of her. The pilot of the Apache off to starboard threw a salute. "Wizard, I'm Surfer, and the crazy person off your port side is Deadeye. Welcome home from wherever you were. Over."

The next forty-five minutes passed without incident. Then, as the superbase appeared in the distance a flurry of orders came her way. Soto was told where to land, how she and her passenger were to comport themselves, and what they were permitted to say—which was nothing.

Hala was seated in the copilot's seat. She was visibly nervous. "All you have to do is tell them the truth," Soto said. "Toplin, ISIS, the Russian team—all of it. And that includes the Wallet ID."

"What about the gold?" Hala wanted to know. "And the briefcase full of money?"

"That too," Soto assured her. "I will give them the coordinates for where the gold is hidden. And they'll find the cash when they board. And Hala?"

"Yes?"

"There's a good chance we'll never see each other again. I want you to know how much I admire your courage. You're a remarkable woman. The little one is lucky to have a mother like you."

Hala smiled a crooked smile. "How do you say? Look who is talking?"

Soto winked at her, turned onto the final heading, and started to descend. About two dozen people were gathered around Pad 2. Soto put the helo down, killed the engines, and opened the door. Three soldiers approached with weapons at the ready. "Hands on your heads!" a sergeant ordered. "And stay where you are."

That was just the beginning. The helicopter was searched, as were both women, prior to being separated. Shortly thereafter Soto was allowed to take a bio break, given some lukewarm food, and subjected to a relentless hotwash in a windowless room.

There were three interrogators, all of whom used their first names, and were clearly spooks. Soto told the story, once, twice and eventually three times. Throughout the interviews Soto was careful to deliver the same information in the same sequence.

Finally, after nearly five hours of Q & A, the man named Mike called the session to a close. "Thank you, Captain Soto. We'll send a team to examine what remains of the Chinook, the cavern, and the location where the gold is hidden.

"By the way, it may interest you to know that the briefcase contained exactly one million dollars U.S. A sure sign of Hala Omar's value to President Toplin. We'll be in touch if we have additional questions."

That was Soto's opportunity to ask the question that had been on her mind. "Was I listed as MIA?"

Mike nodded. "Yes. Your family will be notified that you are safe and sound."

Soto said, "Thank you," and left the room.

Major Albro was waiting outside. "Welcome back, Marie. I'm sorry about your crew. *Our* crew. Do you need anything?"

"Just time," Soto replied. "And a new ride."

Albro frowned. "*Really?* How about a desk job instead? For a month or so?"

"I need to fly," Soto replied. "That's what I do. I'm sorry about losing the *Double Deuce*."

"Go get some sleep," Albro replied. "Lots of it. Come see me when you're ready for duty. I'll find a new machine for you to fly."

***

Santorini Island, Greece

More than a month had passed since Soto and Hala had hijacked the Russian helicopter and flown it to the Tabqa Superbase.

Hala had vanished and was, Soto imagined, somewhere in Washington D.C. where the spooks could talk to her—and the little one would be safe from his or her father.

As for Soto, she was on leave in sun splashed Santorini, and enjoying every minute of every day. Part of that was due to the azure sky, the equally blue sea, and the picturesque buildings that surrounded her.

But quite a bit of her pleasure could be traced to Dr. Casey Milo, or just plain Milo, as his friends called him.

The possibility of a shared vacation had been raised by Milo over drinks at the club, and much to Soto's surprise she'd said "Yes," without a moment's hesitation. As if somewhere deep down the decision had already been made.

And now, three days into the getaway, Soto had no regrets. Milo was romantic, funny, and good in bed. What more could a girl ask for?

Maybe it was a fling. But their conversations frequently strayed into post war fantasy life. What did they want? What would they do? And there was a lot of alignment.

So, Soto was in a good mood as she left the room and made her way down to the hotel's lobby. Milo was out on a boat taking his first SCUBA lesson. And Soto was in the mood for a midafternoon gin and tonic.

It was too early for the happy hour crowd, so tables were available out on the deck, where striped umbrellas threw patches of shade. A waiter arrived, took Soto's order, and disappeared.

The pilot watched a gull ride the wind, thought about the new Chinook waiting for her at Tabqa, and the crew she hadn't met yet.

Could any crew chief be as good as Alvarez? Could any copilot be as funny as Ziggy? No. Memories of them would fly with her.

The drink arrived and Soto took a sip. It was ice cold and very satisfying. Her wallet was on the table. The drink would be charged to the room but a tip was in order.

Soto opened the purse, saw a glint of gold and removed the coin. It seemed natural to give it a spin. Light flashed off the disc as it revolved. A team had been sent to find the gold and retrieve it. All but the smaller stash hidden in the crevice. *Why didn't I tell them about the rucksack?* Soto wondered.

Because I made a promise to Bone. Half for his family, and half for me. A hundred thou? Maybe. Just enough for the down payment on a war surplus Chinook.

The coin slowed, and was just about to fall, when Soto caught it. *I made a promise, Sergeant Bone. Hooah!*

AUTHOR'S NOTES

I knew I wanted to write a braided novel about a Chinook pilot, an army master sergeant, and Russian President Toplin's young mistress. And I knew wanted to place the story in Syria. But little did I know when my research began that the U.S. has been fighting in that country since 2013, when President Obama put the CIA in charge of arming anti-government forces in Syria. An effort that is still underway as I write this in October of 2022. At the moment the U.S. has about a thousand sets of boots on the ground.

Meanwhile Iran continues to exert its influence in Iraq, Syria, and Lebanon—even as the Kurds, ISIS and Al-Qaeda battle each other for territory and resources.

That's the situation when my fictional WW III series begins, and the jumping off point for the events that take place in **RED DOG**.

I thought, "Hey, what if ISIS and al-Qaeda were to merge?" That seemed to be fanciful.

But, after spending thirty seconds on Google, I discovered that such a possibility was being discussed in journals like Foreign Affairs, the Small Wars Journal, and a site called digitalcommons.dartmouth.edu as far back as 2017. My version of what occurred at the first merger meeting is of course entirely fictional.

***

Tell Abyad is a real city. And, by sharing part of a description lifted from Wikipedia, I hoped to communicate the craziness that the locals have been forced to live with over the years.

"After the Syrian civil war started in 2011, Tell Abyad was captured by the Free Syrian Army in September 2012. On June 30, 2014, Tell Abyad was captured by the al-Nusra Front and the Islamic State of Iraq and the Levant (ISIL), who raised their flag at the border crossing with Turkey.

After ISIL defeated the Kurdish forces, the YPG and Kurdish Front, ISIL fighters announced from the minarets of the local mosques that all Kurds had to leave Tell Abyad or else be killed.

Thousands of civilians, including Turkmen and Arab families, fled on 21 July. ISIL fighters systematically looted and destroyed the property of Kurds and resettled displaced Arab Sunni families from the Qalamoun area (Rif Damascus), Deir ez-Zor, and Raqqa in abandoned Kurdish homes.

According to Liz Sly of the *Washington Post*, "ISIL also collected a tax from the Christians, a so called Jizya of about 100$ every six months. While ISIL controlled the border towards Turkey in Tell Abyad, it was a major source for supplies coming in from Turkey."

So, the level of competition, confusion, and conflict described in **RED DOG** understates the chaos, if anything. Sometimes truth *is* stranger than fiction.

***

The "Women's Place," or Almakan Alaman in the story, is modeled on the very real village of Jinwar in northeast Syria, which opened in 2018—and is similar to the women's village of Umoja, in Kenya.

I made passing mention of "an old French Foreign Legion fort." For those readers who are interested in the Legion, back in 1921 the 4e REI participated in French operations to seize control of Syria. The Syrians never catch a break. Not then, and not now.

***

As regards the incident in which a soldier goes crazy inside the *Double Deuce*. That segment was inspired by a flight I was part of back on the night of April 9, 1964 or 65. (Like most 19- or 20-year-olds I didn't take notes.)

An off-duty marine had been injured in a traffic accident near Beaufort, S.C., and brought to the navy hospital there, where doctors decided that his injuries were so severe that he should be transferred to the larger hospital in Charleston.

Our hospital didn't have a helipad. So, the normal practice was to transport critically injured patients to the nearby Marine Corps air station by ambulance, and fly them out from there.

But this poor guy was so messed up that the chain of command decided to land the chopper between a flag pole and the front door of the hospital.

I don't recall what kind of helicopter it was. But I do remember that there was no more than four feet between the rotors, the flag pole, and the hospital. Because a dozen people came out to watch.

That was bad enough. But it was night as well, night vision goggles weren't a thing, and all that the pilots had was ambient lighting. They succeeded and the crowd dispersed.

Because I was on duty in the emergency room, I was selected to escort the patient to Charleston. He was in a stretcher, with an IV in his left arm. I don't remember him being sedated. And, if he wasn't, that would make sense. Because the greater the degree of sedation, the greater the risk of respiratory depression.

Anyway, since the patient was only semi-conscious, I thought the flight would be a no-brainer. All I had to do was keep the drip going, check vital signs, and shoot the shit with the crew chief.

The crew consisted of two pilots and the crew chief. The passengers included myself and my patient.

The side door had been removed, and I remember feeling chilly as the slip stream pushed cold air into the cargo area. About halfway through the flight the marine ripped his IV out of his arm, got to his feet, and made for the open door.

The fact that he could stand, never mind hobble, was nothing less than a miracle. Fortunately, the crew chief and I were able to intercept him. The marine fought like a madman. It took both of us to get the marine back on the stretcher and restrain him.

At some point during the battle, we accidentally broke some of his fingers. That's what I was told hours later, after delivering the marine to Charleston, and flying back to Beaufort. If you read this buddy, I'm sorry… We didn't mean to hurt you.

Then, on the return flight, rather than land at Marine Corps Air Station, and send me to the hospital in a security truck, the pilots decided to land between the flag pole and the hospital all over again! Just for the fun of it.

Did I have a vote? Hell, no.

I returned to the emergency room where the duty Chief Petty Officer was waiting. It was early Easter morning by then. "Welcome back, Dietz," he said. "It's time to set up the chairs for the sunrise service. Get your butt in gear."

If you can't take a joke, don't join the navy.

***

Back to Syria. The Dead City of Abaz is modeled on the Dead City of Serjilla. It's located in the Jebel Riha, about fifty miles southwest of Aleppo, and encompasses about seven hundred archeological sites.

The settlement was founded in 473 within a natural basin and prospered by growing grapes and olives. It was abandoned in the seventh century, when Arabs conquered the region. As depicted in the book, the ruins of Serjilla are still very visible. There are plenty of images online.

Thank you for reading **RED DOG**.

ABOUT THE WINDS OF WAR SERIES

At the conclusion of **RED DOG**, significant progress had been made against the Axis. But, in order to win the war Allied strategists, know that they will ultimately have to bring China to its knees. In order to accomplish that it will be necessary to defeat North Korea and Russia along with Kazakhstan and Mongolia.

At that point China will be effectively surrounded. And, having been cut off from the rest of the world politically and economically, China will be forced to either capitulate or become the new hermit kingdom.

In **RED LINE**, the ninth volume of the *Winds of War* series, WIII continues to rage, as Allied forces attack North Korea.

ABOUT WILLIAM C. DIETZ

For more about **William C. Dietz** and his fiction, please visit williamcdietz.com.

You can find Bill on Facebook at: www.facebook.com/williamcdietz.

Printed in Great Britain
by Amazon

19952041R00150